# Five Legends, Five Guitars
# Pam Van Allen

ISBN 978-0-9600731-1-5

First Edition

## Disclaimer

The material in this book not derived from my own observations or imagination is taken from information that is available to the public and is cited in the bibliography, with the exception of personal communication. Furthermore, I claim no expertise in music analysis or critique, I have only described what came through my ears, so there are undoubtedly errors. Nelson, Lucky, Lefty, Otis, and Charlie T., Jnr. are inspired by George Harrison, Bob Dylan, Roy Orbison, Jeff Lynne, and Tom Petty, but they don't represent the real people. Rather, they are characters I developed based on my perception of their public personae. I named my characters after the pseudonyms used on the first Traveling Wilburys album. Because of this, I can say:

This book is a work of fiction. Characters and incidents are the product of the author's imagination or are used fictitiously.

I have obtained permission to use photos whenever possible. In some cases, I was unable to obtain permission. If the owners of those photos would contact me, I would be most grateful.

## Acknowledgements

Volumes of gratitude are extended to my beta readers:
Clifford Jordan, Robert Cook, Robert Mackey, Jon Baril,
Michael Patrick Kirwan, and Christine Karper-Smith.
Cover Designer & Artwork: Kyle Lechner
Editors: Shannon Winton (content), Brian Paone (line)
Proofreader and copy editor: Samantha Hamilton
Special thanks to Jeff Slate, who took time out of his busy
schedule to help an independent author.

This book is dedicated to the fans of
Otis
Nelson
Lefty
Charlie T, Jnr.
& Lucky

in both universes.

Every word was written with love, respect and admiration
for the five Wilburys in Pam Van Allen's universe.

# TABLE OF CONTENTS

# FOREWORD
## FOR READERS UNFAMILIAR WITH THE TRAVELING WILBURYS

In 1988, five famous musicians who were already friends came together to record an album—George Harrison, Bob Dylan, Tom Petty, Roy Orbison, and Jeff Lynne. Many of you are familiar with some or all of them individually, but you may not know that together, they formed a group called the Traveling Wilburys.

Perhaps because of their fame, the Wilburys chose to issue their album under pseudonyms, posing as sons of the notoriously fertile Charlie T. Wilbury. They became Nelson, Lucky, Charlie T. Jnr., Lefty, and Otis for their first album of heartland rock. Reuniting in 1990, they recorded another album but changed their aliases again, possibly in recognition of the loss of Roy Orbison.

If you haven't heard these albums, they are worth any music lover's time to seek out.

Pam Van Allen
December 2018

## A NOTE FROM THE NARRATOR:

Horseshit is the name of this game. A passel of facts tenuously linked together by long intervals of horseshit make up this story. If you have a hankering for the real story of the Traveling Wilburys, don't buy this book. If you enjoy an amusing bit of fiction intertwined with truth, read on. Keep in mind, this story is only fiction in your universe. In my world, it all happened, just like I'm telling it. You hold in your hands a work of partial truth, according to the definitions of your universe.

My name is Mavis Wilbury, a female member of the family. I don't know much about making music, but I love listening to it.

I compiled this book from numerous sources. I had the opportunity to conduct several interviews in my universe, mostly with Otis and Charlie T., Jnr. I grieved when cousin Charlie T. passed away while I was writing. Lefty passed away before I ever spoke with him. I only met Nelson in my universe on a couple of occasions, and that was before I started the book. Nelson departed this lifetime before I could interview him specifically for the project; although, we did talk about the Traveling Wilburys once. Lucky allowed me to interview him briefly only once.

People who reviewed the early drafts of this book said I'm not a skilled interviewer. They said I didn't have a clear idea of why I was talking to the Wilbury brothers, and I didn't ask them the right questions. I don't have a journalism degree or anything fancy, but I wanted to tell the story of how my distant cousins congregated and made a really good album. I figured the best way to do that was to ask them and put all their stories in a book.

The Traveling Wilburys got together and did something spontaneous and real that is rare in the music business. They didn't even know if they could release their album because they didn't go around and ask permission from their respective record companies beforehand. The half-brothers made music together for the love of the music and the love of each other. I thought that story should be told while those that remember it are still around.

Woven throughout the narrative are the results of the interviews. Some of the conversations are reproduced word for word. Everything I recorded in my universe, you would call "fiction." So what's fact in my world is fiction in yours, and vice versa. Got it?

Information from a number of books, magazine articles, and YouTube interviews went into the research for the book. You would call this "nonfiction" because it came from your universe. Especially helpful was the wonderful Genesis publication *The Traveling Wilburys, Deluxe Edition* (2009). Check out the bibliography if you want the origins for the "true" parts of the story.

Remember, the events take place in an alternate universe to the one where I'm releasing the book. The characters have different names and abilities, but their personal histories match up reasonably well with the people you know in your universe. There are clearly deviations; consider them literary license.

Why did I release my book in your universe instead of mine? Simple. I didn't want to get my ass sued. Besides, I didn't want to have to explain how I know certain things because Wilbury powers are kept secret. On your side, it's just a nice, made-up story, right?

I figured if I came through a portal and published a book about people who don't live here, no one would care. You don't need to know anything about the portals, so don't ask. Refer to the following table to determine who a person from my universe resembles in your universe. The "Legends" are shown in bold type.

Cast of Characters

| Alternate Universe | Your Universe |
| --- | --- |
| **Nelson Wilbury** | **George Harrison** |
| **Lucky Wilbury** | **Bob Dylan** |
| **Charlie T. Wilbury, Jnr.** | **Tom Petty** |
| **Otis Wilbury** | **Jeff Lynne** |
| **Lefty Wilbury** | **Roy Orbison** |
| Lefty Wilbury, Jr. | Roy Orbison, Jr. |
| Buster Sidebury | Jim Keltner |
| Ayrton Wilbury | Dhani Harrison |
| Bill | Bill Bottrell |
| Jane Wilbury | Jane Benyo Petty |
| Bugs | Alan "Bugs" Weidel |
| Carolyn | Carolyn Dennis |
| Desiree | Desiree Dennis-Dylan |
| Ray Sidebury | Ray Cooper |
| Ian Sidebury | Ian Wallace |
| Barbara Wilbury | Barbara Jakobs Orbison |
| Olivia Wilbury | Olivia Arias Harrison |
| Sandi Wilbury | Sandi Kapelson Lynne |
| Richard | Richard Dodd |
| Jim Sidebury | Jim Horn |
| Don | Don Smith |
| Neal | Neal Preston |

In my universe, there are legions of Wilburys. Buried deep within the Wilbury gene is the potential to perform magical feats, but some event of intense power must activate the ability. About one percent of Wilbury descendants encounter such an event in the course of their lives, so magic remains uncommon. Magically enabled Wilburys hide their powers from the public because folks tend to fear and misunderstand the various abilities that have arisen in the family. Most people in my world don't even know about our gifts. Wilburys have maintained it as a closely guarded family secret, although rumors abound when some Wilbury accidentally displays an amazing talent.

Where I'm from, people don't think anything about there being five famous musicians named Wilbury. It's similar to the name Smith of your world. In our universe, we don't assume Wilburys are closely related, just as you don't assume Smiths are.

Their father's traveling explained why the half-brothers hadn't met until they had each become famous. Stepfathers raised the brothers in separate families in widely scattered locations. Admiration of each other's work led them to locate the other artists and discover the family relationships. They wouldn't have become friends unless they found each other simpatico.

Before making the Wilburys album, the half-brothers worked together in pairs or triads on various projects and tours, but all five had never come together. The Traveling Wilburys was an organic event that jelled naturally as a result of respect, love, and friendship. No universe will ever experience its like again.

Mavis Wilbury
December 2018

# CHAPTER 1

## WHEN WE WAS FAB

"Me and you should be in a group," Nelson remarked to Otis, out of nowhere.

Nelson relaxed with Otis in his home studio at Friar Park, near Henley-on-Thames, fifty miles outside London. Lounging in Nelson's opulent studio, they listened to the playback of "When We Was Fab" for Nelson's upcoming album, *Cloud Nine*.

Otis and Nelson had written "Fab" during a trip to Australia about Nelson's time as a member of The Beatles. It was a humorous take on the drawbacks of being one of the most famous people in the world.

A few years earlier, Otis had become disaffected with his group, the Electric Light Orchestra. Touring was a nightmare. ELO studio work, which Otis used to love, had become a grind. He had fulfilled his record contract and dissolved the band. Otis was now an independent record producer for other acts. He had worked with Dave Edmunds and the Everly Brothers. A massive Beatles fan in his youth, he never imagined producing an ex-Beatle.

Otis took a hit off the sweet-smelling, tightly rolled joint. "Great idea. Who should we have in it?" Smoke leaked out his mouth.

"Lucky Wilbury."

The music industry regarded Lucky as the greatest singer-songwriter of the twentieth century. His songs ranged from "Blowin' in the Wind" to "Like a Rolling Stone." The thought of being in a group with Lucky was almost inconceivable. Otis looked at Nelson through an inner haze of marijuana and beer. He decided to play along.

"Then can we have Lefty Wilbury too?"

"I love his songs 'Only the Lonely' and 'Pretty Woman.' Lefty and me go way back. All the way to the sixties, when he opened for us. We'll ask him."

Otis marveled again at what Nelson could accomplish. He scored them backstage access at countless gigs; it made his brain reel.

"We can't leave out our other half-brother, Charlie T., Jnr., or he'll have a fit." Otis dissolved into giggles.

"No shit." Nelson sniggered. "Let's call ourselves the Trembling Wilburys," Their name "Wilbury" had become an in-joke between them with remarks in the studio like: "**We'll bury** these bloody mistakes in the mix."

"Oh, naw, not Trembling. That would mean we're scared … We ain't scared. Tell you what, though. We travel back and forth across the ocean all the time. And our dad, Charlie Truscott, Snr., travelled in his day too. He must have gotten around, fathering so many children in far-flung places. So you see, traveling is a family … thing. I think we should be the Traveling Wilburys."

"Let's keep that in mind." Nelson sighed contentedly and took another hit.

Otis Wilbury told me this version of the Traveling Wilburys' incarnation. He has repeated it to several interviewers. I was astonished at how differently the other Wilburys saw the origin of their group.

I was lucky to score an interview with Lucky Wilbury. Few authors ever manage such a feat. He had agreed to the meeting when he heard my surname. I recounted the Traveling Wilburys founding story which Otis had told me.

"What a bullshit story. That isn't what happened at all." Lucky stared me in the eye. "Nelson contacted me by psychic means, asking to use my recording studio. Then Otis and Nelson parachuted into my yard. It's a fucking miracle they didn't land in the Pacific Ocean, because I live in Malibu, but I saw Otis shooting lightning from his fingers to guide their descent. Nelson hung onto his legs. Lefty arrived in his red classic Corvette, wearing those crimson loafers, and Charlie T., Jnr. arrived in his black Corvette, wearing onyx cowboy boots. I always thought it was funny how their shoes matched their cars."

"I don't understand what you mean by 'psychic means,'" I said, puzzled.

"You know." Lucky waved his hands in the air. "Telepathy! You know that thing Nelson can do with his mind? He goes into a trance, and next thing you know, you can hear his voice in your mind. And usually you have to do whatever the fuck he wants."

Charlie T., Jnr. had a different version when I interviewed him a few weeks later at his compound in Malibu.

"Those guys are all a bunch of liars." Charlie T., Jnr. smiled his easy smile and flashed his sky-blue eyes. "Let me tell you what really happened. The Traveling Wilburys were all my idea. Otis and I were recording my album, *Full Moon Fever*. You know, the album that sold over six million copies, more than any of my half-brothers' records."

"*All Things Must Pass* sold more than *Full Moon Fever*," I interjected.

"What? Well, okay, maybe *All Things Must Pass* sold a couple more copies than *Full Moon Fever*. Anyway, Otis and I were working on my album, and the other brothers asked to be on it, except Lucky. He was busy. We thought we sounded good together. The part about using Lucky's garage studio is true. That was when he wanted to play with us too, because we were up at his house, you see. He didn't want to be left out. I predicted our act would be huge. *The Traveling Wilburys Vol. 1* sold more copies than any of Lucky's albums, and he will eventually release eighty-eight of them."

Lefty Wilbury, Jr. graciously agreed to a brief interview when I dropped by his recording studio in Nashville. I recounted the yarns the others had woven for me.

Lefty, Jr. shook his head. "You know my dad loved all those guys so much, and it meant so much to him to work with them right before he passed away. But they can't keep a story straight to save their lives. Otis was working on Dad's album, *Mystery Girl*, not Charlie T.'s album, when it all came about. Nelson came into town, and the three of them were out to dinner during a break in recording. Nelson said he needed a new song for the flipside of his upcoming single and asked Otis if he would help. They hoped to use Lucky's garage studio the next day."

"Then what happened?" I asked.

"My dad said, 'Well, if you do anything tomorrow, give me a call. I'd love to come by.' Nelson's guitar was at Charlie T.'s house, and he just tagged along."

The fullest account came from Nelson. Perhaps his rings with the most truth.

Nelson's face wore a bemused smile. "Look, this is the way it really happened. The record company said to me about 'This is Love,' 'If you don't have your extended version, then you've gotta give 'em another song.' "So I didn't have an extended version or another song. So I just thought, *The easiest thing is I'll just write a tune and do it tomorrow.* Because it doesn't matter. It's not the A-side. It's not even the B-side. It's the C-side. It's just the third extra one.

"I had dinner that night with Lefty and Otis. So I said to Otis over dinner, 'Look, tomorrow I'm just going to go into the studio and make up a tune and knock it out quick and do it for this thing. Do you want to come and help?'

"Otis said, 'Sure. The problem, though, is going to be getting a studio and an engineer at this short notice.'

"Otis and I went to his house and contacted his previous engineer, Bill. Otis said, 'He's so busy now, you can never get ahold of him.' I said, 'Let me call him.' I called him and he says, 'Fine, I'll come.'

"I phoned Lucky up and he … I mean, sometimes you can phone him and not get through for years, but he picked up on the first ring, and he said, 'Sure, come on over.' I mean, it must have been karma.

"My guitar was at Charlie T.'s house. I went down there, and I said, 'I'm going to do this tune tomorrow.' And he said, 'Oh, great. I was wondering what I was going to do. I'll come along.' So that's it. I just started the tune the next morning, got a few chords. Then we went over to Lucky's.[1]

"Anything anybody else told you about how the Traveling Wilburys got started is horseshit."

---

[1] Quotes from an interview on February 10, 1990 - *Classic Albums* radio by Roger Scott.

# CHAPTER 2

## HANDLE WITH CARE

Nelson was accustomed to getting up early to meditate, but Charlie T., Jnr. enjoyed sleeping late. When Nelson rang the bell at Charlie T.'s Beverly Hills home at 7:30, he was still in bed. His wife Jane answered the door.

"Okay, I'm up," could be heard from down the hall. Shouts of "Shit! God damn it!" followed. Nelson strode down the hall, not waiting to be invited. He caught Charlie T. yanking on a pair of jeans.

"Why we gotta get there so fucking early?" Charlie T. whined.

"Because Lucky told us to arrive at nine, with breakfast. Not everyone keeps rock star hours."

"Is Otis going back to working on my album after we finish this? I can't be putting off the Heartbreakers for too long while I work on this solo album with Otis."

"Yeah, Charlie. This is a one-and-done and you and Otis can get back to it. Just get dressed so we can go. You know how pissy Lucky is when people are late." Nelson snorted. "Course Lucky's late to everything."

The front doorbell rang again.

Nelson said, "That'll be Lefty."

Charlie T. ran a comb through his long blond hair. "Nelson, this ain't gonna be as one-and-done as you think."

"Huh? Why do you say that? It's just a song for an obscure European release. Wait, you're getting something about the future, aren't you?"

"Gotta brush my teeth."

"Charlie T., you can't leave me hanging."

Charlie brushed past Nelson and closed the bathroom door.

Lefty came down the hall. "Got your guitar?"

"Not yet. Jane, where does Charlie have my guitar?"

Jane produced Nelson's guitar from the foyer closet.

Charlie T. exited the bathroom. "We can take my car."

"I want to take my car too," Lefty said. "I just got this new 'Vette, and it'll be fun to drive it on the PCH." He looked back and forth from Nelson to Lefty. "There's no back seat."

Charlie nodded. "Okay, then. I'm takin' my 'Vette too. We'll be the 'Vette brigade."

Nelson smiled. "I'll ride with Charlie T."

Lucky specified waffles for breakfast. Charlie T., Jnr. suggested Roscoe's House of Chicken and Waffles on Gower Street in Hollywood. They served sweet-potato pie that tasted the same as his grandma used to bake. Charlie T. was a Southerner, like Lefty. Otis was born in Birmingham, England, and Nelson was born in Liverpool. Lucky was born in Minnesota. Their father, Charlie T. Snr., never stayed in one place for very long.

Three Wilbury brothers walked into Roscoe's Chicken and Waffles at 8:15 a.m. They found seats and looked at the menu.

"They have chicken sausage," Charlie T. said. "Get that. And eggs with cheese and onions."

Everyone groaned as Lefty sang "Cheese and Onions" from the Eric Idle film, *All You Need is Cash*. Eric Idle was a member of the Monty Python comedy troupe. Lefty loved that film as much as he loved the entire Monty Python canon. The movie depicted a group called The

Rutles which poked fun at Nelson's first group, The Beatles. Nelson had made a cameo appearance, playing a television interviewer discussing theft from The Rutles's business.

Neil Innes, a member of the Bonzo Dog Doo-Dah Band, and friend to Pythons, had written the songs for *All You Need Is Cash*. Neil intended these songs to sound a great deal like Beatles songs. Even Nelson was taken aback by the similarity at first. He chanted "Instant karma's gonna get you" at Eric a few times before calming down and agreeing the songs were both funny and good.

The Beatles didn't own the rights to most of their songs by 1988. The rights to the Lennon/McCartney songs had passed to ATV Music, a subsidiary of Sony Music. ATV Music sued Neil for the close similarities and won. He had to give 50% of his profits from The Rutles songs to ATV Music, as if ATV music hadn't made enough money already by acquiring the songs from Lennon/McCartney.

Lefty sang the first verse to "Cheese and Onions" gleefully. It was a pastiche of several Beatles songs, most notably "A Day in the Life."

Nelson punched Charlie T. lightly on the arm. "Now see what you've done."

Charlie looked around ruefully. "I know. Kill me now. We can't afford to have the roof fall on us."

One of the wooden columns in Roscoe's creaked loudly.

Lefty raised his rolling baritone, while planting his hands palm-down on the table. A thin crack formed down the side of the column. The waitress approached the table, and Lefty stopped singing.

"This order is to go," Nelson said. "It's for eight or nine people."

"We don't do catering." She looked up from her order pad into Nelson's face. "Oh my God. You're Nelson Wilbury."

Nelson smiled his most charming Beatle smile. "Will you do a catering order for me? You see, we're making a record, and we have a lot of people to feed."

"I'll have to go ask." The waitress scanned the table and spotted Charlie T., Jnr. "Are you Charlie T. Wilbury? I love your song 'Refugee.'"

Charlie T. smiled his most charming Heartbreaker smile. "Could you take our order first before you go ask? We're kinda in a hurry."

The waitress nodded and stood ready with her pen. She spotted Lefty and dropped the pen. "Are you Lefty Wilbury? I used 'Pretty Woman' in my wedding ceremony." She bent over to retrieve the ballpoint as Nelson eyed her behind.

Roscoe's was accustomed to celebrities, having been located a few blocks from Hollywood and Vine for more than thirteen years. But the likes of Nelson, Lefty, and Charlie T. Wilbury usually didn't walk in together.

The manager came out to get autographs. The brothers sighed, smiled, and signed all around. They'd do anything to get Lucky his waffles.

Roscoe's packed them up a mess of waffles, two sweet-potato pies, a bunch of chicken sausage, fried eggs with cheese and onions, biscuits and gravy, and corn bread in to-go containers. The waitress packed tiny tubs of butter and maple syrup in plastic bags too. Of course, it wasn't cheap, but it still cost less than renting a studio.

Nelson journeyed in Charlie T.'s Corvette, and Lefty followed in his 'Vette. Otis and their engineer, Bill, had pursued a separate errand in Otis's Mercedes. They arrived severally at Lucky's, laden with food.

Bill and Bugs, Charlie T.'s roadie, carried the plastic bags of food into the mansion. Lucky's cook, Carla, met them at the kitchen door. She began unpacking the bags of food.

"Oh my Lord, you boys brought everything on the menu!"

Charlie T. indignantly corrected her. "We didn't bring any collard greens."

Carla frowned. "How many people you expecting?"

"How many people here are eating?" Charlie T. rejoined.

"Just Mr. Lucky and Ms. Carolyn."

"That makes eight."

"Mr. Lucky don't like to have a houseful of people."

Nelson patted her behind. "So we'll be gone before he has a chance to get crabby about it."

Carla smirked at him.

Driving from Roscoe's to Malibu in traffic consumed a solid hour. The food cooled on the trip, and the task of heating it fell to Carla. She brought a couple of pots of coffee to the dining room. Otis's errand was stopping at Ralph's for orange juice, which Carla put on the table.

Lucky sauntered into the kitchen. "You motherfuckers are late."

"Breakfast is here," Nelson announced, ignoring Lucky's criticism. "Thanks for coming, you lot."

An African-American woman walked into the dining room. "Hi, I'm Carolyn. I'm so pleased to meet you, Nelson. Lucky talks about you all the time."

Nelson shook her hand, and Charlie T. held out his hand. "I was with Lucky in Australia the night your baby was born. Congratulations on your marriage."

Carolyn was taken aback. "Nobody is supposed to know about the baby or our marriage."

Charlie T. tilted his head and flashed his crooked smile. "I toured with Lucky for two years. It's hard to keep a secret on the road."

Lucky chimed in. "I never told you about the baby or getting married."

Charlie T. shot a shut-the-hell-up expression at Lucky. "I sussed it, man. You know."

Lucky stared at Charlie T. for a long moment. "Oh, you mean you used your powers and saw my future. It's okay. Carolyn knows about the Wilbury powers. She's cool. Why didn't you ever tell me you knew? It's hard keeping secrets from your brothers."

"I'm telling you now, okay?"

Back in the kitchen, Carla wiped her forehead with a dishrag as she took a pan of waffles from the oven and slid in another one. "You coulda got breakfast burritos at Lily's in Malibu and not made me work so hard," Carla grumbled.

"Lucky wanted waffles," Nelson objected.

Carolyn laughed. "Lucky was fucking with you. Don't you know him well enough by now?"

Everyone sat down to breakfast.

Bugs looked at Nelson. "So what's the plan?"

Nelson chewed a mouthful of cornbread. He tried to keep to a vegetarian diet whenever one was available. Belief in reincarnation discouraged one from eating other sentient beings, like chickens.

Otis chimed in. "Nelson has part of a song written. We have to finish writing the song and record it, all in one day. We need acoustic and lead guitar, bass, drums and percussion. We have to hear the song before we know what else we need."

"That seems like a tall order," Bugs observed.

Nelson swallowed his cornbread. "We can do it."

Bill wolfed down his breakfast and opened the garage door to survey the equipment Lucky had collected. All sorts of odds and ends were piled helter-skelter, including a twenty-four-track tape recorder, a small mixing board, and some assorted recording gear he had bought off Dave Stewart of the Eurythmics when Dave had upgraded his home studio. Most of it lay in disarray on the garage floor or in shelves and cabinets. A makeshift sound booth stood in the corner.

Otis hurriedly finished breakfast and joined Bill to piece together a recording studio from the disparate parts.

On April 5, 1988, five music legends sat on the grass at Lucky Wilbury's Malibu mansion under the California sun—or four music legends and Otis Wilbury. Otis hadn't quite achieved his legendary status, but he was well on his way. Nelson, Lefty, and Charlie T. Wilbury already thought of him as a legend. Lucky didn't know him from jack.

Charlie T. informed Otis he would ascend to full legendary status when he produced the final Beatles songs. Otis looked at him like he was crazy.

"There ain't gonna be any more Beatles songs. John's dead."

"You'll see," was all Charlie T. would say.

Nelson played the chords he had written and hummed the rudimentary tune. "That's all I have so far. Now let's write the rest."

"What's this song called?" Lucky asked. "What's it about?"

Nelson scanned the yard and spotted a tour crate sitting just inside the garage with an orange sticker pasted across it. He read off the sticker. "It's called 'Handle with Care.'"

Lucky nodded. "That's a good name. I like that."

"Let's start off with a bit of violence." Nelson improvised the first line.

Otis added a line.

"Yea!" The line was a winner!

Lyrics started flying through the air like cannonballs.

"If I love you, will you come around?"

Everyone shouted, "Nay!" No one liked that line.

"From the mountainside, my love resounds."

"Nay!"

"It's just a flesh wound!" Lefty yelled; he loved quoting Monty Python.

"That doesn't even rhyme," reproved Charlie T.

"Let's go to your place and fool around."

"Nay!"

Charlie T. suggested a line about a woman who was the "best thing."

"Yea!"

Nelson contributed what became the tagline for the song.

"I think we've exhausted the 'ound sound," pronounced Nelson. "Let's try a different verse."

"You are so chimerical," Lucky suggested.

"What the bloody hell does that even mean?" Nelson asked.

"Your question is rhetorical." Lucky didn't like it when people questioned his lyrics. He had also found a rhyme for "chimerical," a superpower in itself.

"Nay!"

"This jacket is affordable," "But, baby, you're desirable," and "Your boobs are so remarkable," were all rejected.

Lefty couldn't resist any longer. He had resumed quoting Monty Python. "'I have a very gweat fwiend in Wome called Biggus Dickus'"

Lefty continued in the worst British accent anyone had ever heard. "'He has a wife, you know? You know what she's called? She's called 'Incontinentia.' 'Incontinentia Buttocks.'"

"Knock it off, Lefty," Charlie T. scolded. "We're trying to work here."

Lefty looked crestfallen. "We had enough lines that ended in 'able. Just thought I'd interject a little humor." Lefty belted a song from *Monty Python's Spamalot* in his rolling, resonant tenor. A bird dropped from the air, dead. Lefty's singing had stopped its little heart.

Otis looked at the casualty and whistled. "This bird has flown."

Lefty saw the dead bird as an opportunity to quote a plethora of Python in his terrible British accent. "'He's off the twig! He's kicked the bucket; he's shuffled off this mortal coil, run down the curtain and joined the bleedin' choir invisible! *This is an ex-parrot!*'" Lefty let loose one of his high-pitched giggles.

Charlie T. and Otis laughed too.

Nelson tried to distract Lefty from the Python skit. "I know the *Spamalot* song." Nelson sang and Lefty joined in, a bit more softly. Everyone else rolled their eyes.

"Lefty really does have the best voice in the world," Otis observed, "even if he's singing silly Monty Python songs with it. Let's write a lonely bit just for him. How about this?"

Otis sang new words in a Lefty-like tune.

Nelson grinned. "That sounds like something Lefty would sing." He turned to Lefty. "Lefty, sing this bit for us."

"How does it go? I was busy humming 'Always Look on the Bright Side of Life' from *Monty Python's Life of Brian*, so I didn't hear it."

Otis sang the part for Lefty again, and Lefty belted it right out. A huge branch fell off the tree behind them when he hit the longest note.

"Gotta remember not to sit under any trees when Lefty sings," muttered Nelson.

"Jesus, Lefty, how do you keep from literally bringing down the house when you do concerts?" Charlie T. asked.

"Well, my sound technician sets up the mics and the boards so it filters out the frequency that does the most damage. If I don't sing at full volume, it doesn't happen either, so I don't sing loud at concerts. The only time I sing at full volume is on recording takes. Funny the recordings of my voice don't break stuff, isn't it? We always have the filters on."

"Me and Bill will have to figure out the settings, but we don't want you destroying Lucky's house. Can you tell us the frequency?" Otis asked.

"Oh, sure. We might have to call my engineer for the details."

Lucky spoke up. "Let's get back to writing this song. Now, we need to follow that Lefty part with something less pretentious." Lucky snapped his fingers, trying to think of the next line. "So far the theme has been getting help in sticky situations."

Charlie T. chimed in with a line about leaning on somebody.

Nelson enthused, "Okay, that's good. Now where do we go?"

"I've been fucked up, and I've been fooled." Otis started the next verse.

Nelson immediately objected. "Wait, this is going on a single. You can't put 'fuck' in it."

"Well, why not? I had a song played on the radio in the seventies that had 'fucking' in it."

Lefty sang "I Bet You They Won't Play This Song on the Radio" from the *Monty Python's Contractual Obligation* album, complete with sound effects. Everyone ignored him.

Nelson raised his voice to speak over Lefty. "That's only because the radio presenters couldn't understand what the fuck you were saying—you had your voice so drowned out by the violins and cellos and synthesizers and shit."

Otis looked a little hurt, hunching his shoulders and frowning. "Then say 'fobbed off' instead of 'fucked up.'"

"What's 'fobbed off' mean?" Lucky asked. "I swear, I don't know what you British guys are talking about half the time."

"It means to trick someone in order to cheat them," Otis explained. "I don't think it's British slang."

Lefty stopped singing.

Lucky frowned. "Well, I never heard it before."

Nelson interrupted. "Let's just write these lyrics."

A few more lines flew through the air, followed by "Yea" or "Nay." All five together sang the chorus line.

"That was easy," Lefty said. "Now for another verse."

Lyrics once again filled the late spring morning. Lines like "So many times I've been chastised," "I had a woman much despised," and "It's a pain in the ass being idolized" were rejected.

The songwriters got into a bit of a tiff when Lucky introduced "You'd wanna see me paralyzed" as a suggestion.

"Didn't you already use that one, Lucky?" Charlie T. looked over at Lucky suspiciously. He had toured with Lucky as leader of his backing band for two years and knew most of the words to his songs.

"So what? It's still a good line," Lucky said defensively, frowning and squinting his eyes.

"You cannot just reuse a line, especially a line from a song as famous as that one." Charlie T. wasn't surrendering to Lucky.

"Who says I can't reuse my own lines? I thought of 'em! I can reuse 'em if I want!"

"You aren't the only one writing this song. It's going on Nelson's record. Maybe he doesn't want a plagiarized line in his song," Charlie T. said gently but firmly.

"You're saying I plagiarized?" Lucky was increasingly indignant.

"Nay!" Lefty yelled, thinking Lucky had offered another line.

Nelson extended his arms to curb the heated discussion. "We've got enough good lines for the third verse anyway. Where shall we go from here, Lucky?"

Lucky forgot all about the fight once Nelson appealed to his lyrical talents.

They tossed around a few more lyrics. Lucky excused himself to check on the baby and returned with a couple of new verses.

"How'd you write that so quick?" Nelson asked.

The group accepted one verse in full and rejected part of another as "too Lucky." Charlie T. finished Lucky's final verse with a flourish about the smell of success.

"Yea!"

All five repeated the single tagline together.

"Okay, we've got the lyrics done," Nelson proclaimed. He looked at Otis. "We're producing this thing. Now what?"

"Now we lay down backing tracks. We're in a hurry, so we'll have to play most of the instruments at once instead of layering them like I usually do."

"No problem."

Lucky broke in on the producers. "We aren't going to sing at the same time too?"

"No, it's my record," Nelson answered. "I'm singing it. Except for that bit Otis and I wrote for Lefty."

Otis tapped Nelson on the shoulder and pointed to a corner of the resplendent garden. "Can I see you over there?"

The half-brothers approached the wall, out of earshot from the others.

"Okay, what do you want?" Nelson asked.

Otis whispered to Nelson, "Look, we've got some of the best singers in the world here. Lucky was number seven on *Rolling Stone's* Best Singers of All Time list, and Lefty was number thirteen."

"They rated Lucky higher than Lefty? No way! Lefty is the best singer in the world! Who was number one?"

"Aretha Franklin."

"Where were we on the list?"

"We weren't on it."

"Then it's a bollocks list anyway, but I get your point. We need to use everyone we've got."

"Who sings what?" Otis asked.

Nelson thought a moment. "Lefty sings that bit we wrote for him, and everybody sings the second bridge Charlie T. and Lucky wrote. We'll feature Lucky and Charlie T. on the first line the first time and then you and Lefty on the first line the second time."

"Isn't it a little cheeky to make Lefty sing when he just thought he was coming to watch?"

Nelson laughed. "We'll make him sing to thank me for mortgaging Friar Park so the Pythons could make *Life of Brian*."

"Sounds like a plan."

Otis and Nelson returned to the rest of the group with big self-satisfied grins on their faces.

"Let's go record some music," Otis said.

"First, let's have lunch," Lucky suggested.

Carla served a lavish lunch of bar-b-cued chicken, beans, and salad. Carolyn and the baby joined them.

"When did you two get married?" Nelson asked, being the only one with balls enough to bring it up.

"You know, man, it's a total secret we're married, so I'd appreciate it if no one mentioned it."

Everyone sitting around the table shook their heads.

"Oh, no. Very hush-hush like," Otis said.

"What's the baby's name?" Lefty asked.

"Desiree Gabrielle," Lucky answered.

"Oh, that's pretty." Southerners always said "Oh, that's pretty" when you asked a baby's name and a girl's name was given. "How old is she?" Lefty continued the baby conversation.

Carolyn answered this time. "She turned two in February."

"Wow, they are really fun at that age," Lefty said, still following the script for Southerners while discussing babies. "I never had any daughters. All I ever had were sons." Lefty shifted a saddened gaze to the table top.

Nelson asked again, "When did you say you got married?"

Lucky drilled Nelson with a glare. "We got married five months after she was born, okay?"

Nelson laughed. "That's no biggie. I married my old lady a month after our son was born."

Otis laughed too. "My wife was five months pregnant when I married her."

Charlie T. chimed in. "Mine was pregnant when we got married, except we didn't know it. That future escaped my vision."

Lefty looked around the table. "Am I the only one here who knows anything about birth control?"

Nelson smiled. "Our dad, Charlie T., Snr., obviously didn't, and it's a damn good thing or we wouldn't all be here."

Lunch was over, and the brothers were ready to record. They had only brought electric guitars, but they also needed acoustics.

"Lucky, do you have a couple of acoustics and a bass around here?" Otis asked.

"I want the chiming sound that comes out of a twelve-string acoustic," Nelson said.

"I've got a nice twelve-string, but I get to play it," Lucky replied and went to his music rooms to rummage around. Lefty and Charlie T. followed him.

The three returned with a Fender twelve-string, a Fender bass, and a Gibson J-50 acoustic.

"May I play the J-50?" Lefty asked. "It's just like one of mine."

Charlie T. surveyed the room. "We don't have any drums or anybody to play bass. We gotta have some rhythm on this track."

Otis took command of the problem. "Don't worry, Charlie. Who's the professional producer here? We'll play to a click, and then I'll put the drums and bass in later. You know how I work by now. How many of your songs have I produced so far?"

Charlie T. glowered at Otis. "Five."

"And they were bloody brilliant, weren't they? 'Free Fallin',' huh? 'I Won't Back Down,' what?"

Charlie T. looked at the floor. "Yeah, they're brilliant."

"Otis, I'll do the lead and your rhythm guitar first pass," Nelson suggested. "You can handle the bass now."

Otis didn't bat an eye. He tossed his guitar to Nelson, who caught it by the neck. Lucky tuned the twelve-string.

Lefty didn't buy it so easily. "How's Nelson going to play two guitars at the same time?"

Charlie T. chuckled. "You ain't recorded with Nelson before, have you? Watch this."

Another pair of arms snaked out from beneath Nelson's jacket. He tuned both guitars simultaneously.

"If he'd ever done that in public, *Rolling Stone* would have rated him higher than eleventh on the Greatest Guitar Players of All Time," Otis observed.

Nelson looked up from tuning. "Otis, why are you so concerned with those *Rolling Stone* lists?"

"I guess because I'm not on any of them." Otis stuck out his tongue.

"Everyone knows *Rolling Stone* hates prog rock. Think nothing of it," Charlie T. said.

"ELO wasn't really prog rock, not after *Eldorado*. It was classical pop, then disco, then synths."

Charlie T. snorted. "Well, you got pigeonholed, didn't you? *Rolling Stone* also hated ELO because they thought you were candy-ass Beatles imitators. Is your bass in tune?"

Otis almost railed at the accusation of being a Beatles imitator, but thought better of it. It wasn't Charlie T. leveling the charge, and it was passé by now.

Otis ran the fingers of his right hand once across the strings of his electric bass. Small sparks emitted from his fingers. "It is now," he said. He plugged into the direct box with the XLR cable.

Nelson came to Otis's defense. "Otis wasn't a Beatles imitator. ELO carried on where The Beatles had left off. John even called them 'sons of Beatles,' which he meant as a huge compliment. Otis did things with ELO we never managed, and we had George Martin, who was classically trained, helping us. Otis was the sole songwriter and producer. Don't you ever bring up that Beatles imitator shit again. Besides, everyone imitated us."

Nelson fingered a strand of Charlie T.'s long blond locks.

Charlie T. smiled and moved his head away. "Whoa, man. It ain't me. It's *Rolling Stone*. They're a bunch of elitist bastards with their heads up their ass anyway. You wait." Charlie T. looked off into space, above Nelson's head. "In thirty years, Rolling Stone's going to act like ELO hung the moon."

Otis smiled at Charlie T.'s psychic prediction; he hardly believed it, however. "My dad always said, 'Everything comes to him what waits.'"

Everyone else plugged in as necessary. Bill already set up mics for the acoustics.

Lucky watched Otis moving around the studio, preparing to produce and play on the recording at the same time. "You know, Otis, I worked with Mark Knopfler before as my producer on *Shot of Love*. He played guitar on a lot of the tracks, but he never sang or played more than one instrument."

Otis smiled at Lucky. "Well, I dunno. I like to really get inside the recording process. I've been playing multiple instruments, producing and singing on my own records since the late sixties. Don't know any other way to do it now." Otis glanced at Nelson for confirmation.

Nelson smiled as well. "That's how Otis adds his fairy dust. If he doesn't play at least three instruments and sing backing vocals or a bridge, the tracks won't sound nearly as good. Well, he doesn't always sing when he produces, but it's bloody unusual for him not to play a few instruments. I can't do what Otis does. Haven't you listened to *Cloud Nine*? You don't think I made that record sound so good? It was mostly Otis."

Otis dipped his head a little. "Thanks, mate."

Nelson rubbed his half-brother on the back. "It's high bloody time you started getting some recognition for your musical and production abilities."

Otis laughed. "Well, all them gold records go a long way."

Otis assumed his role as producer. He was no longer the underrated musical genius who had revolutionized pop in the 70s without anyone but his musical peers and an ever-shrinking fan base noticing. He was now the top working producer in the world, with a bag of tricks even crazy Phil Spector couldn't match.

Bill started the click track. *Click, click, click.* This would lay down the rhythm for the track in the absence of a drummer. Otis always used a click track, even when he had a drummer in the studio.

"Okay, then. Let's just run through it a couple of times. Then we'll do it for real."

Otis said, "After four ... Four!"

The first couple of bars sounded a bit ragged as the startled guitarists jumped in. Nelson handled both guitars with aplomb and grace while singing a guide vocal.

"Bridge ... Two, three, four, "Otis said. "Okay, second bridge ... Two, three, four. And stop. That was great. Now let's do it just like that with the tape running. One verse, bridge one, then bridge two."

Lucky was confused. "Otis, doesn't it have four verses? Aren't we going to repeat the bridge?"

"Yeah, but I can expand it to four verses from one."

Lucky shook his head. "I just don't work this way."

"This is much quicker and easier, and we're on a tight schedule. Bear with me, okay? It'll be fine." Otis smiled reassuringly.

"Otis, give us a real count in this time," Nelson said. "No larking about."

Otis snickered and started the tape. "Okay, no more clarting about. After four. One, two, three, four."

Everyone played their parts flawlessly.

Bill started the second tape recorder and ran the sound through the board. Otis pointed his finger toward the board and lightning shot from the end of the digit. All the instruments jumped out of their plugs. The clicking stopped. He pointed two fingers at the tape decks and the lightning effect repeated. The tape recorders ran so fast smoke came off them. The whole operation lasted about fifteen seconds.

Lucky jumped up. "What the fuck, man? That is some superpower. How'd you get that?"

Otis pulled the side of his beard with his thumb and forefinger. "In Birmingham, I went from a group called the Idle Race to The Move in '69, '70, something like that. I get mixed up about dates. I only joined because we planned to develop ELO, but The Move still had to deliver some records and play some shows before ELO could take off. The first concert we played, I walked up to the hot mic and touched my guitar neck to the mouthpiece, you know, to make sure the mic was properly earthed. I had this habit because I'd heard of a bloke who was actually killed by touching his mouth to an unearthed mic. Well, this fucker wasn't properly earthed, and it exploded. I was blown backward across the stage and landed on my arse. It melted them strings right off my guitar. Since that accident, I've been able to shoot electricity out of my fingers and control electronics with it. It's real handy in the studio 'cause I can work fast-like. Of course, it freaks most people out, so I keep it a secret. I caused some accidents when I first discovered my powers, but now I control it, no problem."

"What kind of accidents?" Lucky glanced sharply at Otis, concerned for his real estate.

Otis shrugged. "I shorted out the board during The Move's album *Looking On*. The whole desk had to be replaced. Woody—that's Roy Wood, not Woody Guthrie—made up a story about someone spilling a drink on the board and causing it to short, but I don't think they believed him. I've also burnt up a few microphones."

Lucky wasn't satisfied. "What do you mean 'burnt up?'"

"Just sparked them up too much so the wiring fried. I know how to do it now so it doesn't harm equipment." Lucky's concern dawned on him. "I've never set anything on fire."

Lucky nodded, reassured at last.

Bill had an appreciation for Otis's studio sorcery. "Otis is a real professional, Lucky. Don't worry, he won't tear up your stuff. I've made two albums with Otis. He knows exactly what he's doing, and things go much faster and easier because of his abilities."

Otis nodded his appreciation at Bill. "Okay, let's see what we got on this tape thing."

What they had was a backing track with a twelve-string guitar, an acoustic rhythm guitar, an acoustic lead guitar, two electric rhythm guitars, and a bass guitar. The track was three minutes and twelve seconds long. The backing for the four verses and two run-throughs of the two bridges were exactly in place.

"Everything but the drum track," Otis commented.

"Well, it might be nice to have a tambourine," Nelson remarked.

"And some bongos," Charlie T. added.

"I'll be damned," Lucky said.

"Yeah, isn't Otis something?" Lefty gushed.

Nelson pulled their attention back to the percussion. "I plan to call some Sideburys. They can come in tonight and finish up the percussion."

Sideburys are distant relations of Wilburys. They don't have a superpower gene, but they do flock to certain professions in unusually high numbers. One of those professions is studio musician.

"Who do you want to get?" Otis asked.

"You can play drums. I like Ray for tambourine, and he's in town. He usually has someone in tow for bongos."

"Sounds good. You gonna call now?"

"Yeah. Lucky, may I use the phone in the kitchen?"

"Be my guest."

While Nelson telephoned, everyone but Lefty relaxed on the grass with a beer and some grass. Lefty indulged in his favorite vice: Diet Cherry Coke, which Otis had scored for him at Ralph's. He didn't smoke weed at all and only drank alcohol occasionally. He had promised his wife he would quit smoking tobacco since his coronary artery bypass operation ten years earlier, but he still bummed drags off other people's cigarettes. Otis passed him a cigarette instead of the joint. Lefty's idea of indulging was "coke and a smoke."

Sundown was near, but these night owls could work late.

Nelson came outside and flopped next to Charlie T., who hogged the joint.

"Ray can be here in about an hour," Nelson reported. "Gimme that joint."

Back in the studio, Otis was in control again. The other four watched from outside the garage while Otis arranged the two vocal microphones to his liking. Sparks flickered freely while Otis set up mics, so the others gave him a wide berth. He pointed at a microphone cable, and it snaked into the proper plug accompanied by twinkles.

"Two mics for this, I think, Bill," Otis said. He pointed to another microphone cable, and it snaked into a plug.

Otis repositioned the microphones in the garage studio with a lazy, sparkling wave of his right hand. They flew across the room surrounded by an aura and settled into place.

"Okay, you can come in now," Otis called to his colleagues. "Who wants to test the mics?"

Bill ran from connection to connection to test the security of their contact.

Nelson approached the mic on the left. "Testing, one-two. A dinglederry dildo."

"Okay, that one's good. Now the other."

Bill had called Lefty's sound engineer and assembled the filters they needed from the assorted equipment in Lucky's garage. They were hopeful Lefty's voice would not wreak destruction.

Lefty stood next to the mic and sang softly, "*In dreams, I sleep with you.*"

"Nice, Lefty. Okay, got that adjusted. Now, let's run through the song."

Otis vaulted over the small board and took his place at the left mic. Nelson, as the lead singer, stood alone at the right mic. Bill perched behind the console to monitor the dials. Otis had written out the lyrics the brothers had composed in the afternoon. Everyone donned their headphones, and Bill initiated the tape that would record the vocal track.

Nelson sang out.

Bill gave a thumbs up to show the levels were holding.

Lefty sang the bridge specially composed for him.

The force coming from the console blew Bill backward off his chair. Lefty had cut loose with his full vocal power. It cracked the level monitor and shorted part of the console.

Otis sprinted to Bill to help him up. "You okay, mate?"

"Yeah, I'm okay. The force of his voice is just incredible! We'll have to compensate further for that in order to protect the equipment."

Lucky looked at his smoking console. "Can you fix it?"

Bill nodded. "No problem, I can fix it. I can reroute it right now so you guys can finish recording."

Nelson looked at Lefty, who studied the ceiling. "Has this happened before?"

"Uh, yeah. I've broken the glass on the control booth before and shorted out several boards."

Nelson smiled. "In-fucking-credible. Well, we want everything you got. Just give us the full monty when we're setting levels so we know what to expect." Nelson regarded the smoking equipment.

Lefty nodded. "Okay, I'll let you know when I'm gonna put the dog to it."

Otis approached the console and spread his fingers above it. "Allow me to reroute, Bill. I can be a bit quicker, I think."

Bill stepped back.

Otis closed his eyes and raised his chin. Electrical sparks shot from his fingers and danced over the console. Wires jumped from their sockets and into new ones. The console stopped smoking. The whole spectacle happened in seconds.

"Test it now, Bill."

Bill ran a few pulses through the lines. "It checks out. In fact, it works just like it did before. The only problem is that broken glass on the level monitor."

"I'll buy Lucky a new meter," Nelson said. "Production costs."

Bill ensconced himself behind the mixing desk again. "Lefty, if you'll just sing a few lines, this time at your usual level, I'll run through the set up." Bill set the input levels at their lowest.

This time Lefty sang the lines he would be singing for the song, a cappella, with his eyes closed, visible from the side of his dark glasses. As he sang, his feet lifted off the floor. He floated in midair and slowly twirled around. He completed the lines and sank down.

"That's very nice, Lefty, but can you hang on to the mic while you sing?" Otis asked. "We aren't going to get an even tone if you're turning around like that."

Lefty looked down at his feet. "Was I floating? That happens sometimes too. I put weights in my shoes to keep it from happening at live shows. That's why I stand so still during concerts."

Bill motioned to Otis. "We have to put Lefty on a separate mic and balance his vocal input in the mix."

Otis nodded. "Good idea." He pointed at a third mic and sparkled it into the corner of the garage. The cable snaked to the console and plugged itself in.

Bill checked the connections and levels. "Perfect."

Otis returned to his place at the mic with Charlie T. and Lucky. "Everyone ready?" He pointed to Bill to start the backing track.

Nelson sang the verses the brothers wrote earlier.

This time, the rehearsal went off without a hitch. Everyone came in at the right time. There was a tussle at the mic when Otis, Charlie T., and Lucky all sang the bridge. Otis settled it by moving to the end of the three, stepping backward and leaning in, since he was the tallest.

When Nelson finished singing the last verse, he said, "I'm happy with that. Is everyone happy with that?"

No one disagreed.

"Okay, let's record it."

Bill rewound the backing track and pressed the record switch on the second deck. The Wilbury brothers took their places at the mics. Nelson led off the singing, and the others came in on cue. Lefty floated a few inches off the ground with no spinning. He held on to the mic. When complete, they had a wonderful song.

Ray and Ian Sidebury had arrived while the Wilbury brothers were laying down the vocal tracks. They waited in the driveway until the take was complete. Nelson and Otis met them in front of the door.

"Great to see you lot again," Nelson said to Ray, giving him a warm hug. "Haven't seen you since we worked on *Cloud Nine*." He turned to Ian. "Who's this then?"

Ray returned Nelson's hug. "This is Ian, drummer extraordinaire. We've been hanging out in L.A., and when you said you needed someone for bongos, I knew he was your man. He's worked with Stevie Nicks and Don Henley. He also worked with your neighbor, Alvin Lee."

Ian nodded. "It's a genuine pleasure to meet you, Nelson," Ian said. "You too, Otis. "I'm a great admirer." Ian shook hands all around. "This is Lucky Wilbury's house, isn't it?"

Nelson nodded. "Yeah. Have you worked with him before?"

"On *Street Legal* and the 1979 Budokan residency. What an experience, even if the critics hated the live album."

"Fuck the critics," Nelson deadpanned.

Ian chuckled. "Who else is working on the record?"

"Charlie T. and Lefty Wilbury."

"Wow, what an honor."

Ray was more accustomed to Nelson's friends, since he was one of them. He got right down to business. "What's this song for?"

Nelson answered. "It's a C-side for 'This is Love,' the next single off *Cloud Nine*. Warner Brothers wants to put it out on a twelve-inch in Germany and the UK, and there needs to be a third song for it."

Ray nodded. "And what's the plan for percussion and drums?"

Otis took over. "It's a mid-tempo number, so I'll lay down a nice steady beat. There are two bridges, and I'll add some filler rolls when the song changes to the bridges. I like a hi-hat to match the click track."

Ray listened intently. "Got space for a bit of tambourine?"

Nelson smiled at his friend. "That's why I invited you here."

Ian leaned in. "And you specifically requested bongos."

Nelson kept a straight face. "Well, Charlie T. did, and it sounded like a good idea to me."

"How do you want 'em?" Ian was deadly serious about bongos.

Nelson looked him in the eye. "Not too loud."

Bugs and Bill unloaded the equipment from the van in the driveway and moved it into the garage. Bill assembled the drum kit according to Otis's instructions. Ray whispered to Ian not to be alarmed by Otis's powers; of course, as a Sidebury, Ian knew the tales of the Wilbury family's feats.

Otis pointed his fingers at the microphones and waved his hands. Sparks flew. Two mic stands shimmied toward the drum kit and collapsed to the proper height to pick up the sounds from the snares, tom toms, cymbals, and bass drum. Except for Ian, they'd all worked with Otis before, so there was little alarm at the prestidigitation. Otis indicated Ray and Ian should sit close to the third mic with their percussion instruments.

"We don't have a lot of extra mics. Sorry mates," Otis apologized.

Bill asked Otis, "You don't want the mic closer to the snare?"

"No, it sounds too clicky. I'll compress the drum sound even further when we mix it."

The brothers reconvened in the garage. Bill cued the tape for the newcomers. The two percussionists tapped their toes and bobbed their heads in time to the song.

"Yeah, catchy tune. This is terrific. I'm ready," Ray asserted.

"Let's run through it," Otis said.

Bill handed headphones to Ian and Ray as Otis took his place behind the drums. Bill switched on the tape they had recorded earlier and started the click track. Otis could be heard counting on the recording. The chiming twelve-string, the warm acoustics, and the descending chords on the electric rhythm guitar began. Otis played the drums. Ian and Ray held off on their instruments. The moment hadn't arrived.

The first bridge came. Otis did a drum fill. The second bridge came. Otis did a different drum fill. Ray added a bit of cowbell—nobody knew where he had found a cowbell. Nelson flashed him a thumbs up. Ray shook his tambourine. Ian beat on his bongos. No one heard him.

The song faded out, and Otis said, "That was fantastic. Can you do it just the same again? Let's roll the tape."

Bill cued the tape, and the three prepared themselves. The sound of Otis counting came through their headphones, and they played just at the right time. Three minutes and twelve seconds later, they had completed the recording of percussion and drums.

Nelson frowned. "I wasn't planning to put an electric lead-guitar line in this song, but it really needs one. Otis, can you make me a seven- or- eight-second extended section after the fourth verse—'I've been fobbed off'?"

Otis pointed a lazy finger at the tape machines. "Yeah, sure."

The tape decks smoked and spun, and Bill cued the newly recorded tape at the extended section.

Nelson, fiddling with his electric guitar, played some licks. "How does this sound?"

The resulting passage wasn't slide guitar, but the country flavor seasoned it.

Otis commented, "It's too bloody bad I don't have all the EQ modules from my 16-track Raindirk desk I use at

Walsh Hall. It has great sweeping ability. I could turn that into a slide sound."

Nelson smiled. "I'd rather keep it real."

Otis recorded and dropped in Nelson's new guitar solo. Nelson also recorded an extended solo over the fade out at the end.

Otis jumped up. "Okay, I think we've done it! Now all we need are some cellos and violins!"

Nelson cleared his throat. "Are you out of your mind? A: you aren't in ELO anymore. B: this tune doesn't need strings. C: forget about it."

"Oh, sorry. I just had a little flashback. I don't use strings anymore, well, except when … Never mind. Sometimes you just have to slap me back to reality. Thanks, Nelson. But we do need more percussion. Ian, would you add some tom tom?"

Otis looked at Nelson, who nodded.

Ian cocked his head and frowned at Otis. "I thought you were doing drums for this track."

Otis nodded. "I did, but I want you to add a tom tom bit." He felt badly that no one would ever hear Ian's bongos. They had just been for show to appease Charlie T.

Ian took his place behind the drum set and donned headphones. He laid down a nice easy tom tom beat.

Bill cued the tape and played it back. All five Wilburys listened critically. The Sideburys watched for reactions to their work. Ian hoped his bongos would be turned up louder in the final mix.

Otis smiled hugely. "That sounds great! We've done it!"

Nelson shook his head. "No, it's lacking one final element."

"What's that?" Charlie T. asked.

The five men looked at each other.

Otis and Nelson said simultaneously, "Harmonica at the end."

Otis looked over at Bill. "Play the last bit back, please."

Bill rewound the tape to the exact spot where the singing ended and the fade-out guitar solo began.

Nelson nodded. "Yeah, a harmonica would lend it the perfect folksiness we're looking for. Lucky, you want to do the honors?"

Lucky snorted. "That's so overused; Lucky Wilbury playing the harmonica. Can't someone else play it?"

Lefty spoke up. "I can play mouth harp."

"Lucky, you know what kind of harp it ought to be. I got no clue. Could you pick one for us please?" Otis asked.

"I'd use a G harp." Lucky went in the house and came back with two harmonica boxes. "Try these."

Lefty wiped the first harmonica with a paper towel and blew into it, getting a feel for it. "Cue up that section, would you please, Bill?"

Bill, prepared for the order, hit Play.

Lefty blew into the harmonica, improvising along with the chord structure. "Let me try the other one." He wiped the second mouth harp and repeated the process of playing over the recording. "Which one do y'all like better?"

"The first one," Otis answered.

"The second one," Nelson said.

"I'll be the tie breaker," Lucky interjected. "The first one's better."

Bill cued the tape again, and Lefty practiced with the harp until Otis and Nelson gave him a thumbs up. Lefty recorded a take everyone felt happy with, and Otis dropped it in.

At last, the recording was complete. Some final mixing was needed for all the levels to be right. Bill cued the tapes for mixing purposes, and Otis pointed his finger at the board. Lightning shot into the mixing console. The levers and buttons clicked and whirred, and the tape spun and smoked. The mixing process took Otis the longest. He checked and reviewed the mix a few times before the final version suited both him and Nelson. The whole procedure took at least eight minutes from start to finish.

Bill cued the completed tape for playback. The song sounded flawless. Congratulation and backslapping circled the room. Bill dubbed some cassettes for the primary and session musicians to take with them.

"Okay, we're done, everybody," Nelson said. "Thanks a million. Let's get out of Lucky's hair."

The next day, Nelson and Otis sat in the Warner Brothers corporate offices. They had an appointment with Lenny Waronker, head of artists and repertoire for Warner Brothers Records. Nelson planned to play the song they had written and recorded the previous day. They would find out if it was good enough to be the C-side for "This is Love." Charlie T.'s admonition about the song not being so one-and-done came back to him. He had forgotten to bother Charlie T. about what he meant.

When the brothers arrived with the tape, Mo Ostin, the head of Warner Brothers Records, was in Lenny's office as well.

*I guess it's sink or swim*, Nelson thought. *Either they accept it or we have to do another.* Still, Mo had accepted the incredibly slap-dash "I Don't Care Anymore" as a B-side for "Dark Horse." "Handle with Care" was better than that.

"I got my brothers together to do this song," Nelson explained. "Otis co-produced *Cloud Nine*, so I asked him to co-produce and play on it. He's also producing Lefty's album, so Lefty came along. Charlie T., Jnr. had my guitar at his house, and he came along. We used Lucky's studio, so he's on it."

Nelson put the tape in the cassette player. Bill hadn't even edited out the count at the beginning. When the song ended, Nelson looked to the label executives for their reactions.

Mo Ostin jumped out of his chair. "You can't use this as a throw away! You might as well use it for the group you're always talking about because you're all playing on it. There's your first single; go ahead and make the rest of the tracks."

Nelson was a little taken aback. "Do you mean I have to do another song for the twelve-inch?"

"No, no. We'll use something off one of your other albums. Do you think you can get your brothers to do an entire album?"

"We had a lot of fun. I think they might want to do a whole album … I really want to. But Otis is working on albums for Charlie T. and Lefty. They'd have to put their projects on hold. Lucky is going on tour this summer, so he doesn't have much time. It'll take some convincing."

As Nelson and Otis exited the building, Nelson elbowed his brother. "This is the group we wanted to form, the Traveling Wilburys!"

# CHAPTER 3

## I'D HAVE YOU ANYTIME

Lucky Wilbury is the most enigmatic of the half-brothers. He rarely grants interviews, and he wasn't happy about giving me one. "Just because you're family, Mavis," he said. "I kinda trust you."

"I'm only interested in the public history of the Traveling Wilburys," I reassured him.

We sat at the kitchen table of his Malibu home where "Handle with Care" had been recorded in the garage. Carolyn and the baby were long gone. So was Carla. Carolyn and Desiree had moved to Tarzana shortly after the half-brothers recorded their album, and the marriage ended four years later. No one knows why Carla had left, but she would probably say, "Mr. Lucky a handful." Maybe she went with Carolyn and Desiree.

Lucky had aged quite a bit since he had recorded the history-making album with his brothers. He sat hunched in a denim jacket and baggy jeans, wearing a hat, and regarding me with some suspicion. We sipped spice tea and ate slices of vegan chocolate cake.

"Of all the Wilburys in the world, it's really something that the five of you ever found each other. You know I'm putting this book together about how you guys made the album. Your relationships are reflected in the music. I'd like to hear the story of how you met Nelson."

"It was so long ago," Lucky began and stared off into space.

I waited. Soon he said, "I first met all four of them in New York in '64, '65 something like that. There's a famous story where I turned them on to weed, but they had smoked it before we smoked it together. That story was bullshit. We talked and played some music. Smoked some dope. I figured that was it. Nelson and I were astounded to discover we were half-brothers. Wilbury is a common name, after all."

I knew Lucky was speaking of Nelson's other group, not his four Wilbury half-brothers. I let him tell the story in his own way.

"The marijuana smoking wasn't the important thing. It was the music. We listened to each other's music. They learned from me, and I learned from them. We influenced each other. I changed my music because of The Beatles, and The Beatles changed their music because of me.

"Nelson came to my place in upstate New York after my motorcycle accident. It was, I don't know, 1968. I was a recluse, withdrawn, afraid. I didn't want to talk to nobody. He pushed me, gently, persistently. He started playing his guitar. 'Let's write a song,' he said. He started playing what he called his naughty chords: the major seventh, diminished, and augmented chords he liked so much. He turned them into a song. 'I'd Have You Anytime.'" Lucky lit a cigarette and looked at the floor.

"Those lyrics seem to affect you," I said.

"Yeah, he was talking directly to me. He wanted to know me. He wanted me to let him in. I wasn't good at letting people in. I'm still not good at it." He glanced at me briefly.

"What did you do?"

"I answered him with some more lyrics. I told him I would hold him in my arms. I didn't mean anything sexual. I meant I would try to open myself up and let him in as a friend. He was a tenacious motherfucker. When he wanted you as his friend, he didn't let up. We committed to each other during that visit. We agreed to be friends for life. We did a lot for each other through the years."

"Like what?" I prompted.

Lucky shrugged. "I appeared in his Concert for Bangladesh. It was really hard for me. I wasn't really ready to perform again after my hermit stage, but he dragged me out. The Isle of Wight had been a disaster and I had retreated again. It was good for me. Got me going again. And he needed me to appear for his Bangladesh fundraiser to make it bigger. Attract more attention. He wrote 'Old Brown Shoe' as an homage to me. He showed up for my Thirtieth Anniversary Concert Celebration, his last major appearance. We did some recording together before and after the Traveling Wilburys. We hung out at various times no one else knows about. We were travelers together on the spiritual river."

"Any more light you can shine on the relationship between you and Nelson?"

Lucky sat back in his chair and looked me full in the face for the first time during our conversation. I felt he was saying words he had said before. "He was a giant, a great, great soul, with all of the humanity, all of the wit and humor, all of the wisdom. He had the spirituality and the common sense of a man with compassion for people. He inspired love and had the strength of a hundred men. It was an honor to be his brother."

I paused a beat. "What about your other half-brothers in the group? Do any of you go way back? I know you toured with Charlie T., Jnr."

Lucky retreated to his hunched position. "I went by Lefty's house north of Nashville when I was recording *Nashville Skyline* in '69. He wasn't home."

"Did you first meet Otis when Nelson introduced you for the Traveling Wilburys album?"

"Naw. I met Otis in Tokyo, when we were both on tour there. Musta been late seventies. I was sitting on an amp in the wings of the Budokan, watching him sign autographs for dozens of Japanese fans. He was so ... generous, you know? Talking to each person and signing a personalized message on their thing they had brought in. I would never give autographs like that. I would scribble my name and turn to the next person. Now I don't sign autographs at all except to sign my paintings and prints. Anyway, at the Budokan, some of the fans started asking me for my autograph.

"Otis saw me over there and borrowed a piece of paper from one of his fans. He headed over in my direction and got in line to ask me for my fucking autograph. Can you believe that? He was my fan."

"Out of the other four, who would you say you are the biggest fan of? Nelson, Otis, Lefty, or Charlie T.?"

Lucky reclined into his kitchen chair again until it reared back on its legs. He smiled for the first time during our visit. "Well, you've really got me there. I admire each one for different reasons."

"Come on, Cuz. Don't gimme that bullshit. Of your half-brothers on that album, whose work do you admire the most?"

Lucky removed another cigarette to buy time. He lit it slowly and blew smoke through his nose. He used his index finger to push his ever-present hat back on his head and crossed his legs. "You aren't gonna leave until I answer you, are you, Cuz?"

"I wouldn't be that rude, but I sure would like to know. It's okay if you want to give me reasons why you admire each one."

"Naw. I'm ready to pick one. It's Lefty. With him, it was all about fat and blood. He sounded like he was singing from an Olympian mountaintop. After 'Ooby Dooby,' he was singing his songs in three or four octaves that made you want to drive your car over a cliff. He sang like a professional criminal. His voice could jar a corpse; always leave you muttering to yourself something like, 'Man, I don't believe it.' He's one of the original troubadours who set a course for the future of music. His singing carried the emotions of mankind."

# CHAPTER 4

## YOU GOT IT

Nelson and Otis sat in Charlie T., Jnr.'s living room. Charlie T. strummed an acoustic guitar as Nelson explained the events at Warner Brothers. "The record company thinks this is way too good to go on the back of a twelve-inch for two countries, so Otis and me were thinking; why don't we form a group and make an album?"

Charlie T. balanced his guitar against the sofa. He leaned forward in his seat, placing his elbows on his knees, his hands hanging. "Yeah, that sounds like a real good idea." He had felt the genuine magic while doing the first track. Besides, he couldn't get Otis to finish his solo album, and he needed to make some money. Anyway, he had foreseen "Handle with Care" wouldn't be the last track the half-brothers would record together, by a long shot. He decided to play the skeptic.

"Lucky has to start his next tour on June 7. He usually wants at least two or three weeks to rehearse with a new band. It's April 9 now. How are we gonna convince Lucky to squeeze a whole album in? We don't even have any songs, do we?"

Nelson shook his head. "I don't have any finished songs, but I have a few ideas. I figured we could all write them together on the spot, like we wrote 'Handle with Care.'"

"Lefty and I are working on his album right now," Otis added. "We've got one more track to do. He's got them other producers coming in after me. How are we going to convince him to suspend work on his solo album and record with us?"

Charlie T. glowered. "You not only have to convince Lefty. You have to convince Barbara to abandon a potential big money-making project like his album. You know his wife handles all his business affairs."

Nelson looked at his brothers. "Who do you know can talk anyone into anything?"

Otis and Charlie T. answered simultaneously. "You!"

"Baby, it's me." Nelson grinned. "Just give me a little time, and I'll have both of them eating out of my hand."

Otis tugged his beard with his thumb and forefinger like he did when he was nervous. "Lefty is playing a concert in Anaheim tonight. He gave me some comps. Let's go out there and see if we can convince him to join the group."

Nelson asked Otis, "What kind of car do you drive?"

"A Mercedes. Why?"

"Is it big enough for us and our wives to fit in?"

Otis sucked air through his teeth. "Cor, it would be a tight squeeze. If you want us all to ride together, we should rent a van. But why do you want our wives to go?" Otis angled his head forward and peered over the top of his shades, looking puzzled.

Nelson cocked his head in response and smiled. "It's part of my strategy."

Bugs telephoned and found a Toyota van they could rent the same afternoon. Bugs picked up the van and came back to Charlie T.'s house to collect Otis and Nelson. Charlie T. and Jane took off on their own errand. Bugs dropped Nelson off at Hotel Bel-air, Nelson's usual L.A. residence. They picked up Nelson's wife and son, Olivia and Ayrton. They dropped off Ayrton at Otis's house in Beverly Hills and picked up his wife, Sandi.

Sandi was both irritated and pleased with her husband. As she climbed into the center passenger seat of the van, she complained about the short notice. "You could have let me know yesterday we were doing this. Otis, Liv's nanny is off this week, so Ayrton is going to be here at our house playing with La-la and Weencie. Our nanny is watching them. But never mind about that. I'm so excited about going to this show."

Olivia folded her long legs behind Bugs in the center passenger seat next to Sandi. "Thanks so much for your help with Ayrton, Sandi. I'm excited about the gig too."

Charlie T. and his wife, Jane rendezvoused with the other four at the Hotel Bel-Air. Nelson came to the lobby when Olivia called him on the house phone.

"Why do we have to leave so early?" Jane asked as she climbed into the most rearward of the passenger seats. She sniffled as she bounced into place.

"I have to talk to Lefty before the show," Nelson answered. "He'll be more amenable before he hears the applause."

"I'm getting hungry. When do we eat?" Olivia asked. She had never been on a tour with her husband. They met at a party during his North American *Dark Horse* tour in 1974, but she hadn't attended any of the gigs. The outing was unkindly labelled the "Dark Hoarse Tour" because Nelson's throat was raspy and sore throughout his performances due to laryngitis.

"There's always snacks backstage, Arias," Nelson reassured her. One of his nicknames for her was her maiden name.

The band members knew they had some songs to write in the near future for the album they were planning to make. As a method of preparing, Nelson brought some yellow tablets for everyone to write on. He told them to jot down anything interesting they saw on billboards or any unusual events which occurred. They could refer to their notes when they were stuck for song ideas.

"I've been doing this for years," Nelson told them.

"'Every day is Judgment Day.' That's a good one," Otis called out. He scribbled on his pad.

"'Every dog has its day.' That's a cliché." Charlie T. wrote it down anyway.

"'Let Rondo Chevrolet be the end of the line.' Hmm, catchy." Nelson's pen scratched away.

After two hours of stop-and-go L.A. traffic, the van arrived at the Celebrity Theater. Everyone piled out at the rear entrance. Nelson approached the security guard. Bugs parked the van.

"Pardon me. We'd like to visit with our friend, Lefty, before the show. We've got comps too." Nelson said in a matter-of-fact tone. He did this all the time.

The security guard looked surprised for a moment. "Sure, Mr. Wilbury. Let me get you some backstage passes and your comps."

"The comps are in my name," Otis added.

The security guard looked Otis up and down. "And you are?"

He sighed. "Otis Wilbury."

The security guard flashed a light in Otis's face.

Otis squinted, despite his shades.

"Could I see some ID, Mr. Wilbury? Are you Nelson's brother or something?"

"Or something," Otis answered, pulling out his passport. "Lefty only left us four comps. What can you do about getting three more for Bugs, Nelson, and Olivia?"

"It won't be a problem to get comps for anyone in Nelson Wilbury's party. Charlie T. Wilbury is with you too? Welcome, welcome." The security guard flashed a huge smile at Charlie T. and Jane as they ambled up to the door.

"Hey," Charlie T. responded with a smile and a nod.

Another security guard escorted the group to the Green Room, where food and beverages were plentiful, as Nelson had promised. Olivia grabbed some cheese and crackers. Otis and Sandi procured glasses of red wine. Charlie T., Jane, and Nelson helped themselves to champagne.

"Hey, you lot, let me speak to Lefty alone when he gets here."

Everyone nodded. They were happy to stand by the food table and wait for Nelson to work his magic.

Lefty swept through the Green Room with his wife, Barbara and a couple of members of his backing band. "Hi, fellas. I didn't expect to see all y'all here tonight! It's nice that you brought the ladies."

"Let me have a word with you, Lefty."

"Sure, Nelson. Let's go to my dressing room."

Barbara started to follow the two men, but Nelson stopped. "Barbara, would you mind if I had a word with your husband alone?" He looked deeply into her eyes.

Nelson focused and sent a message into Barbara's mind. *You're hungry and thirsty. You're hungry and thirsty.*

Barbara stopped in her tracks. "You, know, I think I'll go talk to Otis about the album he and Lefty are making together. He's at the refreshment table, isn't he?"

Olivia joined Barbara and Otis. "It's wonderful Lefty is getting so much attention."

"Yes," she agreed. "We really thought Lefty's career was winding down and he'd be playing his greatest hits in small clubs for the rest of his life." Barbara filled her plate with cheese and turkey cold cuts and cracked open a Diet Coke.

"I credit Otis with Nelson's number-one record off *Cloud Nine*, 'Got My Mind Set on You.' He's a brilliant producer," Olivia enthused. "You know Nelson's previous two albums didn't sell well at all. He had given up recording for five years and was inspired to work again when he met Otis and heard what he could do with his tracks."

Barbara chewed and swallowed. "The song Otis and Charlie T. wrote with Lefty is fantastic. 'You Got It.' I was there while it was recorded. I think it will be a big hit."

Jane and Sandi joined the group. Otis departed when his wife approached.

"You know they recorded something with Lucky the other day?" Jane added. "Charlie toured with him for years. I think it's fabulous these music legends are all working together."

"Otis has written songs with some of the best songwriters on the planet," Sandi commented. "Including Brian Wilson. He has such a talent for melody. You can't help but sing along to the songs he writes."

Barbara studied the group of women. "You know, maybe there is some other project our husbands could do together that would benefit them all. Don't you wonder what Nelson and Lefty are talking about?"

Nelson put his arm around Lefty's shoulder and escorted him down the corridor. "You and me go way back, don't we?"

"Yeah, we met back in 1962 when we were on the same bill in England. You were the only one in your group who didn't insist I give up my top billing."

"I didn't think it was right, Lefty. You were the big star back then, and The Beatles were just getting started."

"Of course, it worked out, because most of the audience would have left after The Beatles played, and I would have been embarrassed if I'd been last on the bill."

"Oh, I don't think that would have happened. Those crowds were cheering for encore after encore from you. Anyway, I want to talk to you about something important."

They reached the dressing room door, and the two men entered the comfortably furnished room. Nelson quietly locked the door behind them and crossed to the sofa against the wall.

"Have a seat, Nelson." Lefty pointed to the sofa. "Can I get you something to drink?"

"No, thanks."

Lefty settled in the adjacent overstuffed armchair. "What's on your mind?"

"Well, I've been thinking a lot about this. You know the little song we recorded a few days ago? Mo Ostin at Warner Brothers loved it."

Lefty smiled. "That's great news."

Nelson closed his eyes for a moment. He went into a meditative state. He formed a picture in his mind of Lefty recording with the Traveling Wilburys. *Wilburys for the future. Wilburys for the future.* He opened his eyes again.

"They especially loved your voice on the song. 'Lefty's voice made the song,' they said."

"Everybody loves a compliment from the bigwigs." Lefty's grin grew larger, and he straightened his posture.

Nelson crossed his left foot over his right knee. "Warner Brothers wants us to do a whole album as a group, and we need you, Lefty."

"I don't know, Nelson. I'm working on this album now. I'm really hoping it's going to cement my comeback. You know, I got into the Rock and Roll Hall of Fame last year, and I had a television special featuring my music called *Black and White Nights*—did you see it? I really feel like I'm on the comeback trail."

*Wilburys for the future. Wilburys for the future.*

"Lefty, you've never been gone. Making this album with the rest of us will only increase your success. It won't take but a couple of weeks because Lucky is going on tour in June. We'll be finished by the middle of May."

"I don't know, Nelson. You know I have to talk to Barbara about it."

"Let's get her in here, then."

Lefty unlocked the door and headed down the hallway, looking for his wife. He found her still at the food table, talking to Olivia and Sandi. Jane, Otis, and Charlie T. sat on the Green Room sofa.

"Baby, will you come to my dressing room for a minute? Nelson has an interesting proposition."

"Sure. I've been dying to know what you two are talking about."

Barbara and Lefty entered the dressing room. Barbara sat on the sofa a couple of feet from Nelson, who smiled at her, and Lefty returned to his chair.

"Hi, Barbara. What did Lefty tell you about my proposition?"

"Nothing yet."

"Did he play you the tape of the song we recorded up at Lucky's?"

"Yes. I thought it was wonderful."

"So did the execs at Warner's. They want a whole album. Everyone else is on board, and I've come to ask Lefty to join the group and make the album."

"You want Lefty to make an album with you, Lucky, Charlie T., and Otis?"

"Right."

"This would be just like the album he made with the county superstars called *Class of '55*. You made that album with Johnny Cash, Carl Perkins, and ... and ..."

"Jerry Lee Lewis." Lefty finished his wife's sentence.

Nelson nodded. "I have a copy of that album. It is excellent. Carl is a good friend of mine. I've met Jerry Lee a few times too. The man is a powerhouse. And Johnny Cash is a legend."

"I think this would be another wonderful opportunity for Lefty. It puts him on an equal footing with more of the greatest names in the music business."

Nelson cocked his head and crinkled his eyes as he smiled. "Well, Lefty's always been on equal footing. He *is* a music legend."

Lefty smiled and nodded at his wife, who smiled back. "Nelson, it looks like I'm joining the Traveling Wilburys."

"Excellent! When will you be available?" Nelson waved his hands and moved his feet. He smiled hugely, looking excited.

Lefty had been gazing at his wife, lost in thought. "Uh, what?"

"I said, give me some consecutive dates between April 20 and May 20 when we can get together and do this." Nelson dropped his hands to his lap, still grinning.

"Since I have to put my solo album on hold, I'm available any of those dates. Hey, Nelson, will you play on a track on my album if I do this?"

Nelson nodded enthusiastically. "Yeah, sure. Love to."

"I'm glad Otis and Charlie T., Jnr. are here. I'm adding the new song we wrote together to my concert set tonight—'You Got It.' I know the record is a long way from being released, but I really think it's going to be big.

I want to start getting it out there. The band's version doesn't sound as good as the version Otis produced, but it's a great song any way you play it. We even brought some tympani for the performance. Otis loves those damn things." Lefty imitated Otis playing the tympani by making fists as if he were holding drumsticks and pounding on large kettle drums.

The three brothers and their wives enjoyed the concert from backstage. They celebrated their victory of Lefty joining the group with champagne from the Green Room. When Lefty passed them on the way back to his dressing room, Nelson got down on his knees and paid homage to Lefty for how great his performance had been. He hugged his old friend.

"I can't wait to record with you, Lefty. This is going to be so much fun. I'll call you as soon as I get the dates from Lucky."

Charlie T. and Otis hugged Lefty as well. They piled into their rented van, exultant.

Nelson distributed the yellow tablets again.

"Oh, man," Charlie T. whooped. "I'm happier than a pig in shit. Don't make me take notes!"

Otis was copying a billboard. "You'll wish you had something to work from when we are stuck for a song."

"My brain is full of shit to write songs about. There won't be any problem." Charlie T. threw his pad on the van's rear floorboard.

Olivia turned to her husband. "You wanted us there to help you get Barbara on board, didn't you?"

Nelson nodded. "I know Barbara is Lefty's business manager. Even if I could talk Lefty into joining, she could talk him right back out of it after we left if she didn't approve. I needed you ladies to help her understand how joining the Wilburys would help Lefty's career."

Sandi leaned forward from the rearmost seat. "Why didn't you let us in on the plan, Nelson?"

Nelson grinned a big shit-eating grin. "I had complete confidence in the inclination of a wife to brag to others about the abilities and accomplishments of her husband, even if she is mad at him."

Sandi's eyes widened. She shouted, "What?"

Otis leaned across Charlie T. to tap Sandi on the knee. "Did you brag about me? I'll be buggered!"

Sandi ignored him.

Jane twisted in the Toyota's front seat. "What did you say about bragging on our husbands? You mean you set us up?"

Simultaneously, Jane yanked the yellow tablet from Nelson's hand, and Sandi yanked the same object from her husband's hand. They both hit Nelson with the tablets while Nelson raised one set of arms to protect his head. Seated on and strapped in the van's center seat, he was surrounded. Surrendering, he raised his second set of arms to protect his face.

"I'll teach you to use me in your schemes!" Jane shrieked, but she laughed at his multi-armed appearance.

Nelson and Olivia laughed too.

Olivia patted his knee. "They saw your extra arms in the 'When We Was Fab' video and probably figured they were a Wilbury power."

When the playful hitting stopped, Nelson began chanting, "*Lefty Wilbury is in our band! Lefty Wilbury is in our band!*"

Everyone in the van, including the women, took up the chant. *Lefty Wilbury is in our band!*

# CHAPTER 5

## NOWHERE TO GO

Nelson dialed Lucky's number on the hotel's black telephone. "Pick up, pick up," he whispered under his breath as he listened to the ringer tone. He plopped down on a nearby chair.

No answer. This must be one of those days Lucky wasn't answering his phone. Nelson would have to contact him psychically.

Striding across the room, he assumed the lotus position on the large floor cushion in the Hotel Bel-Air suite's master bedroom. He lit some incense and began to meditate. Deeper and deeper he went, to more and more transcendent levels of consciousness. Psychic connections weren't the purpose of meditation, but Nelson had discovered he could do this long ago, when he had telepathically contacted his former fellow band member, John, while he was doing a bed-in. The contact was purely by accident—a byproduct of the depth of Nelson's meditative trance, like astral projection.

"Yoko and I don't want you in bed with us, mate," John had chastised him.

"Believe me, I don't want to be in bed with you either," Nelson had said, severing the psychic connection.

He pictured Lucky in his mind, hoping he wasn't sitting on the toilet when he got through.

Lucky was sitting at the kitchen table, feeding the baby, when Nelson established the connection. Nelson decided to play it cool and monitor for a few minutes. Maybe he could find out whether Lucky was interested in joining the group before he started putting on the pressure.

"Nelson, is that you?" Lucky was on to him.

Nelson knew Lucky had his own psychic abilities from their long friendship. He had acquired them at that place in the woods Lucky had shown him twenty years ago. Lucky enjoyed projecting an air of mystery, even to his friends and family members, so he had never fully explained to Nelson what he could do.

"Yeah. Hi, Lucky. You didn't answer your phone."

"I'm busy, man. I'm not at your beck and call. Get the hell out of my head, and I'll call you after lunch."

Thinking his sell job was not off to an auspicious beginning, Nelson broke the connection. He expected Lucky to be a hard sell. After all, Lucky was one of the most successful acts in show business. He was near or at the top of almost all those *Rolling Stone* lists Otis was always prattling about: greatest songwriter, greatest song, greatest singer, greatest album, greatest musical influence. The damn magazine had taken its name from one of his songs.

Lucky didn't need to be bothered doing a little album with some musicians who just wanted to hang out and have a good time. Yet, the Wilburys weren't the Wilburys without Lucky. He brought a certain *je ne sais quoi* to the overall composition and sound of the group.

Besides, Nelson looked up to him. Even though Nelson wanted to be the leader, he didn't want to be the only one everyone fawned over. Otis doted on Lefty too, so the problem was already sorted. But with Lucky in the group, another musical great would be present to take more pressure off Nelson.

Nelson also knew the Wilburys needed Lucky's ability to write lyrics off the top of his head. This work had to be cranked out quickly, because the albums Lefty and Charlie T. were making with Otis couldn't wait very long. The other four were also lyricists, but the process of toiling over the words was time consuming. Lucky was able to generate reams and reams of brilliant song lyrics seemingly without putting in any effort. When they were stuck for a lyric, all they would have to do is say, "Oh, Lucky, would you come up with a line for us, please?" He would be able to look at what they already had and rattle off something pleasing and perfect without even thinking about it.

Beyond any of the practical reasons, Nelson wanted to be in a group with Lucky, writing songs and recording them. He had jammed with Lucky many times, and they'd done *The Concert for Bangladesh*, but he hadn't experienced working with his friend to create a product. Nelson wanted to see what they could forge together.

For the rest of the morning, Nelson fretted about how to get Lucky to join the group. He thought of several bribes he might offer, but Lucky probably wouldn't accept any of them. He could afford just about anything monetarily. What he really needed at this stage in his career was an infusion of creativity and a good album.

Olivia sat in their hotel suite's living room, tutoring Ayrton in arithmetic.

"Hey, Arias. When you two take a break, can I bounce a few ideas off you?"

"Sure, honey. I was about to get Ayrton his lunch. Would you like anything?"

"No, not right now."

Ayrton sat on the floor next to the coffee table with a sandwich and a glass of milk. He preferred to be in the room where his parents were. Olivia sat close to her husband on the opulent white sofa.

"What would you like to talk about?"

"I've been thinking about how to get Lucky to work on this project with us."

Olivia snickered. "You mean you recruited Lefty before you recruited Lucky?

"Well, yeah. Why not? I've been friends with Lucky forever. I don't think he'll say no. It's just he's under a time crunch, and I want to make sure he agrees to doing it now rather than later."

"What are you going to say to convince him?"

"Tell me what you think of this approach. I can offer Lucky lead vocal on more songs than anyone else. We can record Lucky's songs first so he can get the hell out of Dodge for his tour. I'll let Lucky off the hook for the publicity appearances, which he passionately despises. What do you think?"

"That doesn't sound like much enticement for a performer of Lucky's stature. Would you do it if the tables were turned?"

Nelson stared at his wife. She always knew just the thing to say to derail him.

"Hell, no."

"What would it take for you to join if you were in Lucky's shoes?"

Nelson shifted on the sofa and crossed his legs. "Lucky needs what I needed when I started working with Otis. An infusion of creativity and the heart to make a good album. You remember I made those two awful albums in a row and didn't want to record anymore?"

Olivia nodded. "I remember. You concentrated on film producing instead."

Ayrton joined the conversation. "Those albums weren't awful, Dad."

Nelson smiled at Ayrton. "Thanks, son, but your opinion is a bit biased. The public thought they were awful, judging by their sales.

"I met Otis and started playing music and writing songs with him, and he built a fire under me. Lucky's written a couple of songs with Charlie T. while they toured together, but nothing that set the world on fire. "Got My Mind Made Up" and "Jammin' Me"—the last one was a big hit, but it sounded like a Charlie T. song, not a Lucky song, so not much infusion of creativity there.

"Otis produced some songs for Dave Edmunds and restarted his career. He produced my last album and restarted my career. Now Otis is producing albums for Lefty and Charlie T. We've heard cuts off both those, and you know how phenomenal they are. Lefty's career really needs an infusion of power that Otis can offer. When I told Lefty last night 'you never left,' I was just being kind. Lefty has been absent for a long time, and he has only recently been on the comeback trail. This album he's making with Otis, Bono, Elvis Costello, and T Bone Burnett will seal the deal. Charlie T. told me he foresaw Lefty would be back in the top ten with 'You Got It.' It'll be his first solid hit since the sixties."

Ayrton finished his sandwich and ran off to play in his bedroom.

"What makes you think Lucky's career is on the rocks like Lefty's?"

"Come on, Arias. We've listened to his last two albums. *Empire Burlesque* from three years ago was overproduced, and *Knocked Out Loaded* was one of the worst albums Lucky ever made. He played me some of the songs from the album he's releasing next month, erm, *Down in the Groove*. Same shit, different verse. He worked on it forever, and it's still terrible. He's lost touch with his songwriting muse. Lucky told me himself his last few albums were made up of 'bits and pieces,' or something like that. He didn't even write all the songs on them."

"Nelson, you record covers."

"Yeah, but I'm not Lucky, the songwriting genius, am I? Last year he was in that shitty movie, *Hearts of Fire*, and made the mistake of going out on the road with the Grateful Dead. The audiences and critics loved the Dead, but they hated Lucky. He's almost exactly where I was when I quit recording, except he hasn't been failing as long as I did. I suspect working with Otis would be just the bump Lucky needs, like a line of cocaine. And not just Otis. Working with all four of us might get Lucky's juices flowing again."

"Would that be enough motivation for you?"

"If I was sure it would work."

"Just figure out how to convince him then. That's your specialty." Olivia patted her husband's knee. She stood to tutor her son for the afternoon.

Lucky wasn't familiar with Otis, and he would have to take Nelson's word about the magic he could perform, especially since it wasn't even Wilbury magic.

Nelson's phone jangled well after lunch.

"Well, what do you want?" Lucky's voice inquired testily.

Nelson rapidly entered a meditative state and started repeating in his mind, *Wilburys for the future. Wilburys for the future.*

"Enough with the Jedi mind tricks. What the fucking hell do you want, Nelson?"

"I want you to make an album with the Traveling Wilburys, Lucky."

"I thought you'd never ask. I think it will really get my creative juices flowing to work with you guys, after these shitty albums I've been making. I've been listening to the stuff Otis produced. While his style isn't really my thing, he brings a lot to the table, song-writing-wise, and he seems to be a good collaborator. Of course, Charlie T. is great. I've always loved Lefty, and was waiting to make sure you got him signed on. You did, didn't you?"

"Yeah."

"I have ten days starting Sunday, May 8. Can we do it then?"

# CHAPTER 6

## DIRTY WORLD

Dave Stewart's house in Encino, with its studio out back in the guest house, became the new recording location. Dave was half of the Eurythmics. He had also co-produced Charlie T., Jnr.'s album, *Southern Accents*, and had co-written three of the songs on it. He had performed on Lucky's album, *Knocked Out Loaded*. Dave and his wife, Siobhan, were out of town, so the Wilbury brothers had free run of the studio and the house.

Dave had nicer equipment than Lucky and an actual sound booth. Dave's studio was more sophisticated than Lucky's garage, but it wasn't a slick record company studio.

After they laid down the basic tracks, Nelson, Otis, Lefty, and Charlie T. would fly to England with the tapes and record the overdubbing in Nelson's state-of-the-art home studio. Every Tom, Dick, and Harry who ever had a hit record had a home recording studio at this point in history. Lucky needed to stay in L.A. or they would have recorded the album at Friar Park.

The guest house, built on higher ground than the main house, had a bedroom and bathroom upstairs with a bath, living room and kitchen downstairs. The sound booth, lined with green mover's blankets, stood off the kitchen and occupied part of what used to be the living room. The control booth was carved out of about half of the living room. This meant the remaining living room area was quite small, with a narrow hallway connecting it to the kitchen. The entrance to the studio was through the kitchen/dining area. A roomy front porch offered comfortable seating. The studio was pleasantly but sparsely furnished. Gold records the Eurythmics had earned and other music awards Dave had won hung on the walls. Dave and Siobhan displayed framed photos of friends and awards ceremonies as well.

Two skylights allowed sunrays to flood the sound booth and the control enclosure, giving a cheerful brightness to the rooms during the day. The yellow curtains on the kitchen windows sported humorous cartoons of Porky Pig, the *Looney Tunes* character. They billowed in the early afternoon breeze.

Otis, Lefty, Nelson, and Charlie T. sat in the kitchen dining area with Richard, the engineer, and Bugs, the roadie. The dining table resided in storage during their recording sessions, and they placed the chairs in a circle around the coffee table from the living room. Otis had enlisted Richard, who had worked on *Cloud Nine* and was engineering Lefty's album.

Lucky had yet to make an appearance, and he wasn't answering his phone. Nelson said, for the third time, "Oh, Lucky's late."

Otis fumed. "Bollocks. What if he changed his mind and he isn't coming?"

"He's coming," Nelson said. "He was very enthusiastic. I didn't even have to psychically squeeze him or offer him top billing or anything."

Charlie T. rounded on Nelson. "You were gonna offer him top billing?"

"If I had to, then renege on it later."

"Oh, that's better." Charlie T. unpuffed from his self-righteous posture.

Hearing a car in the long driveway, they jostled each other to get a look out the window, pushing aside the

Porky curtains. Lucky steered up the driveway in his white Ford van.

"At last," whispered Lefty. He didn't like for people to be late.

The four rushed to their chairs and assumed a casual air.

Lucky walked through the door, looking like he owned the place. He put his guitar case on the stove and unsnapped the clamps. "Hi, everybody. Ready to get started?"

Nelson stood. "I want to get something out in the open before we start working. We know that you're Lucky Wilbury and everything, but we're just going to treat you and talk to you like we would anybody else."

Lucky eyed the group. "Well, great. Believe it or not, I'm in awe of you guys, and it's the same for me."

Charlie T. smirked, and Lefty giggled. Otis looked incredulous.

Richard got behind the control console, and Lucky took Richard's chair. He strummed his guitar to check the tuning and twisted a couple of pegs. Everyone else took their guitars in hand.

Nelson played some minor chords. "Yeah, let's get started. Who's got an idea for a song?"

"I wanna do a song that sounds like Prince," Lucky said enthusiastically.

"Prince who?" Lefty asked.

"You know, that androgynous black singer. 'Party like it's 1999?' *Purple Rain*?"

Lefty laughed. "I'm just messing with you, man."

Lucky strummed chords loudly on his guitar. "Love your body so sexy, ooh baby. I love your mind so dirty."

"That sounds pornographic. I love it," Charlie T., Jnr. said. "How about 'Oh baby, you're such a pretty thing. I can't wait to introduce you to my new cock ring.'"

"Maybe we shouldn't go so far," Nelson said, ever the mother hen for purposes of the airwaves.

"We'll clean it up later. Just go for broke right now," Otis said. In the early days of ELO, Otis had often labelled demos with obscene titles.

Lucky took over again. "Your hood don't need no wax job, it's smooth enough for me. If you need my oil stick dipped, I'll do it for you free."

Charlie T. took up the refrain. "If you let me drive your dump truck, I'll park it where the sun don't shine."

Nelson grinned an evil grin. "Well in that case, how about this? 'Every time I touch you, my ass stands up on end. My dick begins to quiver, and my mind begins to bend.'"

Otis took a turn. "Oh baby, I'm on my elbows and knees. Life would be an easy lark if I only had you to please."

Lefty shook his head. "I'm from a different generation than you guys. I just can't write lyrics like that. Here's my contribution. 'Oh baby, spin around and say goodbye. You go to the beauty parlor now and I'm going home to cry.'"

Lefty's age didn't keep him from contributing risqué words, it was his strong religious faith. About three years before, he had rediscovered the Christianity of his youth in Wink, Texas. Since then, he had become a regular church goer. He made life choices according to the teachings of Jesus. Somehow, the obscene Monty Python lyrics didn't seem inconsistent to him. They were just too much fun. Besides, someone else had written them.

"Don't change, Lefty," Otis said. "We love you just the way you are."

Lefty continued. "I have another idea. Let's end it with a list of things he loves about her. They can be, um, open to interpretation."

"What kind of things?" Lucky wanted to know.

Blank stares ensued.

"Trembling Wilbury?" Nelson suggested.

More silence.

Nelson spied a stack of magazines on the low table: *Vogue, National Geographic, The Week, Auto Sport, Bon Appétit.* He handed a magazine to each group member.

"Look through these to get ideas about what he might like about her. Make them ridiculous. Hey, Richard, we need you to take notes." Nelson threw a yellow pad to Richard, who produced a pen.

Soon all five men were thumbing through the magazines and calling out short phrases from articles and ads which caught their attention. They made no effort to edit since they were brainstorming. Later they could eliminate some particularly witless offerings. The entire list consisted of forty-nine entries with examples like:

Added stiffness

Quest for fire

Latest lap

Clothes that stretch

Electric dump valve

They tweaked "electric dump valve" and "Quest for fire" to make them funnier. Eventually, they rejected almost all the choices from *Vogue, National Geographic,* and *The Week* and accepted almost all from *Auto Sport and Bon Appétit.* Lefty made a master list boiled down from the initial list in bold red Sharpie, his preferred writing instrument.

Satisfied with the list of attributes, Nelson perused the legal pad with the written verses. "Now let's compose a tune for it."

"It's already got a tune," Lucky said.

"I meant a better tune," Nelson replied.

"I'd rather work on the chords."

Nelson relented. He knew they didn't have time to argue. "Okay, let's work on the chords."

He passed the yellow pad to Charlie T. and asked him to notate the chord progression. Otis played the simple E to A progression Lucky had used from the start, but he added a slightly surprising C# minor and a Bsus4, which blew everyone's mind.

As Otis played, he hummed a tune using Lucky's initial melody but sounded decidedly less monotonous. Although aware he could fashion a superior melody than the ones Lucky had been writing lately, Otis knew better than to challenge the greatest songwriter in the world. However, if he only changed Lucky's tune a little, maybe he would approve.

Waving his hand, Lucky stopped the proceedings. "Otis, are you fucking with my tune?"

Otis played a mischievous riff on his guitar. "Well, maybe a little. Nelson said he thought your tune could be improved."

Lucky's eyebrows frowned above his shades. "Nelson told me you could write a good melody line."

Otis looked at Nelson and bobbed his head. "I'm honored, Nelson."

A few moments of silence ensued. Otis and Lucky took the measure of each other in a staring contest. It was an odd one since they were both wearing sunglasses.

Lucky broke the silence. "Okay, Otis. Let's see what you can do."

Otis breathed a sigh of relief.

After everyone agreed they had made good progress on the song, they were ready to eat. Part of Bugs's job as roadie was finding food for the group. He had commandeered enough basic supplies for an army and called a different catering or delivery service every day. He lived in L.A., the home base for Charlie T.'s band, his primary employer, so he knew who served the good food. Today's caterer had delivered before the group was ready to eat, and Bugs stashed the food in the fridge, to be reheated later. One of the catering team said she would return to pick up the plates and serving ware.

The brothers went to the big house for dinner. Bugs and Richard pulled plates covered with tinfoil from the refrigerator. The Wilburys had mentioned it in the song they had just written, immortalizing it as "the big refrigerator."

Lefty's wife, Barbara, arrived just in time to help prepare the lunch, assisting Bugs with the food. She was younger than her husband, but she shared his values about traditional sex roles.

"I hope my wife doesn't show up," Otis joked.

"Otis," Barbara chastised him. "You shouldn't say such things about Sandi. She's a lovely lady. And a wonderful mother to your two daughters."

Otis looked at the ceiling and shook his head. "If you only knew."

Barbara wagged her finger at Otis.

"Lemme tell you about the time Sandi left some X in her night table drawer and Laura found it. When she came home, our five-year-old daughter was tripping out of her mind, lying naked on her mother's fur coat. She wasn't properly supervised by Sandi or the nanny Sandi had hired."[2]

Barbara frowned. "Where were you, Otis?"

Otis pulled his beard. He hadn't seen that question coming. "I was in Germany, recording ELO's last bloody album."

"Things aren't going too well with my old lady right now either," Charlie T. said. "She behaved herself at Lefty's show, thank goodness."

"Arias went back to England." Nelson added. "We don't like to keep our son out of school for too long."

Opening the oven, Barbara checked on the heating food and slid a fresh batch into the microwave. Bugs set delectable salads on the table. Barbara piled servings of turkey sandwiches and warmed candied yams in the middle of the nine place settings. Bugs brought out bottles of wine to supplement the bottles of already opened beer. A sumptuous feast spread before them, and the working day was only half over.

Just as everyone gathered around the table, Buster Sidebury arrived. Otis and Nelson had invited him to play drums for the evening's recording session. Barbara set another place. Nelson teased him. "You always arrive in time to eat."

Buster laughed. "Yeah, I'm good at that."

Lucky came around the table and warmly shook Buster's hand. "Ain't seen you since you worked on *Empire Burlesque* three years ago."

---

[2] Interview with Laura Lynne on Facebook, June 30, 2017

"How the hell are you, Lucky?"

"About the same. You?"

"Doing great."

As they ate, Buster contemplated the recording set up. "Where am I going to put my drums?"

Otis had been thinking about that. The guest-house kitchen didn't have the square footage to accommodate a full drum set. "Don't worry. We can work it out. We might have to lay down more than one drum track or finish the drums at Friar Park."

Buster laughed. "I never worry about production when you're around, Otis."

"I always do the drum track first, so doing it after will be different for me," Otis responded.

When everyone finished eating, Bugs and Barbara cleared the plates and washed the dishes; Richard helped them dry.

"We still have to clean up these obscene lyrics," Nelson said.

The Wilbury brothers sat at the dining table and changed enough words to the new song so it would bear airplay without removing all the innuendo.

In the kitchen, Buster retrieved his drumsticks and addressed Charlie T. "When Dave records here, where does he put the drums?"

"In the main house. They just run a snake."

"So I'd be far away from the rest of the guys?"

"Yeah, they always overdub the drums."

Jim, with his horn, and Ray, with his tambourine, rang the doorbell. Ray also carried a cowbell, just in case. They sat at the dining table to watch the lyrical revision.

Otis reared back in his chair. "I don't think we ought to clean this up entirely. Let's put 'fuck' at the very end."

Nelson sighed. "Why are you so insistent about using fuck in a song?"

Otis grinned. "'A working class hero is something to be.'"

Nelson rolled his eyes and shook his head.

"How about this after the list of likes?" Otis started singing. *"Dirty world, dirty world, it's a fucking dirty world."*

Lucky stepped in. "I like it, but let's not say 'fucking dirty world.' Let's say 'ucking dirty world.'"

Otis nodded. "Or we could do that."

Jim and Ray helped Bugs and Buster set up the drums in the living room of the main house. Running an eighty-yard microphone lead from the board across the lawn wasn't something Otis wanted to do by zapping. The grass in the yard might catch fire from a spark. Richard and Buster had to piece several leads together that would stretch the distance, and it took some time.

Barbara went home to greet her children after school. Her older boy was a senior and could fend for himself, but she liked to supervise the younger, who was still in junior high school.

When he was producing, Otis usually skipped demos, but in this case, he wanted to get the feel of the studio— its equipment, acoustics, ambient noise, quirks, and poltergeists. Otis played the studio as much as he played his instruments.

He called a quick producers' meeting with Nelson before they started recording for the day. "There's a lot I don't like about this studio. You know I like a dry sound, and this place has a lot of bounce because of the walls and the ceiling. We can put some more quilts up to calm down the bounce, and we can use EQ post to take some more out. We can't get much separation in here because of the environment, but I guess that's okay. We aren't recording a bloody orchestra."

Nelson nodded as he listened to his co-producer talk. He hadn't usually worried much about the ambience of the recording space, and let the chips fall where they may. "I'll leave that to you, Otis."

Otis assumed his role as producer. "Bugs, can you find some more of these quilt thingies to damp down the reflected sound and hang them in the booth? And the kitchen opposite the windows?"

Bugs looked over at Charlie T. "Don't look at me, Bugs. Otis is in charge. Just do what he tells you."

Bugs looked back at Otis sheepishly. "I guess that's clear enough. Yes, sir. I know exactly where to get those things, and I'll have them on the walls within the hour."

"Thanks."

Otis turned to the other musicians. "Okay, everyone know the chords? Richard, cued up? Let's go. Let's just do one verse, and I'll expand. After four."

Richard started the click and hit Record. Otis counted in. Five acoustic guitars played. Lucky did the guide vocal for the first verse. Otis planned no backing vocals on the demo.

Lucky flubbed the guide vocal twice, but the recording was a demo, so it didn't matter. Otis used the first take. He planned to overdub the rhythm section of bass and drums together just to save time.

Richard started to reroute the cables for the second run.

Otis warned him away from the board. "Stand back, Richard. Let me see what this board can tolerate."

Otis held out his hands, fingers extended, and his lightning danced across the soundboard and the cables. Cables flew through the room, rearranging and rerouting themselves. A couple of mic stands zoomed toward the living room, surrounded by sparkles. The end of the snake elevated itself to plug into the newly placed mics.

One of the caterers ambled into the studio, looking for a missing platter. She froze in the doorway, eyes open wide, staring through the control room's soundproof glass at the sparks skipping across the recording equipment and out the control booth's door. She grabbed the fire extinguisher by the stove. "Quick, there's a fire!"

Lefty grabbed her by the arms. "Relax, it's just Otis."

"What do you mean, 'It's just Otis?' The house is burning down!"

By this time, the flickers had died, and the cables had rearranged into the new configuration. Otis checked the levels with his bass guitar, completely oblivious to the young lady's consternation, as he couldn't hear her through the control room's double-pane glass while wearing headphones. Richard had gone to the living room to check that the cables had plugged themselves in properly.

Otis spoke loudly through the talkback mic to the kitchen. "Play a riff. Then we'll test the drums."

When he looked up, Otis saw the caterer struggling against Lefty, who wrestled with her to prevent her from rushing into the control booth to spray the soundboard with fire retardant. Otis's mouth fell open. "What's wrong?"

"She thought there was something wrong with the equipment," Lefty shouted.

Otis spoke through the talkback mic. "Oh, no, everything's fine. What do you need?"

She stopped struggling, but her face continued to reflect her emotional state. "But sparks were coming out of everything. I thought sure there was an electrical fire."

Otis removed his headphones and stood at the door of the control room. "No, no fire. I was just resetting the equipment. We're doing a level check now. If you don't mind, could you go tell Buster in the main house we're ready to set his levels for the dual mics on the drums? I don't know how to communicate with the drummer when he's over there. Just say, 'Otis says hit your snare.'" Otis smiled his most charming rock star smile at the hapless young lady. "Please?"

The caterer stared at Otis indignantly for a moment. Despite herself, she couldn't resist his smile and his soft British accent. She stomped off in the direction of the main house to deliver his message. She grabbed her platter and skedaddled away from the guest-house studio as quickly as she could, planning to tell her boss not to deliver to this particular bunch of crazy musicians again.

Nelson stuck his head through the opened control room door. "Woah, mate. That was a close one. We don't want the non-Wilburys seeing what you can do, now do we?"

Otis crossed his arms and hunched his shoulders. "How was I supposed to know a caterer would be wandering around in here while we were working?"

The recording team didn't need Lucky, Charlie T., and Lefty while Otis captured the drums and bass. Lucky had gone upstairs. Lefty relaxed on the porch, softly singing "The Penis Song" while Charlie T. accompanied him on ukulele.

The song listed the advantages of having a penis and gave several slang names for the male organ.

Nelson joined them on the porch. "You're wasting your fantastic voice on that twaddle."

"I wish there was a companion piece called 'The Vagina Song,'" Lefty commented.

Bugs sat down with the brothers. "Lefty, I thought you were a nice man and didn't talk about things like that."

Lefty smiled. "Well, normally I don't, except when it's Monty Python."

Nelson continued his expression of disapproval. "The Pythons are all great friends of mine, especially Eric. I bailed out their movie, *Life of Brian*, by mortgaging my house. At the last minute, EMI decided the film's subject matter was sacrilegious and withdrew their funding. I wanted to see the movie, so I put Friar Park up as collateral against a loan. Another Python, Terry Jones, described it as the "world's most expensive cinema ticket.""[3] A wide grin erupted on Nelson's face. "Course, the film made money, so it turned out to be a good deal for me. I got a film production company out of the deal." He touched his palm to his chest.

Charlie T. foresaw some things psychically he didn't tell his brothers, to spare their feelings. He didn't mention Nelson's movie business partner, Denis O'Brien, would betray him and rip him off to the tune of twenty-five million dollars over a period of years. The chicanery was going on even now.[4] Charlie T. could see Nelson was having too much fun being a movie producer to ruin it.

---

[3] http://www.theguardian.com/film/2011/oct/30/george-harrison-little-malcolm-handmade (retrieved 4-18-18)

[4] http://en.wikipedia.org/wiki/Denis_O'Brien_%28producer%29 (retrieved 4/2/18)

His foreknowledge sometimes caused him pain for those close to him.

Charlie T. ambled to the big house to watch Buster's drumming.

Now Lefty sang "Always Look on the Bright Side of Life" from *Life of Brian*. This time he sang it in his full-operatic singing voice. A crack formed in the kitchen window.

Nelson tapped Lefty on the shoulder. "Brother, you've got to be more careful. I can't have you destroying Dave's place."

"I know. I'll pay for any damages."

"No, that's okay. It all goes under production costs. But can't you control the damage your voice causes at all?"

Otis stomped out of the kitchen, followed by Richard. "Lefty, I always like to hear you sing, but we are picking up your voice through the door. Can you keep it down? Anyway, we're finished with that part of the track. I can loop the last bit Lefty ruined. Now, I'm going to put on some keyboards and see how it works."

Otis turned to Nelson. "I'm going to leave the snake to the drums where it is. We're probably going to be using them drums every day. Don't want anyone tripping over it though. Think there might be some way to anchor it?"

Bugs hopped up and looked for bungee cords and stakes to make the drum snake in the grass safer.

Otis returned to the kitchen and pointed at the mixing console. Sparks flew, and cables jumped from the bass and the direct box and into the Casio keyboard Bugs had set up.

Lefty watched the whole thing happen through the window. "How does he do that?"

Nelson shrugged. "It's part of his superpower from nearly being electrocuted in the seventies. It's one reason why he's so fast at turning out tracks. We don't have to muck about with the equipment. The downside is that he wants to lay twenty or thirty overdubs, so sometimes you have to drag him away from the studio when he wants to keep working on the same song. You've heard the stuff he did with ELO. He'd make two cellos and a violin sound like five bloody orchestras. He'd make an orchestra and three guitars sound like an avalanche of sonic images. He told me he did so many overdubs once, he pulled the tape off the reel and he could see right through it. Had to throw out all that work. Doing this album will be good practice for him because we only have nine more days. He can't do fifty overdubs."

Nelson's demeanor turned serious. "But I need to discuss with you the damage your voice causes. Don't worry about this little cock-up—this studio is hardly soundproof. But still …"

Lefty returned Nelson's glare, and dropped his gaze to the porch flooring. "I feel real bad about causing destruction, Nelson. I've tried to control it and just can't."

"Maybe I can work with you psychically. What have you tried?"

Lefty looked up again. "The only thing that works is keeping my volume low. Then I can't sing out and use the full range and power of my voice. It's a damned-if-you-do, damned-if-you-don't situation."

Nelson touched Lefty on the shoulder. "Tell me about a time when you were able to sing at full volume and your voice didn't cause damage."

"How did you know? Oh, yeah. You're psychic. There was this one time I was on a picnic in the woods with Claudette, my first wife. I was playing my guitar and singing a song I had written for her—'Claudette.' Have you ever heard it?"

Nelson nodded.

"Instead of causing damage, my voice had the effect of building something. We looked over at the bank of the stream we were next to, and mud and water were forming a life-sized statue of a woman as I sang. The rhythm and tempo of my singing seemed to be what was affecting the dirt and the water as they formed the shape. I was so surprised I stopped singing, and the water and dirt stopped moving and fell to the ground where they were. I don't know for sure, but it might have been the emotions I was feeling that brought about creation instead of destruction."

Nelson nodded again. "That makes perfect sense to me. You were probably feeling love for Claudette."

"And happy about being with her and having just written that song for her. The boys hadn't been born yet. It was just us. It was one of the happiest times of my life. Then she died. People I loved started dying. My career went into the toilet. I never felt that happy again, Nelson."

"Happiness is something we create for ourselves, Lefty."

"I'm just starting to understand that. Maybe there is a way to use my voice for creation rather than destruction."

"Don't you feel happy when you're singing Monty Python songs?" Nelson asked.

Lefty cocked his head and sat silently for a moment. "I feel amused, not the kind of deep contentment I felt by that stream with Claudette. It was a spiritual moment."

Nelson nodded again. "Maybe you'll discover it now that you've reconnected with the Lord."

Lefty heaved a deep sigh. "I hope so."

Back in the studio, Otis had finished laying down a keyboard track. Richard cued the tapes for mixing. Otis placed his hands over the middle of the soundboard, three feet above it. Sparks danced through the slides and dials. The whole desk rocked. The tapes spun rapidly. Richard retrieved the completed mix and cued it for playback. Otis walked through the house to gather everyone for the first listen.

The half-brothers congregated in the sound booth, or near enough to the open sound booth door to hear the monitor speakers.

"Okay, you know this demo is gonna be a little rough. It's just to find out what we can do in this studio," Otis explained.

The tape started, and everyone liked what they heard. Lucky had flubbed a few vocal lines. The drumming and bass playing sounded flawless. The keyboard had been played properly, but Nelson declared it wasn't the right instrument for the track, and Otis agreed.

"Why don't we try a sax?" Otis suggested. "Let's use Jim. He's already here."

"No need to muck about with the demo anymore," Nelson asserted. "Let's just do it for real."

"Guitar players into the kitchen," Otis announced. "Okay, let's get to work on the backing track."

The acoustic guitars went down easy, then the Sideburys arrived from the main house. The drums, tambourine, and bass went on smooth as silk. Jim and Otis spent a few minutes developing a subtle horn part to play during the second verse.

Once he'd had a chance to sing the lyrics all the way through, Lucky suggested a few more changes to them.

No one objected, deferring to his status as the best lyricist in the world.

On the final pass, all five brothers sang backing vocals, standing around the single mic. "*Ahhh-ohhh. Ahhh-ohhh. Ahhh-ohhh.*" Otis had worked these out while they were recording the backing track. Backing vocals comprised another of his natural-born superpowers. He could conceive, arrange, and direct perfect backing vocals at the strum of a chord.

At last, the time had arrived to sing the "He loves your ..." lines. These lyrics would be dropped in after Lucky's lead vocal. They taped the list of funny phrases to the mic and all gathered around. All five sang "*He loves your ...*" in a separate take, augmented to multiple repetitions by Otis's flashy superpower. Afterward, they would take turns going down the list and singing the items.

"Let's practice it first," Lucky said.

"Are we going to sing it or say it?" Otis asked.

"I think we should sing it," Nelson suggested.

"Okay, let's sing it," Charlie T. agreed.

Richard started the backing tape and hit Record on the second deck.

The half-brothers continued around the circle until it reached Lefty. In his operatic tone, he sang, "*Trembling Wilbury.*"

Multiple wacky phrases ensued until Lefty finished up.

Otis removed his headphones. "I don't like my words. I can't sing 'em without laughing."

"I don't like my words either," Charlie T. said.

"Okay, let's switch up the order we sing them in," Nelson said. "I'll start this time. We'll go the other way round. Everybody got it?"

Richard restarted the backing tape.

The half-brothers sang the silly phrases in a completely different order around the circle, yet somehow "Trembling Wilbury" again fell to Lefty.

The giggles ruined the take.

"Lefty got 'Trembling Wilbury' again!" Nelson said, laughing.

Lefty nodded. "No matter which way we went, I got the dumb line. It's like some kind of conspiracy."

Otis pointed at his brother and guffawed. "It was just meant to be, I think."

In the end, they decided to use the first take of the "He loves your ..." list. They all hated "clothes that stretch," so Nelson dropped in a better phrase. By midnight, the brothers had a song in the can. They listened to it two or three times; afterward, they took an hour to unwind and play some music they wouldn't record.

Those studio mics were notorious for picking up the sound of people sucking on joints. Lefty avoided the joints and asked for puffs off cigarettes instead. "Ghost Riders in the Sky" rang out into the night.

## CHAPTER 7

## JAMMIN' ME

I sat down with my cousin, Charlie T. Wilbury, Jnr., for a chat about his recollections of making the album. I also wanted to pump him for information on the earliest origins of his relationships with his half-brothers before they became a band.

"In all of Wilbury lore, there is no one else like Charlie Truscott Wilbury, from whose loins sprung a horde. How many children do you reckon he fathered in all?"

Charlie T. cocked his head and smiled a lopsided grin. "Well, Mavis, I never really thought about that. How many half-brothers and half-sisters could I have out there? My daddy got around, you know, and he was really, uh, virile. And he could literally charm the pants off women. That was his superpower. Hundreds, I suppose."

"How did you come to be named after the senior Wilbury, father to you all?" I asked with a twinkle in my eye.

"Oh, you know. Our daddy usually didn't stay around for the birth of his children, but he happened to be in Gainesville when I was born. He saw enough of himself in me to insist that my mom name me after him. I imagine there's lots of Charlie T. Wilbury, Jnrs. running around, but we haven't bumped into them yet. I always wondered why he insisted on the British spelling of 'Jnr.,' though. But I never got to ask him.

"Did you see him much afterward?"

Charlie T. guffawed. "Only when he thought Mamma had some money."

I rapidly changed the subject. "Tell me about how you met your brother Lucky."

"I heard Lucky's music growing up in Florida as a teenager and suspected he might be a brother. My mom would tell me about all the nefarious things Charlie T., Snr. would do, sleeping with women all over the country and the world—boozing, gambling, doing drugs, you name it. A half-brother from Minnesota wasn't such a farfetched idea.

"I met him in '77 or '78 in L.A. Me and Bugs got comps to one of Lucky's shows. We had a flat tire on the way, and both of us got out on the road trying to change the tire, so we got to the concert covered with grease and dirt. We got to the venue and found our seats just as the show was starting. Then a guy came up to us where we were sitting and said, "Lucky would like you to come backstage." So we went backstage and had a brief conversation. I said to Lucky, 'Who's your Wilbury daddy?' He said, 'Charlie Truscott, same as yours.' Then we knew we were half-brothers."

"How did you become his backing band?" I asked.

"We were both on the Live Aid bill in Philadelphia in July, 1985. Even though he had Keith Richards and Ron Wood playing behind him, he didn't feel like the music was solid. He wanted a tight, disciplined band to back him for Farm Aid a few weeks later. He had heard us play, so he asked us if we would back him. We went down and rehearsed. We rehearsed a lot. We played a lot of different songs. He loved the Heartbreakers. He could just throw something out, and the Heartbreakers were good at grabbing it and going for it. We rehearsed Lucky's tunes and learned more songs than we needed.

"He would lead the rehearsals. He would just play us a little bit of the song he wanted to do, and he would play it on guitar, so we could see what the changes were. And then we'd just start to play.

"So we backed him up at Farm Aid, and it went really well. And then afterward in the trailer, Lucky said, 'Hey, what would you think of doing a tour? I've got a tour of Australia I want to do, and what would you guys think of doing that?' And we'd all been huge Lucky fans, and we were very intrigued by the idea of playing with him. So off we went. And that went on for two years."

I sat back in my chair and rested my hands on its arms. "But you guys were a huge act. Headliners. Didn't it feel like a demotion to back up another headliner?"

"We did our thing in between legs of the Lucky tour, so we didn't feel creatively stifled, if that's what you mean. Look, I learned so much from Lucky. He gave us a kind of courage that we never had, to learn something quickly and go out on stage and play it. You had to be pretty versatile because arrangements could change, keys might change, there's just no way of knowing exactly what he wanted to do every night. You really learned the value of spontaneity and how a moment that is real in a concert is worth so much more than one you plan out."

"You must have gotten to know Lucky well over those two years. What can you tell me about him as a person?"

"One of the nicest things about Lucky is that he's an honest guy. Really, really honest. Not someone who would ever lie. Not someone who would brag about his accomplishments either. And I enjoyed all those years of working with him, and I think in addition to our family ties, we had a genuine friendship. Still do. We had a lot of long talks.

"I'll tell you this about him: I saw a lot of people giving Lucky a wide berth, being afraid of him or afraid to say what was on their mind. Trying to anticipate what he was might say or do. I always found that if I asked Lucky a direct question, I would get a direct answer. So maybe our friendship wasn't that difficult, because I made up my mind that I would treat him like anybody else. Though I was certainly in awe of his talent. But people are just people. And I don't remember ever asking him a question when he didn't give me a direct answer."[5]

I shifted gears. "When did you meet your brother Nelson?"

"I first met him in 1974 when I came out to Los Angeles. I hadn't been out here very long. I was working at Leon's (Russell), and there were a few nights doing sessions with Nelson and Ringo. It's a scary thing meeting Beatles, but Nelson was so nice to me and included me in everything. We found out we were half-brothers same way me and Lucky did. Nelson said, 'You must be Charlie Truscott's son. He's my father too.' Then our paths didn't cross again until years later. This was '87, when the Heartbreakers were touring England with Lucky.

"Nelson came one night to see us in Birmingham. That was the first time I met Otis too. Lucky was busy with something, and so me and Nelson wound up just talking. I reminded him that we'd met years earlier in L.A., and there was some kind of weird click. It felt like we had known each other all our lives, and in a very personal way. We wound up just hanging a lot. I have a great photo somewhere; it was my birthday, and Nelson brought a little cake to my dressing room. In the photo, there is me with Nelson and Otis, Lucky, Roger McGuinn, Benmont Tench, and Mike Campbell—all of my favorite people

---

[5] Adapted from an interview with Tom Petty by American Songwriter, January 24, 2012 http://americansongwriter.com/2012/01/tom-petty-on-bob-dylan/

right there, and it was so sweet. That night there was a surprise hurricane in the UK, and my life never felt the same again after that hurricane blew through it."[6]

Charlie T. disappeared into the walk-in closet of the building he used as a studio on his Malibu estate where we met for our interview. I heard him rummaging through boxes. He returned with the photo in his hand.

From left to right: Lucky, Charlie T, Jnr., Benmont Tench, Roger McGuinn, Mike Campbell, Nelson, Otis
Photography Credit Unknown

"Don't we look like a fine bunch of fellows?"

I smiled as I reached for the photo. "All the Traveling Wilburys are there except Lefty."

---

[6] http://www.beatlelinks.net/forums/showthread.php?t=33896 (originally appeared in Rolling Stone but no longer retrievable)

As I handed the photo back to Charlie T., I remarked, "You said before your Wilbury power is seeing the future."

"Yeah."

"You must have known Lefty was going to pass away not too long after y'all finished the album."

Charlie T. lost his cheerful demeanor and frowned. "Look, I don't like to talk about that. I've tried warning folks when I knew something bad was going to happen, and it never made a damn bit of difference. I finally realized I couldn't change fate. Nelson says we have to be here now. Exist in the moment. Make the most of today. Eat, drink, and be merry, for tomorrow may never come. The only difference is, I can see whether it's coming or not. You have no idea what a pain in the ass knowing that is."

## CHAPTER 8

## LAST NIGHT

Nelson awoke earlier than usual that morning. He meditated for half an hour and looked at the hotel breakfast menu in disgust. The Hotel Bel-Air always offered the same thing, with meat on the side. Today he was hungry for something different. After checking his watch to ensure there was time for breakfast out, he remembered The Griddle Café, a Los Angeles landmark. They had the best pancakes in Southern California.

Finding a parking place was difficult in that part of Sunset Boulevard, so rather than driving up and down the street, Nelson parked about a half a mile away and set off at a brisk pace. A few passersby seemed to recognize him, but no one stopped him.

Halfway to his destination, Nelson spotted a street musician playing a ukulele. *Nine-thirty in the morning is a bit early for busking.* He stopped to listen nonetheless. The musician was male, wearing clean but shabby clothes and playing the uke like Nelson had never heard before. He accomplished glissandos and arpeggios that should not have been possible on an instrument with such a short neck.

After this warm-up, the street musician launched into an introduction familiar to Nelson—one of his own songs, "Flying Hour." He had written the song in the late seventies, but his record label had rejected it for two consecutive albums. "Flying Hour" had been released for the first time three months ago as part of a luxury, limited-edition book/record set that cost a small fortune. Nelson smiled at the musician, wondering how he had come by a copy. The musician caressed his instrument, coaxing sweet strains from it uncharacteristic of the ukulele.

Nelson stood on the curb, daydreaming about how he had written the song with Mick Ralphs of Mott the Hoople and Bad Company. A clock tower stood on his thirty-two-acre spread near Henley-on-Thames outside London. On the clock was a poem, placed there by a previous legendary owner of the mansion and its grounds, Sir Frank Crisp. The poem read:

> *Past is gone — thou canst not that recall*
> *Future is not — may not be at all*
> *Present is — improve the flying hour*
> *Present only is within thy power.*

With the song, Nelson had meant to convey what was lost by not living in the present. The past is gone, and we may not have a future. The only choice to bring value and meaning to living is to hold our consciousness in the present. Nelson attempted to live every waking moment by this philosophy. He often failed, but its driving principle was the one he returned to, over and over again.

*By recalling the genesis of the song, I'm living in the past, not the present. I want to be here now.*

Nelson dropped a ten-dollar bill in the player's ukulele case and trekked on to the café.

The Wilbury day started between noon and 1:00 p.m. The guys thought it was pretty early, since the group had been up until 3:00 a.m. the night before, getting high and playing ukuleles and guitars. The weather was so nice that everyone took their guitars outside to the little porch.

"Who's got an idea for a song?" Nelson asked as the half-brothers sat around the porch.

Charlie T., Jnr. spoke up. "I came up with a little something last night, and it's called 'Last Night.' See what I did there?"

Lucky knocked on Charlie T.'s skull with his knuckles. "Yes, Charlie T., we all see what you did there. Now, play us the song."

All Charlie T. really had was a one-line refrain. *"Last night, talking 'bout last night,"* which he sang over and over a few times.

Otis chuckled. "That ain't a song; it's a line on a loop."

Charlie T. crinkled his nose at Otis. "A what on a what? Well, you guys are going to help me turn it into a song, aren't you? We have all this songwriting virtuosity here. We must have written a hundred top-forty hits among us, but who's counting? Come on, let's get busy on the chords for the verses."

"Let's just do a three-chord progression with some sevenths thrown in," Nelson said.

They all started experimenting with different chords. It didn't take long.

"Okay, that's done," Charlie T. said. "Now for some lyrics. 'There at the bar, I got out of the car.'"

Lefty added, "She was long and tall."

"Or 'She was short and fat,'" Nelson suggested.

The air filled with laughter.

Nelson tried again. "She gave me a thrill."

"She was over the hill," Charlie T. interjected.

More laughter resulted.

Despite the horseplay, Charlie T. had been taking notes. He consolidated the better ideas into the first verse and read it out loud.

"Okay."

"That's great!"

"Yeah, that's a good'un."

He tried the second verse he had scribbled. "Her hair was dark, she was discreet; she danced lightly on her feet. She gave me a thrill there on Blueberry Hill."

Nelson pondered. "Well, the first two lines are good, but the second part will probably bring Fats Domino's attorneys down on our heads. I've had enough of being sued over copyright infringement after the 'My Sweet Lord'/'He's So Fine' fiasco."

Otis tipped down his head and regarded his brother over his shades. "That started off in 1971, didn't it? When Bright Tunes first sued you? And it's still dragging on?"

Nelson nodded ruefully. "A right royal pain in the arse. I never want to go through anything like that again."

Charlie T. leaned toward Nelson. "I'm sorry to tell you, it won't be completely over until 1998."

Nelson frowned at Charlie T. "Another ten years? What bullshit. Still, 'My Sweet Lord' has done a lot of good in the world, and I'm glad I wrote it, even if I did 'subconsciously plagiarize' it, as the court already found. There's no use wishing it didn't happen now, but I've learned not to do it again."

Charlie T. continued his predictions about Nelson's legal woes. "Speaking of doing good in the world, your lawsuit will become the template for hundreds of copyright infringement cases in the future. Lots of artists will be saved the headache of going through what you've had to endure. Many more people are gonna settle out of court when they see the gain for the guy doing the suing is minimal and the loss for the guy accused of doing the ripping off is huge in the end. The truth is, lots of songs sound alike. People can't just sue each other all the time because there's a resemblance. But if it's the same song …"

Nelson nodded at his brother. "I like the idea of reducing suffering in the world, so I'll take that prediction. Still, one copyright infringement lawsuit was enough for this lifetime."

"So no Blueberry Hill, eh?"

"You can quote song titles without getting sued," Otis advised. "It's called an homage. I wrote a song called 'Beatles Forever' and didn't get sued. Oh, wait, I never put that song out."

Nelson batted his eyelashes at his friend. "Afraid Yoko might come after you?"

Otis gulped. "Maybe a little."

"Otis, my brother, you're going to write more songs that contain homages and not get sued for them in the future," Charlie T. predicted.

"Oh, really? Which? Maybe I can go ahead and write them now for this album."

Nelson stamped his foot. "No fucking way."

Charlie T. snickered. "Tell you later."

Lefty had been lost in thought about Charlie T.'s ability to predict the future. He interrupted the conversation. "Charlie, have you always been able to foresee things?"

Charlie T. looked at his half-brother with a bemused expression. "No, Lefty. That started happening when I was about ten years old. You see, my stepdaddy was pretty abusive. He'd bang me around a lot when I was a kid. Whipped me with a leather belt, a switch, his hand—really whatever he could grab. One day he was so drunk and got so mad at me that he threw me up against the wall in our house, and my head hit the brick fireplace. I saw stars and heard birds chirping, and then I blacked out. My mamma picked me up and put me in bed. She cleaned the blood off my head. When I woke up the next morning, I had visions of the future. Things a ten-year-old shouldn't have to see. I had to grow up real quick then."

The room was silent.

"We have to work on this song." Nelson tried to get the group back on track. "Who's got a line instead of 'She gave me a thrill there on Blueberry Hill?'"

"She could lower a boom on him," Lucky suggested.

Charlie T. raised his eyebrows. "What kind of boom is she going to lower, Lucky?"

"Let's do it like a shakedown," Lucky replied. "The guy thinks he's met this beautiful woman who's going to sleep with him, but it turns out, she robs him."

Otis strummed some augmented chords. "Well, let's have 'em fuck first."

Charlie T. nodded. "So the boom she lowers can be a blow job."

Lefty frowned. "I don't think we have to spell that out. Let's just leave it up to the imagination of the listener."

"Okay, so we'll do the musical equivalent of panning the camera away from the action. Let's do a bridge," Nelson said and strummed an A-minor chord.

Nelson felt really proud of his brothers. These guys had been front men, solo acts, and a member of the greatest show on earth. He marveled at how little struggle for control there was among them. He was adding a certain amount of mental leavening to mellow out the proceedings, as well as doing his level best to keep his own ego out of it. Most of the unanimity arose from the willingness of each man to participate in the cooperative effort and really listen to each other. They all showed tremendous respect for each other.

Nelson smiled. He hadn't had this much fun in a long time.

Otis leaned back on the leather couch in the part of his Beverly Hills home known as The Barn. He crossed his long legs at the ankles. To my surprise, he lowered his shades for a moment and winked at me. I blushed and got flustered. I reminded myself we were blood relations.

"Ask your questions, Mavis" he said, smiling.

It took a moment to regain my composure. I wanted to conceal my longtime admiration for Otis, so I adopted an aloof attitude for this interview. I didn't want to blunder and botch my chances at a future invitation. His memories and insights were critical for this book. Oh, hell. I might as well admit I wanted to be in the same room with him, too.

"As the producer and co-writer of the track, what can you tell me about the recording of 'Last Night' back in 1988 with the Wilburys?"

"Blimey, that's almost forty years ago," Otis said.

"Actually, it's thirty years ago."

He was showing his well-known difficulty with timelines.

"Forty years, thirty years. It's still a long bloody time ago. I don't remember many specifics. Let's see. That was mostly Charlie T.'s song."

"Was a demo done first?"

Otis wrinkled his forehead as he thought. "I think so. I guess that was one of the first songs we recorded, and we were still getting used to the equipment. Nelson and me wanted to play around with how it would sound, even though we didn't have much time."

"How did you do the drum track?"

"I think we did some basic snares at Dave's, and then Buster finished it off at Friar Park. Same with Jim's horn."

"How about the bass line?"

"I don't think there was any bass on that one until Friar Park. No, maybe there was." Otis's face became more animated. "Oh, I'll tell you something about 'Last Night!' Buster was playing the refrigerator shelves in the intro on that one. He was playing them on 'Rattled' too."

My fannishness finally broke through. "You were so modest about writing 'Rattled.' That was obviously your work, but, in interviews you said all you did was sing it."

"Well, I wrote bits of it. We had agreed we all would share songwriting credit for all the songs."

"Each of you has such a strong voice as a songwriter that it's hard to hide it in the songs that weren't equal collaborations."

"Thank you." Otis showed me a shy, closed-mouth grin.

I pressed on, not realizing I was embarrassing him. "You wrote the tune and most of the words to 'Not Alone Anymore' too, didn't you?"

"I wrote that with Lefty. It was an equal endeavor."

I could tell he once again downplayed his contribution to the song. "In my opinion, that's the best song Lefty ever sang. Also, the best-produced song he ever sang."

Otis sank a little lower on the couch. "Thank you. It was my favorite thing I ever did." Otis has said this about several songs he has produced.

I finally realized how uncomfortable he was with all the compliments. "Let's talk some more about 'Last Night.' Who sang lead vocals?"

"Charlie T. and Lefty sang lead vocals. Lefty wrote the words to one of the bridges. Besides, we wanted to use

Lefty whenever we could because we just liked to hear him sing."

"And who did the backing vocals and the chorus?"

"Everyone did backing vocals on all the songs, unless someone couldn't make it for that day. We took no production notes until we got to Friar Park, so the details are lost to posterity. Why do you want to know all this?"

"I want to lend a note of authenticity to a work of fiction."

Otis regarded me sympathetically. "Since this interview is also fiction, that's going to be hard to do."

Otis and The Barn dissolved in a wash of fangirl fantasy.

# CHAPTER 9

## CALIFORNIA BLUE

The world grieved when Lefty Wilbury passed away on December 6, 1988 at the age of 52. He died of a heart attack at his mother's house in Tennessee. Although he lived long enough to see the great success of the Wilburys album, he would never know his own album, *Mystery Girl*, recorded with help from Otis, Nelson, and Charlie T., would also be a winner. He would become one of four performers to posthumously have two albums in the Billboard Top 5. Jim Croce, Elvis Presley, and Michael Jackson are the other three.

My interview with Barbara Wilbury, Lefty's widow, almost didn't happen. She had been extremely difficult to reach by phone or by email, and she hadn't been feeling well for the last few weeks. Her sons and stepson are extremely protective of her; they would allow me a fifteen-minute phone interview, no more. I chose my questions carefully.

I led with an easy question. "How did Lefty begin working with Otis?"

Barbara's voice sounded strong. "We had a telephone call from management that said Otis Wilbury was trying to reach Lefty Wilbury. Well, we weren't sure if they were half-brothers or not. There are many Wilburys in this world. We allowed the number to be given to Otis. Maybe three hours later, the telephone rang, and I said, 'Hello,' and nobody said anything. I said, 'Hello' again, and *click!* I knew it was Otis intuitively. Then somebody called again. There was a moment of silence on the line, and then somebody said, 'It's Otis Wilbury. Could I talk to

Lefty Wilbury?' And I said, 'Yes, he's waiting for you.'"
Barbara laughed at the memory.

"It sounds like Otis was quite nervous about talking to Lefty."

"Yes, he was. Otis told me later that Lefty was a teenage idol of his. He used to listen to Lefty's singing on the radio as a kid and just marveled at it."

"What happened next?"

"Otis came to our home in Tennessee and stayed for a few days. Our two sons were young then, and they got into a wet paper towel fight with Otis while he was waiting to meet with Lefty. They smacked him right in the face with a paper towel. He was such a good sport about it.

"Otis really wanted to do an album with Lefty. That was the beginning of *Mystery Girl*, the record. Within six months of having Otis to the house, Lefty said, 'I'm gonna take her on again.' He meant recording.

"Otis and Lefty learned then that they shared the same father, Charlie T. Snr. They told each other funny stories about their father, and it had to be the same man. Neither had grown up with their real father, but their mothers had told them all about the scoundrel he was.

"They tried to write some songs together, but things just weren't clicking. They agreed to get together again, but it didn't happen until we moved to Malibu. Once we got settled in California, Lefty called Otis at his home in Beverly Hills and said, 'I'm here, and I'm ready to work.'

"Otis also invited their other half-brother, Charlie T., Jnr., to join them in the songwriting. They came up with 'You Got It' the first time they collaborated. I think that's quite an accomplishment."[7]

Barbara's answer to the easy question had taken up my fifteen minutes, but she had told me what I wanted to know.

---

[7] Adapted from an interview with Barbara Orbison in *Mr. Blue Sky: The Story of Jeff Lynne & ELO*, video available in the Jeff Lynne's ELO at Hyde Park boxed set

## CHAPTER 10

## CONGRATULATIONS

Charlie T., Jnr. woke in the morning on the third day of recording hankering for a new guitar. The day before, Otis had described a twelve-string Ovation guitar he used on the *Eldorado* album and tour. He spoke lovingly of its resonance. Charlie T. decided he wanted one. Before heading to the recording session, he stopped by Guitar Center on Sunset Boulevard. He parked his 'Vette across the street and dodged cars as he crossed the six lanes of traffic.

Once he had survived the speeding cars, Charlie allowed himself to focus on his wider environment. In front on the huge music store, he noticed a street musician playing, of all things, a Gibson Flying V. He used a tiny amp sitting on the sidewalk with a wireless pickup. The Flying V was the guitar Charlie T. had made famous, incorporating it into his band logo. He decided he could spare five minutes to listen to the street performer and sauntered to the far outside corner of the store to see how well this guy could play.

The guitarist could play all right. This fellow was as good as Hendrix, Clapton, and Charlie's own lead guitarist, Mike, all put together. He tore up that Gibson. "Shredding" was putting it mildly. Completing the selection, the itinerant guitarist started a slower song Charlie T. recognized as one of his own—"Runaway Train," from his most recent album, *Let Me Up, I've Had Enough*. Charlie had strummed a twelve-string on that song. Next time he performed it, he would use the Ovation twelve-string he planned to purchase today.

The lyrics of the song reflected the losses Charlie T. had experienced in his life. He had written the song years after his mother died, but she had been on his mind while he was writing it. He had foreseen her death, just as he had foreseen the death of everyone he cared about. He thought it was odd that he couldn't foresee his own death but was glad of it. Knowing when someone would die and not being able to prevent it was a heavy burden to carry. Charlie T. tried to stay lighthearted and live every day to the fullest, but sometimes the weight oppressed him.

"Why are you playing that song, man? I'm on an upswing right now. I don't want to be brought down. You've got me thinking about a friend—who's gonna die soon." Charlie T. gazed at the sidewalk and reflected on the time Lefty had remaining, the pain he had experienced, and a life well-lived.

The guitar player ignored Charlie T. He produced a slide from nowhere and turned the tune into a blues riff. Charlie T. sang a couple of verses with him. He walked away when a crowd formed on the sidewalk and someone asked him for an autograph.

Back at the guest-house recording studio, Nelson and Charlie T. arrived on time from their respective errands, but Lucky was late again. The other four brothers sat on the porch, in the beautiful spring weather, strumming their guitars and trying to think of a song. Otis was playing with an E-A-B progression he thought he could turn into a rockabilly song.

Nelson noodled with some chords based on a raga, or Indian motif. He was determined to get at least one song about God somewhere on this album. Lucky had become a born-again Christian a few years ago but settled down to practicing a mixture of Christianity and Judaism. He was past proselytizing, so he wasn't writing as many songs about being saved. Plenty of Lucky's songs were washed with spirituality, which Nelson appreciated; he just didn't like being told he was going to Hell if he didn't accept the Lord Jesus Christ as his Savior. He worshipped the Lord Krishna, and venerated several thousand gods in the Hindu pantheon.

Lefty jotted ideas on a yellow pad for a song based on William Blake's "The Sick Rose." The poem was about a love that had become corrupted. The rose was red, like his lover's vagina, and the worm was the taint of her wandering desires. Lefty planned to call his song, "Winged Victory." Love would triumph in Lefty's version. He had the words to the poem in front of him:

> *O Rose thou art sick.*
> *The invisible worm,*
> *That flies in the night*
> *In the howling storm:*
> *Has found out thy bed*
> *Of crimson joy:*
> *And his dark secret love*
> *Does thy life destroy.*

Charlie T. relaxed in the shade on the grass with a joint stuck in his new guitar's strings at the machine head, strumming the chords to "A Mind with a Heart of Its Own"—a song he was working on for his solo album.

Up the driveway crunched Lucky's white Ford van. Out jumped Lucky, waving a piece of paper. "I've got most of a song done. That's why I'm late."

"Look who's here. Lucky Wilbury!" Nelson said.

Lucky ignored Nelson. He unpacked his guitar, haphazardly tuned it, and sang, *"Congratulations … That's the chorus. I've got a couple of verses too."*

The song had the usual droning two-note tune Lucky had been using lately. Otis and Nelson caught each other's gaze behind Lucky's back. There was enough light for Nelson to see Otis's eyes through his shades. He had one eye open wider than the other, looking askance.

Nelson smiled. "This is great, Lucky. Thanks for working on it at home. You've saved us a lot of time in the studio. Let's see what we can do with the melody."

Lucky raised one shoulder. "What's wrong with the melody?"

Nelson turned on the diplomacy. "Well, you know, Lucky, it's only got two or three notes. Let's just jazz it up a bit."

"The words are great!" Otis added. "I wish I could do lyrics like you, Lucky."

"Yeah, in your dreams," Lucky grumbled. Somewhere in the back of his ego, he knew all four of the others were better tunesmiths than he had been lately, but he could still run circles around them when writing lyrics, with both hands tied behind his back. On second thought, he needed one hand free to use his superpower. He also knew Otis was buttering him up so he would accept changes to his tune more readily. These words weren't *that* great.

Otis strummed the chords Lucky had played for the chorus. He looked at the lyric sheet Lucky had put on the table. Instead of playing the D major Lucky had written down, Otis went to a D minor, and back to the G6. That made the chord progression less monotonous, at least.

"This is backwards from how I usually work," Otis commented. "I usually do all the chords and a few tunes in my head and let the music suggest lyrics to me. Trying to get music from lyrics is a bit awkward."

Charlie T. had finally joined his brothers from the shaded yard. "Seems like you're doing okay at it."

Otis pointed to the last line in the verse. "I'm stuck on this bit here."

Charlie T. strummed. "Simple. Got a melody yet?"

Nelson nodded. "Yeah, for the chorus." He sang, *"Con-gra-tu-lay-tions."*

Otis nodded. "Way better than Lucky's."

Lucky sang "Isn't It a Pity" to mess with Nelson while he tried to sing the second line.

"That's the same two-note melody that Lucky brought in here," Otis objected.

"How do you expect me to compose a brilliant melody with him singing an old song of mine in my ear?" Nelson spluttered.

Lucky snickered.

Nelson tried again. *"Con-gra-tu-lay-tions."*

The next line was a descending melody.

"That's better," Otis said. "Still somewhat monotonous, but better. I'll give the verses a go."

Otis applied his melodic ability to the verse and composed three different variations, which he sang sequentially for Nelson, Charlie T., Lefty, and Lucky.

"How the fuck do you do that, man?" Lucky asked, with a tinge of jealously.

"I just do it. I've got another one I can offer you now," Otis said. He sang a fourth melody, completely different from the other three, and just as pleasant and catchy.

"I like the fourth one," Charlie T. said.

"I like the second one," Lefty argued

"Sing them all again," Nelson requested.

"Yeah, sing them all again," Lucky agreed.

Otis studied the lyric sheet written in Lucky's spidery handwriting and started over with the first tune he had shared. When he finished the fourth choice, he added a fifth that had come to him in the midst of singing the others.

"Did you sing five that time?" Lefty asked.

Otis nodded. "Yeah, just thought of another."

"Stop it, just stop it. We could be here for a week with you thinking of different tunes," Nelson chided his brother.

Otis looked crestfallen. "Just trying to get the best one."

Nelson shook his finger. "You know you're a perfectionist. This is one time there's no room for perfection."

Otis surveyed the men in the room. "Well, which is it?"

"Four," Nelson replied.

"Four," Lefty agreed.

"Four," Charlie T. said.

Lucky said, "Two." He liked to be obstreperous.

Nelson nodded. "Four it is then. Could you run through that one again, Otis? Just so Lucky can get a handle on it."

Otis and Nelson decided to do a demo of "Congratulations" as well. They were still finding their bearings with the equipment. There had been a few surprises on the first two songs, especially Lefty floating.

"Let's run through it with the acoustic guitars and a click track," Otis said.

The legends trooped into the kitchen with their guitars.

Nelson tapped his fingers on his guitar. "When we're ready to add the vocals, I think we should all sing 'Congratulations,' then Lucky should finish with each chorus line. Lucky, most of this song is yours. You sing the lead on the verses."

"Okay." Lucky loved being in the spotlight.

"This is just a rough run through. We'll work out the *oohs* and the *aahs* for the backing vocals later." Otis started the click track. "Strike up on your guitars once Richard gets the tape going. I'll count to four."

Richard had been listening, so he started the tape. Otis counted in. The five musicians strummed their guitars, playing one chorus and one verse. Richard had already cued the two tape decks, anticipating what Otis wanted.

Otis entered the control booth and turned one chorus and one verse into a full backing track.

"Okay," Otis looked around. "We're ready to do the vocals for the demo."

Five vocalists donned headphones. All came in on cue for the portions sung in chorus. Lucky sang his solo parts. Richard rewound the tape. Everyone crowded into the control room to hear the playback.

"Great."

"Turned out nice."

"Can we use that?"

"No," Otis said. "We need to work with the sound levels. I'm peckish. Let's eat and then do another one."

Charlie T. chuckled. "You're 'fetish?' What did you just say?"

Otis smiled. "It's how we say 'hungry' in Brum."

At the dinner table, Nelson held his checkbook. "I need to pony up some money for all the food we are eating. How much have you spent so far, Bugs?"

Bugs produced his account book. "About two hundred. I took it out of the Heartbreakers' funds."

Charlie T.'s head spun around. "You did what?"

Bugs looked askance. "I knew Nelson would be good for it. You think he was going to rip us off?"

Charlie T. shook his head. "Well, no."

"How much more you think we're gonna need?" Nelson asked.

Otis spoke up. "Why should you pay for all the food, Nelson? We've all got dosh. Why don't we split it?"

"Don't worry, I can take it out of sales and production costs, along with Lucky's level meter that Lefty blew up."

Otis seemed satisfied. "Okay, then."

Nelson looked back at Bugs and started writing a check. "How about a thousand?"

Bugs grinned. "Your autograph on that check is probably worth more than the amount."

"You want somebody else to write you a check?" Nelson asked, sneering.

"No, no, I'm saying I'll sell the check and get more than a grand."

"I don't think my autograph is worth that much these days. Maybe a hundred and fifty." Nelson continued writing.

"It'll go up to about twenty-five hundred in the future," Charlie T. muttered.

Nelson pretended not to hear him and tore the check from the book. He handed it to Bugs, who stuffed it into his wallet and thanked Nelson.

With the meal complete, the group trooped to the guest house. Ray had arrived during dinner and managed to grab a few bites before all the provisions returned to the big refrigerator.

Otis looked at Nelson. "Shall we do it just the same, then?"

"Sure. It sounded like it was almost there, didn't it? Let's fool with the levels a bit."

Otis entered the sound booth. "Okay, you lot, play some guitars."

Nelson picked up his guitar in one hand and Otis's guitar in the other hand. Two more arms protruded from underneath his shirt. He was wearing a tee-shirt today, so he ended up showing a large swath of skin. The two big-body acoustic guitars were awkward to play at the same time. Nelson maneuvered and adjusted them until he had them situated in a playable position. Lefty and Lucky watched him incredulously while he jostled. Charlie T. picked his teeth.

"How long have you had those other arms?" Lucky asked. "I saw them before and didn't ask because there was too much other stuff going on at the time."

Nelson scowled slightly as he regarded his half-brother. "I woke up with them one morning, about fifteen years ago. It happened after a particularly heavy recording session with Ravi. I thought they were permanent until they retracted during my morning meditation. They're related to my ability to control my body and mind through meditation."

"Why can't other people who meditate do that trick?"

"Maybe they can, and you just don't know it."

The four guitarists played the intro to "Congratulations" on their five guitars. Otis poised his long fingers over the control console and shot sparks. Gentle lightning danced over the soundboard. Knobs whirled, and levers spun, making subtle adjustments to the equipment.

"Perfect," Richard announced.

Otis returned to the kitchen to reclaim his guitar.

Nelson retracted his extra arms and pulled down his shirt.

"Guess I should keep a jacket handy when I'm going to do that," Nelson commented to Otis.

"No, mate, just take your shirt off altogether so's everyone can see how them extra arms work. You know they're all curious."

"Have you got any other extra parts that come out when you need them?" Charlie T. asked.

Nelson answered without missing a beat. "Why don't you ask my wife?"

Lucky, Otis, and Charlie T. fell out laughing, but Lefty looked mystified.

"Okay," Otis said. "One chorus and one verse, same as before."

They repeated the process as for the demo, with Lucky singing guide vocal. Twenty minutes later, the brothers had a backing track with guitars and a click track.

"Let's do the backing vocal tracks now," Otis called out. He was on a roll.

"No, let's have a beer." Charlie T. was thirsty. He didn't like to sing when he was parched.

"Yeah, time for a beer," Lucky said.

Pretty soon everyone except Lefty was sitting in the kitchen, holding cold beers. Lefty held an icy Diet Cherry Coke.

Nelson clicked his tongue at Otis. "What time do you think we'll be finished with this?"

"It's nine now. I think we can lock it down by eleven thirty, maybe eleven, as long as we don't try to do more than drums and bass here."

Nelson nodded. "We can add anything else we think it needs at Friar Park. I'd like to try to stick to the schedule of one song a day."

With the beer break over, the five congregated in the sound booth, wearing headphones. They had to sing into the same mic, so they formed a half-circle around it. That left Richard to handle the level check.

*"Oooo-oooo-aaaah,"* the legends sang.

Richard fiddled with the knobs and levers. "Otis, I'm not getting it."

Otis was standing closest to the door so he could have easy access to the soundboard. "Let's try again."

Richard tinkered with the adjustments on the soundboard for another two or three minutes as the brothers sang and watched him.

"What's the problem, Richard?" Lucky asked, removing one side of his headphones.

"I don't know, man. I just can't get it set right."

Otis sighed. "Let me do it. Start over, mates."

He moved to the board, hanging his cans around his neck. Otis shot a thin stream of sparks from his finger into the control board.

Instantly, Richard gave the thumbs up. "It's like she won't respond to anyone but you."

"Sometimes electronics are like a woman," Otis said. "They get a taste of a dick they like, and they don't want any other dick. Sorry, man."

Lefty launched into his favorite Monty Python ditty, "Penis Song."

Nelson broke in. "Not now, Lefty. We'd like to finish this song before midnight. After that, you can sing 'Penis Song' to your heart's content. I'll even call Eric Idle, and he'll come over here and sing it with you."

Lefty looked around. "You would do that for me, man?"

"I would do anything for you, Lefty. Now, let's sing this song. I mean let's sing 'Congratulations,' not 'Penis Song.'"

Lucky, Lefty, and Charlie T. went home after the backing vocals were done. They weren't needed to lay down the bass and drum tracks. The snake still ran to the living room of the main house, so Buster took his place behind his kit and tested sound levels. Ten minutes later, they had a drum track. Buster was one of the best session drummers in the business. He didn't fool around, and he knew what was needed.

All that was left was for Otis to record the bass line. Nelson said good night around 11:15 p.m. and left Richard and Otis in the studio alone. Otis liked recording this way the best. If his brothers would let him, he'd play every instrument himself and work alone with the engineer.

# CHAPTER 11

## RATTLED

At the start of Wednesday, May 11—the fourth day of recording—it was Otis's turn to deliver part of a song. He had some chords, five tunes, and rough lyrics he had stayed up most of the night writing.

Otis and Charlie T. rode together in Charlie's 'Vette to the recording studio. Otis poured out his heart to his younger half-brother on the way.

"You know, Charlie, you're the only other member of the Traveling Wilburys I feel like is my equal. We're the two youngest, and we've had about the same number of hits and sold the same number of records. Your songs are only a little better than mine. It feels natural and a good match to write songs with you."

Charlie T. nodded. "Thanks, Otis. It feels natural to write songs with you too, but I don't know about my songs being better than yours. And ELO had more Top 40 hits than the Heartbreakers have so far, although I'll end up with more than you just from sheer persistence." Charlie T. shook his head. "But the funny thing is you'll co-write five of my most popular tunes. We'll sell more records than you, but your manager fucked up your record sales figures so bad there's no telling how many records you really sold. Probably way more than us."

"I never had a number one, except 'Xanadu,' which I didn't sing."

Charlie T. laughed uproariously and slapped the steering wheel. "Neither did I. And I won't ever, so you got me on that one. Isn't life funny?"

"Whatever. Anyway, don't tell the others what I'm about to tell you, okay? It's kind of personal."

"Won't say a word."

Otis took a deep breath. "Lefty was the first pop singer I ever idolized. I remember listening to 'Only the Lonely' under the covers of my bed on the old crystal set and would imagine my voice coming out of the radio. His singing was so good he sounded like the opera singers my dad played all day long on the radio, but Lefty was doing popular music. I knew I could never sing opera, but maybe, just maybe, I could sing pop, like Lefty ... though I wouldn't ever be as good as him. Working with Lefty is like a dream come true. I get butterflies in my stomach every time I sit next to him, singing and playing." Otis grew quiet and pulled his beard.

Charlie T. glanced from the road to Otis for a moment and nodded. "Yeah, I know what you mean. I'm the youngest of the group, and I idolized those guys too, especially Nelson. But he acts like a regular guy and doesn't expect to be treated special. He makes me feel comfortable."

Otis looked back at Charlie T., nodded, and returned his gaze to the road. "I want to feel comfortable around Nelson, but every time I look at him, the word *Beatle* pops into my head. The Beatles hit the scene in the UK when I was fifteen. I had a guitar by that time. It weren't much of a guitar, but I worked out them chords to The Beatles songs, and I formed this half-soaked group called the Andicaps. I completely idolized The Beatles. I ate, slept, and breathed The Beatles. I couldn't wait to get out of school so I could play full time in a band and be just like 'em."

"Yeah, man, me too. I was fourteen when I started The Sundowners. Then the Epics, then Mudcrutch after I got out of school. Mudcrutch is as bad a name as the Andicaps." Charlie T. giggled.

Otis glanced at Charlie. "Nelson was my favorite Beatle. His guitar playing inspired me to become a lead guitar player. I learnt all the lead licks on all The Beatles' records. I even copied the lead line from 'Dear Prudence' for '10538 Overture,' ELO's first hit. I jangled it up and played it faster, but it were all the same notes as 'Dear Prudence.' Another homage." Otis snickered. "I wonder if Nelson has cottoned on to that?

"And Lucky. I first heard Lucky's songs when a friend from Shard End back in Brum played 'Blowin' in the Wind' on his mono record player. This was about a year after The Beatles took off in the UK. At first, I thought of Lucky as a sort of anti-Beatle. He was folk and protest, one lone guitar and voice … but he wrote songs with incredible lyrics that touched my heart and soul. Then he went electric and became more like a solo Beatle, but with those poetic lyrics still pouring out of him.

"Lucky was the only artist who could come close to writing songs as good as The Beatles. On the other hand, Lucky was nowhere near The Beatles in putting a track together. Most of Lucky's message was in the lyrics, not the music. The Beatles revolutionized how music was made."

Charlie T. brought the car to a stop at a red light and turned to Otis. "I've always been amazed by Lucky's lyrics. I don't know how he wrote those songs, you know. It's like he was touched by some supernatural force. It must be his Wilbury superpower, but he's never let me in on it. I feel really honored that he asked me and the

Heartbreakers to tour with him. That's been one of the highlights of my life."

"Those tours must have been incredible. Yeah, I'm really curious about Lucky's superpower too. He's got to have one. And now, here we are, in the same room with Lefty, Nelson, and Lucky, recording with them. It feels really big-time-Charlie. How did I get here? Even though we're all brothers, we grew up in different families. We were strangers most of our lives. Sure, I've got slews of gold records and won music industry awards for songwriting and recording, but none of that seems good enough to warrant working with them three musical ... gods. Them three are the very people who set me on my course in life as a musician. I would never be where I am if it wasn't for them. And they want to work with me. I'm gobsmacked."

Charlie pressed the accelerator when the light turned green and chuckled. "I know. Isn't it something?"

"So I wrote this song about being twisted, shaken, and rattled, thinking about how amazed I am to be working with them, but I made it about a relationship so they wouldn't know I'm starstruck."

Charlie T. guffawed. "I won't tell them about you, if you won't tell them about me."

When Otis and Charlie T. arrived at the studio, Lucky was actually there already, having arrived right on time. The other Wilbury brothers gathered around to listen to the song Otis had mostly ready. He sang melody number three, which he liked best, to the other members of the group.

"How many more melodies you got?" Nelson asked.

"You don't like that one?" Otis rebutted.

"I like it fine," Nelson replied, "but I know you have more."

"I got four more," Otis admitted.

"All right, then. Let's hear them," Lucky said.

Otis sang the other four melodies for his brothers. They voted and chose the one Otis had offered the first time.

Otis sighed and pulled the side of his beard—the surest tell Otis was nervous. "I told you that were the best one. It sounds the most like an old rock and roller."

Charlie T. poked Otis in the ribs. "We wanted to make sure."

"Now, let's work on these lyrics," Lucky suggested.

"Yeah, the lyrics need work," Otis agreed, knowing lyric composition wasn't his strong suit. It could take him days to complete song lyrics. He would start with one set of lyrics and rework it over and over. The finished lines rarely resembled the starting ones. On the other hand, some of his song lyrics had been banged out in the studio while his bandmates waited. Several of his songs had been recorded with unfinished lyrics: "Doo dah dah dee" and "Doo wop, doobie doo doo wop." Despite this relative weakness, he had written some of the finest lyrics in pop.

"Let's leave that 'til later," Nelson said. "I want to get on with a demo for this song."

Otis looked at Nelson. "You wanna do a demo for this one too? I'm feeling pretty comfortable with this equipment."

"Well, I'm not," Nelson responded. "I don't like it that Richard couldn't set those levels yesterday. What the hell was going on? Maybe you should keep your sparks out of the board today and just let Richard do it manually."

Otis pouted a little. "Whatever you say, Nelson. But you know we're in a hurry because of Lucky's schedule. It's so much faster when I just zap it."

Nelson's voice was stern. "Otis, what if the board doesn't work right for Dave and Siobhan after we leave? It would be our fault if you fuck it up with your shortcuts."

"Nelson, you know that's never happened before. The boards I've worked on have always gone back to normal." Otis wasn't going to let his brother push him around despite his immense respect for him. He had more experience as a producer in a wider variety of studios than anyone in the room.

"Then why couldn't Richard set the sound levels yesterday?"

Otis shrugged. "I dunno. I didn't troubleshoot. I just fixed it. It didn't have anything to do with me."

Nelson continued to look doubtful. "I really think we should let Richard do the setups manually."

Otis nodded. "Okay. We'll see how the day goes. That will work today 'cause the song is almost done, but on days we have to write a song and record it too, we're going to be here a long time."

Richard set up the mics for the acoustic guitars in the kitchen. The five half-brothers filed into the kitchen with their instruments and sat down. Otis called for a level check and Richard hustled into the sound booth. This time the board responded to his touch.

"This is a demo," Otis said. "We need to do two verses, a bridge, then the guitars stop playing to allow for some percussion where we're gonna do the 'rattled, twisted, shaken' bit, then another verse, then another bridge, followed by the guitars stopping for the 'rattled, twisted, shaken' bit, and a final verse with the coda. Everyone got it?"

"I don't got it," Charlie T. said "Will you write it down?"

"What happened to one verse and one bridge?" Lucky asked.

"Otis isn't going to zap the board today," Nelson answered. "We decided to give the zapping a rest."

Charlie T., Lucky, and Lefty all talked at once.

"Why the hell do you want to do that?"

"It's going to take forever."

"Why can't Otis zap the board?"

Lucky's voice rose over the din. "We've got this fucking miracle worker who can throw lightning from his fingertips and magic a soundboard into doing anything he wants and he isn't going to use his superpower? What the fuck?"

"I think it's best if we give the board a rest since it was acting funny yesterday," Nelson said.

"How was it acting funny?" Lucky asked.

"You know. It wouldn't let Richard adjust the levels, and Otis had to do it with magic," Nelson said.

Lefty objected. "I saw Richard set the levels today."

Nelson held up his hands. "Yes, Richard was able to work the board today."

"Then, why can't Otis do his thing today?" Charlie T. interjected.

Nelson could see he was about to have a full-blown rebellion on his hands. He wasn't expecting this. All his brothers were recording artists who were used to the vicissitudes of studio life. He thought they would cooperate with his direction, but they were clearly going to argue about this one. Otis's ability had spoiled them, and they wanted to take advantage of it.

"Otis," Nelson said, "Let me see you outside."

Otis and Nelson were co-producers on this album, and they made any production decisions together. The two walked around the side of the big house. When

Nelson looked toward the guest house, he saw three pairs of eyes watching them from the window. They continued walking far enough around the big house so the other three could no longer see them and read their body language.

"What do you think, Otis?" Nelson asked.

Otis pulled the side of his beard again. He was especially nervous today because they were working on his song and he would most likely be the featured vocalist. "I think those three are going to be pissed off as hell if I don't run the board. They've gotten used to my shortcuts, and they want them to continue. Lucky might even walk."

Nelson looked deeply into his half-brother's blue eyes, visible through his shades in the bright sunshine. "Damned if you aren't right. Go ahead and zap the board. Can you keep it to a minimum?"

"Okay, Nelson. Maybe you should tell them that if the board acts up again, there will be no more zapping."

"Good idea." Nelson clapped his half-brother on the back. "I really love working with you."

Otis smiled broadly. "I love working with you too, Nelson."

When Otis and Nelson had returned to the guest-house studio, Otis first addressed the rest of the group. "I'm going to be using my extra abilities on the board, but Nelson has something to add."

Nelson looked from Charlie T. to Lefty to Lucky. "If the board acts up again, we will be doing things the old-fashioned way. Everybody got that?"

The other three nodded. It seemed like a reasonable compromise.

"Okay, one verse and one bridge," Otis said. "Everyone ready? Richard? Got the levels?"

Richard recorded the verse and bridge while Otis sang a guide vocal. They followed the usual procedure and Otis's magical ability produced the acoustic guitar backing track they needed, coming in at three minutes and eight seconds.

Otis looked for Buster. "Let's put some drums on this thing. Where's Buster?"

Buster was nowhere to be seen. He had not come to work that day.

"Can't you just do some vocals while we're waiting for Buster?" Nelson asked. "I'll call him now."

Nelson trotted to the main house to call Buster, and Richard readied the board for Otis's vocal.

Otis felt reluctant to record the vocals with the lyrics half done, but it was only a demo. He'd have to hum and mumble his way through part of it. He used to do this when he'd forget the words during ELO concerts in the 70s, and it was nothing new. In those days, he'd just turn up the volume on his guitar a bit. Forgetting lyrics was one of the reasons he'd grown to hate touring.

Otis stood next to the mic in the sound booth. "These lyrics are only half done you know, so this is going to be rough."

Richard started the tape.

"I don't know what it is. I'm only going to fuck around with it," Otis muttered.

Otis had the unfinished lyric sheet in front of him. He settled the cans on his head and sang "Rattled"—the song he had partially worked out the night before. He changed some of the lyrics as he sang and mumbled others.

Nelson returned from calling Buster while Otis was still singing. He donned headphones and brought a headphone-wearing Lefty into the sound booth with him.

Otis watched them enter, wondering what they were up to.

When Otis reached the part of the song where there was no guitar backing, Nelson leaned closer to the mic. "Rattled, twisted."

Lefty sang over Nelson. "Shaken."

Nelson repeated, "Rattled."

Lefty trilled one of his famous *Rrroooww* sounds, like he had used in "Oh, Pretty Woman."

Otis and Nelson looked at him and grinned. Nelson pointed at Lefty and nodded approvingly. Otis gave him a double thumbs-up.

Otis could barely finish singing the demo, he was smiling so widely. He leaned back from the microphone and said, "Can you believe we have Lefty Wilbury singing with us?"

Charlie T. stuck his head in the door. "Come on, Lefty, you gotta do the growl again."

"Oh, you want me to do the growl?"

"Yeah, yeah. Please do the growl."

"*Rrroooww.*"

Charlie T. hopped around on one foot he was so excited. "I love it. I love it."

An hour later, Otis had laid down the bass track on the demo, and they were still waiting for Buster. The delay from the missing drummer had negated their head start of having part of a song written.

"Let's eat," Nelson said. "Buster said he would be here in an hour and a half from when I called."

Once again, Buster arrived just in time for a sumptuous meal served by Bugs's caterer. Buster had a pair of dowel drumsticks in his back pocket, which he laid on the sideboard behind him. Dowel sticks are between regular drumsticks and brushes, made of small birch rods tied together with plastic and capped on one end. They deliver a softer sound than sticks and a harder sound than brushes. Buster thought they would be perfect for the acoustic sound the Wilburys were seeking. He brought them to dinner to discuss them with the producers.

Nelson picked up an avocado, tomato, and sprout sandwich. "It's about fucking time you got here, Buster. Where the hell have you been?"

"You've been writing songs all day the first two days. I didn't think you needed me until tonight, man. I'm sorry." Buster looked at his plate. He had played with the greats: Lucky, CSNY, Pink Floyd, and all the ex-Beatles. He respected no one more than the Wilburys. He was chagrinned to think he might have let them down.

Otis saw Buster's discomfiture. "Really, Buster, we never know what time we'll need you. Sometimes earlier, sometimes later. Is it inconvenient for you to just hang out? Can you get here at like two-thirty or three o'clock? You might have to sit around and watch us struggle with a song for a while before we need you to play."

"I can get here at one o'clock if you need me to. I'd love to watch you guys write. Are you kidding?" Buster knew he was sitting with some of the world's greatest songwriters.

After dinner, Buster was still bummed by Nelson's tongue lashing. He ordinarily would have helped Bugs with the dishes. Out of nervousness, he used the dowel sticks to bang on the inside of the big refrigerator. Drummers often hit things in time to work out their emotions, and Buster was no exception.

Buster banged a rhythm on the grate above the refrigerator that vented the heat from the coils. He tapped a rhythm on the shelves. He moved the plate of eggs aside to make more room for his tapping and banging. He moved the big platter of enchiladas from the front to the back to see what effect that had on the pitch of the shelf he was whacking and was pleased with the results.

Nelson had come from behind him to get another beer. "Looks like you've invented a new percussion instrument—refrigerator shelves."

Buster laughed and ran his dowel sticks over the empty cups in the door where the eggs belonged. They were almost out of eggs, and Bugs would probably be going to the market today to stock up.

Otis joined them in the kitchen, also intending to grab another beverage. "What'r'ya doing, Buster? Finding the rhythm of the fridge?" Otis stood behind him, nodding his head to the beat of the sticks against the different parts of the big refrigerator. "I like this sound. We should overdub it on the track."

Nelson leaned against the counter. "That's a capital idea, Otis. Let's do it."

"Wait, you guys want me to play a percussion line on the refrigerator?"

Nelson shrugged. "Sure, why not? This album is anything goes, right? We can do whatever the hell we want."

Buster laughed as he continued to tap a rhythm on the parts of the fridge. "You guys are in charge. I'll do whatever you like."

He felt a lot better now that he had found a way to please Nelson.

When Richard and Bugs finished placing the microphone lead, Buster hurried to the big house and donned his headphones. He had already worked out how he would tap on the shelves during the middle bit, when the guitars were silent, and the subtle tapping could be heard. It took two takes, with Buster backtracking to the studio between takes so he could hear how his work sounded and the tape. Bugs snapped some Polaroid pictures that preserved Buster's creativity for posterity.

After finishing the demo, the brothers commenced work on the final version of the words. The workday was almost gone—nearly ten o'clock. Lefty, Nelson, and Otis sat in the dining room of the big house with the rough lyrics Otis brought that morning.

"What are we going to do with these?" Nelson asked rhetorically.

"Where's Lucky?" asked Lefty.

"Where's Charlie T.?" asked Otis.

Charlie T., Jnr. was the fastest and best lyricist after Lucky. The brothers needed both working on this song if they were going to get it done quickly enough to finish the track tonight.

Nelson went looking for the other two brothers. "Oh, *Laa-Keee*." His voice was singsong. "We need you to write some brilliant *lee-rics* for us."

Lucky and Charlie T. trooped in from the patio. "I heard someone say my name. You guys ready to work?"

"Yeah," Otis said, "We need to finish this song so we can wrap up sometime tonight."

Nelson hurried into the dining room as Lucky took the lyric sheet from Lefty, who had jotted a couple of new lines on it.

He perused what the others had written over Otis's original lyrics and grunted. "These are a mess. It's already late. How are we gonna finish this song tonight?"

"Let's get to work on it," Nelson suggested.

Nelson took control. "This is a simple rockabilly song, so the lyrics should be simple. Some of these lyrics Otis wrote are good, so we don't have to start from scratch."

Charlie T. and Lucky made some suggestions for improving the second verse. Lucky's ideas were much more complex than the song required.

*I'm rattled and embattled from wanting your touch.*
*I'm rattled from the emptiness of needing you so much.*
*I prattled like a child going wild over you.*

"Well, Lucky, those are great lyrics, but not for this song. Think folk music. Simple lyrics," Nelson said cautiously.

"Those are pretty simple lyrics for me."

"Simpler."

Lucky hunched over with his elbows on the table and leaned his cheeks on both of his fists. "You want me to write these lyrics or not?"

"Of course. I want you to write the lyrics with the rest of us."

Charlie T. had been scribbling on his tablet. "How does this sound?"

*I'm rattled like a snake from a gypsy pond.*
*I'm rattled like a cake in the oven too long.*
*I'm rattled, baby, over you.*

Nelson chuckled. "You two are really laying on the metaphors. I preferred Otis's original version that wasn't so metaphor heavy."

"When you use 'like,' it's actually a simile, not a metaphor," Lefty corrected.

Lucky dropped his hands from his cheeks to the table. "My lyrics are better than Charlie T.'s."

Charlie T. leaned on the table. "Well, yes, brother, they are, but not for this song."

"We're not using either one of those verses," Nelson interrupted. "Lucky, can I see you in the kitchen, please?"

Lucky frowned. "What for?"

"Indulge me, please."

Once in the sizeable kitchen and out of earshot of the other three, Nelson put his hand on his half-brother's shoulder. "I have complete faith in your ability to flick out brilliant lyrics in a twinkling."

"Okay … And?"

"We aren't getting anywhere with this song, and we are in a hurry."

"Then use Otis's original, shitty lyrics."

"I know you can do way better than Otis's original, shitty lyrics if you just put your magic finger to work."

Lucky grunted again. "You're determined to make me use my superpower, aren't you?"

"Why do you want to keep it secret from our other brothers?"

"You know I've always kept it hidden. I showed it to you up in Woodstock because we had gotten so close during that visit. I knew I could trust you after I took you to the cave and the entity shared its power with you like it did with me. I'm surprised you didn't get the same songwriting gift I did."

"No, my songwriting got streets better, but I'm not able to do what you can do. I must not have quite the same Wilbury gene as you."

Lucky stared at Nelson for a long moment. "Okay, I'll do it. The others have showed me their gifts. I'm the only holdout. It does kinda make me feel like a shithead."

Lucky and Nelson trooped back into the living room, and Lucky picked up the original lyric sheet that contained cross outs and scribbling. He paused and looked at the other three, still seated around the dining room table.

"We're all gifted Wilburys here. This stays between us."

Lucky clutched the lyric sheet in his left hand and held his right hand in the air with the elbow bent, index finger extended. He concentrated for a moment and moved his finger to the right. Golden words in spindly longhand appeared from nowhere, floating in the air behind Lucky's finger. Lucky moved his finger in one row after another, as if he were writing lines of a song in the air. He didn't appear to be actually writing words with the finger, but wiggling it randomly.

The words hanging in the air were the verses to Otis's song, in meter and rhyme. The lyrics used Otis's basic ideas, refined in form and fluidity. They incorporated the new ideas that had been written in the margins.

Three mouths dropped open. Charlie T. recovered first. "You didn't tell us you could do that!"

Lucky chuckled. "I hadn't needed to before. How do you think I've written so many long, poetic songs?"

Lefty hurriedly transcribed the golden words floating in the air. The first words were already dissipating. "Lucky, how long do your lyrics usually remain visible?"

Lucky shrugged, finger still wiggling. "About an hour, but they start to fade out before that. I write 'em down as soon as I can."

Charlie T. flashed his blue eyes at Lucky. "Man, I wish I could do that. It would make songwriting a hell of a lot easier."

Lucky scoffed. "Well, I don't do it every time. Just when I get stuck, or when there's some kind of time crunch, like now."

Otis still stared open-mouthed at the floating lyrics. He thought about how hard it was for him to write words. The song he had put together last night was one of the fastest he had ever written—next to "Evil Woman," which had taken six minutes without words—and he still needed his brothers to help him finish it. *If I had this gift instead of my gifts as a producer ... Well, no point wishing for something I can't have. I should be grateful for what I do have.*

"Okay, I got it," Lefty said and handed the new lyric sheet to Otis.

Otis grabbed his guitar and strummed the chords. He sang the new lyrics to test them out. He had trouble with the line Lucky's superpower had written: *"It might look like nothin's wrong but way down in my soul."* He tried singing it a couple of different ways and couldn't make it work.

Charlie T. suggested how to change it so it would parse better.

The brothers trooped toward the studio. Otis waved to Buster and Richard, sitting in the control room, playing gin rummy on a board across two chairs.

Otis turned on the vocal mic and spoke to the control room. "Richard, will you overdub the drum line from the demo to the final version we're working on now? Also, we aren't going to have time to redo the guitar tracks. Would you just double them, so we can get a richer sound? We can get some nice tracking on those guitars. Then we'll do the vocals over it."

"Will do," Richard answered through the talkback mic from the control room. He dropped the cards in his hand and worked with the tape decks.

"What about the bass line, Otis?" Nelson asked.

Otis cast his eyes toward the ceiling, thinking. The bass line he had done for the demo sounded pretty good, probably good enough for the final version. "Let's overdub the demo bass line onto the final version. If you don't like it, we can redo it at Friar Park. Sound okay?"

Nelson nodded. "Then, we're just going to do vocals and backing vocals, and call this one done?" Nelson asked.

Otis nodded. "On the BVs, I'm thinking some *oohs* and *aahs* with doubled voices, the rest of us saying, 'twisted, shaken, rattled,' and of course, Lefty growling. That was bostin."

Nelson clapped his hands. "Let's do this then. You're singing it."

Otis felt nervous. "Rattled" was the only song for which he was performing the lead vocal all the way through for this album. One of his vocal variations, a powerful rock-and-roll style, would fit the rockabilly song perfectly. Still, he felt the others would be evaluating his performance. He was especially nervous about singing lead on a whole song in front of Lefty, the greatest pop singer in the world.

When Otis had started his music career in the sixties, he was too shy to sing at all. Until many other Birmingham musicians told him he was a fantastic singer, he hadn't thought his voice was good enough. By the seventies, he had enough confidence to be the lead singer on every ELO song ever recorded, after Woody had left.

*Just go in there and do your best,* Otis thought.

Otis approached the mic. To jazz up the beginning, he sang *oh yeah* before starting the first verse. Nelson nodded at him through the glass.

Otis flubbed the first and second take, even though the lyric sheet hung right in front of him. He tended to lose his place when he was nervous. He performed the song perfectly on the third take and felt an immense sense of relief.

The brothers sat in the kitchen and worked out the backing vocals. Otis had been too nervous to think about them while he was doing the lead vocals, but Nelson had been developing them. He explained what everyone was to do. They entered the sound booth and recorded the backing vocals without a hitch. Otis was great at directing backing vocals. People who normally couldn't do good supporting vocals, like Lucky, were outstanding at them when Otis was in charge.

The track was as complete as they had planned for it to be by 1:00 a.m. Despite the long day, everyone was energized. They sat around the living room of the big house, drinking, smoking, and reminiscing.

"Hey Nelson," Lefty said. "You remember my birthday party in Soho in '64? Your whole group and your wives and girlfriends were there. My wife and kids were there."

"No, Lefty, I didn't make it to that party. Only Richie and John were there. Richie, or Ringo as he's known to you, told me about it the next day."

"Oh, yeah. Well, I was pretty drunk that night."

"Richie told me you had a huge cake shaped like a bloody guitar. You had a food fight and were all covered with it by the end of the night."

"Yeah, I remember the cake. You know, these days with y'all remind me of the hijinks on the tour with the Rolling Stones in Australia," Lefty said.

Otis loved hearing Lefty talk about his experiences from the early days of rock and roll. "Tell us about that tour."

"Mick Jagger bet me that if I would sing my worst song during one night's show, the Stones would sing their worst song. I went out there and sang 'Ooby Dooby,' and those suckers just sang their regular set. I got all over them for not singing a bad song!"

"It probably would have been 'I Wanna Be Your Man,'" Nelson speculated. "John and Paul unloaded that shit on them early. Then we turned around and recorded it anyway. Poor Ringo had to sing it."

Lucky laughed. "Hey, 'I Wanna Be Your Man' isn't such a bad song. I did a homage to it, as Otis calls it, back in sixty-five. It was called, 'I Wanna Be Your Lover.'" Lucky reached for his guitar and strummed a few chords as he sang.

"I don't think 'Ooby Dooby' is a bad song," Otis added. "I like it."

Lefty shook his head. "I'm not crazy about it."

"Anyway, they gave me a silver cigarette case to make up for it. It's inscribed 'From the Rolling Stones to Ooby Dooby.' So funny."

"That's a great story, Lefty," Lucky said.

Lefty continued. "I met Marianne Faithful on that tour. She was such a beautiful, sexy girl. She talked me into letting her wear my shades and we took a picture. It's one of the few photographs of me without them." Lefty looked around the room. "Hey, Otis. Let me take a picture of you without your shades."

"I'm afraid not, Lefty. I haven't taken my shades off for ten years. I'm not taking them off tonight." Otis smiled and took a pull at his beer and a drag from his cigarette.

"Otis, why do you wear those shades all the time, anyway?" Lefty asked.

"Homage to you, my brother. It's my homage to you."

Lefty laughed. He obviously thought Otis was teasing him.

"Why don't you tell some stories from your touring days, Otis?"

"Cor blimey. I was drunk most of the time and can hardly recall what happened. Anyway, I have this problem with remembering when things happened. Always have. I do know I fished Sharon Arden, who was our tour manager, out of the fountain at a big hotel. She was totally pissed up and probably would have drowned if I hadn't waded out there and rescued her. But I don't remember when or where it was. She married Ozzy Osbourne later on. She had to stay sober with him around. He was always getting into trouble with his drug use and drinking."

Lefty turned pensive. "It's really a shame what happened to Marianne Faithful when she got into drugs. But the most amazing thing about touring back then was the girls. I never thought of myself as a good-looking guy. I mean, y'all probably got a lot more of this than me because you are all good looking. But the girls used to mob me in the early sixties, especially in England. And I had my pick to take back to my hotel room." Lefty shook his head.

Otis laughed. "It's the rock-star magnetism. They think that by fucking us they can somehow become one with the music."

Charlie T. scoffed at Otis. "Naw, that ain't it. At least not with me. It's because I'm so sexy and irresistible. Come on, if you was a woman, could you resist me?"

Nelson turned to face his half-brother. "If I was a woman I wouldn't have any trouble resisting you, you greasy-haired motherfucker."

Charlie T. turned serious. "Yeah, fans can be really frightening sometimes too. I was pulled down into the audience once, and it felt like they were going to tear me apart. My clothes were all torn, and I was bruised up. Bugs got there first, but it was the two of us against hundreds. It seemed like it took concert security forever to get there and get me back up on the stage. Scariest experience of my life. Almost as scary as having my house burn down."

Lefty's eyes opened wide in surprise. "Your house burned down too?"

Charlie T. nodded. "Yeah. Arson."

Lefty looked him in the eye through his sunglasses. "Did everybody get out?"

Charlie T. nodded again. "Everybody."

Lefty sighed in relief. "Thank God for that. Did they catch the guy?"

"Never caught him."

The brothers knew the tragedy of Lefty's home burning to the ground and the loss of his two oldest sons. The youngest had been playing with airplane glue. His parents and his youngest son had survived. Lefty and his wife were in England on tour when the catastrophe occurred.

No one spoke for several moments.

Nelson broke the tension. "The scariest thing that ever happened to me on tour was in the Philippines when President Marcos's wife, Imelda, got mad at us for ignoring her goddamn luncheon invitation. She cancelled all the police protection, and we had to get on the airplane without any help. The citizens were mad at us because we insulted their first lady or empress or whatever she was called. Brian got beat up, and some others in our party were injured getting to the plane. Guess we got the last laugh when they got deposed."

Lucky spoke softly. "It scared me pretty bad when I hurt my hand."

Nelson turned to Lucky. "How'd you do that?"

"I don't want to talk about it." Lucky was flexing his right hand, as if recalling the injury. A scar ran across the palm that no one had noticed before. Charlie T. knew the story, but he protected Lucky's privacy. Lucky had never told the tale publicly.

Nelson cradled Lucky's hand in his. "I guess you were afraid you wouldn't be able to play anymore, huh?"

Lucky nodded. "It still hurts sometimes."

Nelson ran his fingers over Lucky's scar. "That would scare me, too. Play us something now, would you?"

Lucky picked up his guitar and played "Hobo's Lullaby."

## CHAPTER 12

## WINGED VICTORY

All five musicians, even Lucky, arrived on time for the fifth day's session. The Wilburys had put four songs to bed and were feeling pretty cocky.

"Okay," Nelson said, surveying the group seated on the front porch. "Who's got a song?"

"I've been working on this song called 'Winged Victory,'" Lefty answered. "It's based on 'The Sick Rose' by William Blake."

Lucky spoke up. "You mean the *Winged Victory of Samothrace?*" Although Lucky had only attended college for a semester, he had given himself the equivalent of a liberal arts education. He had studied painting with Norman Raeben and had become familiar with modern and classical art and literary works. He knew the *Winged Victory of Samothrace* was a marble statue from the second century BC, carved in Greece. Standing eight feet tall, it is headless and armless, having lost them to the ravages of time or vandalism, like many statues of that era. It had been carved to commemorate a victory at sea.

"Uh, yeah," Lefty answered. "That's the statue in the Louvre. I saw it one of the times I was in Paris. It really spoke to me."

Lucky nodded. "That's the one." Charlie T. asked, "What's 'The Sick Rose' about?"

Lefty smiled. "Love gone wrong. What else?"

Charlie T. cocked his head and raised his eyebrows. "I'd like to hear how you put a bad love affair and a Greek statue together in the same song."

Lefty grabbed his guitar and sang the two verses he had written. His sonorous, rolling tenor filled the afternoon air as he strummed his guitar. He got a little loud at one point, and the branch above their heads cracked audibly but didn't fall. Things only seemed to go awry when Lefty amped up the volume.

Lucky peered up when he heard the noise from the fractured branch. "Lefty, how did you come by the power to break things with your voice? You killed a bird the other day too. And the floating is pretty weird."

Lefty glanced at Nelson. "I've been wondering when y'all were going to ask me about that, dadgum it. Since all y'all have special abilities too, I might as well get it out in the open."

Charlie T. flashed his toothy smile. "So spill it."

Lefty removed his shades and pinched the bridge of his nose with his thumb and forefinger. He replaced his shades and scratched his dyed-black head, and he rubbed his temples.

"We're all waiting," Nelson observed impassively. Lefty had shared a few details about his Wilbury powers with Nelson, but not their origin.

Lefty remained reluctant. "I don't talk about this with very many people. Hardly anyone. I'm afraid y'all will think I'm crazy."

Otis shook his head. "No, we won't."

Lefty scrutinized the circle of seated men and directed his gaze to the porch flooring. "I haven't always had the voice I have now. My voice used to be thin and a little squeaky, even though I could always carry a tune really well. Back home in Texas in senior high school, I was in a group called the Wink Westerners. We used to play gigs in West Texas. There's a whole lotta space in West Texas in between towns, so you can drive for hours and not see a living soul, and it's dark in the country. If you turn off the car lights on a moonless night, you can't hardly see your hand in front of your face. And there's a billion stars in the sky.

"One day, in the summer of '54, the Westerners were driving to a gig out in the middle of nowhere and ..." Lefty stopped in mid-sentence.

Lucky became impatient. "Well, what happened, man? You can't leave us hanging."

"There's no going back after I say this," Lefty said, studying the porch planks again. He opened his mouth and closed it.

Nelson encouraged his friend. "We won't repeat anything you tell us. After all, you know our secrets."

The others nodded.

"Yeah, okay." Lefty looked at Nelson. His words tumbled out. "Our car went dead, and a flying saucer landed next to the road."

Otis and Lucky leaned back in their chairs, and Charlie T. picked his teeth.

Nelson whistled. "Wow, that's cool."

Lefty continued. "My memory of what happened next is hazy. I kind of remember being inside the ship and being strapped to a table, but I'm not sure what they did to me. I don't think there were any anal probes, but, you know, I'm not sure. All I do know for sure is that when we got to the gig the next day, my voice had changed. What happened when I sang had changed."

Lefty drilled Otis with a stare. "All of a sudden, my voice was full, my range increased, and I had this terrific vibrato. And things started cracking when I sang, like wine glasses and pieces of wood. And I was floating above the stage. I had to stop singing to come back down to the ground. I was flabbergasted the first time it happened. I hardly knew what to do. The other guys in the group were all freaked out too. Melvin hit on putting weights in my shoes, and I've been doing that ever since, but it makes it hard to walk or move around on stage, so I stay in one place. I discovered that when I don't sing at full volume, I don't break things. I still can't control it very well, as y'all have seen. And sometimes I need to sing at full volume for the sake of the performance."

Nelson interrupted him. "Thanks for telling us about what happened. Now we know your story. Don't worry about any of us repeating it. Let's get back to your song."

"So you guys don't think I'm crazy?"

Nelson shook his head. "Not at all. I'm pretty sure I've seen UFOs as well, although I don't think I've been picked up by one. We can talk more about it later, but right now we need to work on your song. What did you think, Otis?"

"That was a great tune," Otis enthused. He couldn't say the same for the words; they needed a lot of work.

"I don't know, Lefty. I love a lot of your songs, but that wasn't one of them," Nelson said.

Lefty looked a little downcast. "What's wrong with it?"

Nelson frowned. "Well, it's a good song, but it's a bit posh for our group. I mean, we're supposed to be country boys."

Lefty looked dejected. "Yeah, maybe."

Otis wasn't going to let Nelson dismiss Lefty's tune so hastily. "I say let's record a bit of it and see how it sounds."

Nelson frowned at Otis. "Are you sure we have time for that? What if it turns out we can't use it?"

Otis shrugged. "What if it turns out we can?"

Otis stepped through the kitchen door toward the sound booth. "Don, will you do a sound level for the guitars, please?"

The others followed Otis into the kitchen and opened their guitar cases.

Richard had other obligations starting today, so Charlie T. had asked Don to engineer. Don had worked in Dave's studio before and was quite familiar with the equipment. He had engineered three of Charlie T.'s albums, including the one Dave had produced. He had also worked on Eurythmics albums with Dave and on *Knocked Out Loaded* with Lucky.

Don turned the knobs and moved the levers to the pre-marked spots and spoke into the talkback mic. "Play something."

Nelson said, "That'll Be the Day" and five guitars played the chords to the classic song. After thirty seconds, Don said through the speaker, "Got it."

Lefty placed his song's chord sheet on the low table in the middle of the group. The guitarists leaned over and studied the song's simple progression for a moment.

"Let's play one verse," Otis suggested. "It doesn't have a chorus yet, unless anyone wants to write a chorus right now."

No one had a chorus off the top of his head. Otis had a wordless chorus, but he didn't offer it because he was fairly certain Nelson was going to veto the song in the end.

"Don," Otis said, "I always use a click track from the Oberheim."

"Gotcha," Don said.

It took seventy seconds to record the backing track for the verse. Don was unfamiliar with Otis's methodology, so Nelson asked him to set up two tapes, one for the original recording and one for the transferred results. Don looked puzzled but did as he was told.

"Now, don't freak out, Don," Nelson said. "Otis has his own ways of doing things."

"I've really been looking forward to working with him." Don grinned. "I've heard he's a real wizard in the studio."

Charlie T. snickered. "You have no fucking idea."

Otis took his place behind the soundboard and held his hands at shoulder height over it. "Don't touch the board, Don."

Otis released his lightning into the board, and the levers and knobs clicked and whirred. The tape decks spun and smoked. Don leaped from his chair, knocking it over backward. He sat down on the floor. His eyes grew wide, and his mouth hung open. His skin had grown pale.

Nelson said to the engineer, "I told you not to freak out."

"But he ... I never ... How did ..."

Nelson helped Don up off the floor. "Otis has many gifts. That lightning trick is the most visually impressive. And he can make microphones fly."

Lefty fetched Don a bourbon, neat. Don sipped it and slowly calmed down. He was finally able to speak in complete sentences. "I've never seen anything like that."

Charlie T. could understand Don's distress. The first time he had seen his half-brothers' superpowers, he had been blown away. All he could do was foresee the future.

That wasn't showy at all, but it sure did come in handy, despite its drawbacks.

"Look, Don. I know you've worked with some greats in the music business: Waylon, Aretha, Stevie, and Lucky. You've worked with a bunch of others that aren't so famous. You've seen a lot of amazing things. You've heard a lot of amazing music. But you've never seen anybody like Nelson, Otis, and Lefty. Just relax and get ready for the ride of your life. And don't tell nobody about it."

Don nodded. "Okay. It'll be our secret. Has Otis ever hurt anybody with that lightning trick?"

Nelson emphatically shook his head. "Otis never hurt anybody with anything. He is the sweetest, gentlest man you will ever meet."

Otis had been sitting in the kitchen, drinking a beer and smoking a cigarette, waiting for the dust to settle. He hated breaking in engineers for this very reason. He had worked with the same engineer with ELO, Mack, from 1975 to 1981. After Mack, he had worked with Bill from 1981 to 1986 when ELO split. Bill had done "Handle with Care" for them last month. If he had to use an unknown engineer, he would hide his powers for the reason that was unfolding today.

Don finished his drink and ventured into the kitchen to talk with Otis, sitting a few chairs away. Otis smiled encouragingly at him.

"Sorry I freaked out so bad, man," Don apologized without looking at Otis.

"It's okay, Don. I'm used to it. I wouldn't have used my gift, but we're in a hurry, you know?"

"Yeah, I get it. And I get why you don't want word of this to get out."

Don finally faced Otis. He tried to wink at the musician/singer/producer/composer and failed miserably; his expression looked more like a grimace.

Otis ignored the face Don had made. "Thanks. Ready to record some more music?"

Otis played back the tape to confirm he had correctly doubled the number of verses and the number of guitar tracks. It was perfect, just as it always was.

Lefty entered the sound booth to overdub the vocals. Otis instructed Don to set the sound levels as low as they would go. The special filters were still incorporated into the board where Richard had set them.

"What are these filters for, Otis?" Don asked. "I've never seen anything like them."

"Oh, yeah. They're for Lefty. He has vocal abilities besides just tone and vibrato. The filters prevent his, erm, uh … powers from getting on the recording."

"Oh, okay."

Lefty sang a couple of lines at his lower rehearsal volume, and when recording started, he belted out the verses at his full volume. He rose off the floor a few inches. One of the level meters cracked, but the board held. Don was agape at the exhibition although he didn't lose his shit this time. After Otis's lightning show, levitation was nothing. All five group members entered the sound booth to listen to the playback.

Lucky commented first. "I don't know, man."

"Well, it's a great vocal," Charlie T. remarked, "but it's got a different character than the rest of the stuff we've done for this album."

Nelson shook his head. "This just isn't going to work, Lefty. I respect you a hell of a lot. I don't want you to think I don't like what you've done. But this song doesn't fit on our album. Maybe you can use it on the solo album you're doing."

"Yeah, Lefty," Otis added. "I'd love to work on finishing this song with you; although, the subject matter is a bit over my head. I'll try to keep up, if you explain it to me." Otis had visited the Louvre and had seen the *Winged Victory of Samothrace*. He'd read romantic poetry. He wasn't an ignoramus, despite having left school at age fifteen. He was just building up Lefty's ego.

Lefty slumped, disappointed the other four didn't accept his contribution. "Yeah, I see y'all's point. What else do we have to work on today?"

# CHAPTER 13

## END OF THE LINE

The five sat on the porch in the lovely spring weather, strumming their guitars and trying to think of a song to record in the latter part of their fifth work day.

"I started this song in Hawaii," Nelson remarked. "I've been saving it for a day we were short on time. Since we spent the first part of the day on Lefty's song, let's see what we can do with my half-done song now." He strummed a D chord. "Sounds like a skiffle song, doesn't it?" He sang *"It's all right"* over the D chord.

"What is that, Nelson?" Otis asked.

"I don't know," Nelson replied. "I'm just making it up. I was thinking of a Carl Perkins song. He says that a lot—'It's all right.' Somebody give me the next line." Nelson played an A and a G chord.

Everyone stared blankly at him.

*"We're going to the end of the line,"* Nelson sang. "That was on one of the signs coming back from Anaheim that night we got Lefty to join the band."

"Yeah, that's good, Nelson," Lefty said.

"Let's make the song about that," Lucky suggested.

Nelson smiled. "Lefty joining the band or the end of the line?"

Lucky snorted and pushed the neck of Nelson's guitar down a couple of inches. "The end of the line."

Otis and Charlie T. added a few more lines.

"Who's writing these down?" Nelson asked.

Everyone returned more blank stares.

The legal pad was sitting on the chair next to him. "I guess it's me, then." He jotted down what he could remember of his brothers' contributions.

Otis piped up, "We saw 'Every Day is Judgment Day' up on that billboard in Anaheim too. Nelson and Charlie were there, and so were our wives."

"I'm Brian, and so's my wife," Lefty threw in some Monty Python and giggled in his high-pitched way.

Nelson scribbled as he spoke the lyrics he had just come up with. "He used to pump iron, and now he pumps gas. He used to gas badgers, and now he hauls ass." He laughed as he read the unusual lyrics.

"What the fuck does 'gas badgers' mean?" Lucky asked.

"What, you lot don't gas badgers over here?" Nelson retorted.

"No, we don't gas badgers. What is gassing badgers?" Lucky grew impatient. "That must be another one of those weird British things."

"It's banned now, but the British government used to throw these cyanide bombs down badger holes to exterminate them."

It was Charlie T.'s turn to be puzzled. "Why'd they do that?"

Nelson looked at his compatriot, Otis, in exasperation. He couldn't believe the Americans had never heard of this or didn't have a similar procedure themselves.

"Don't you lot have badgers?" Nelson asked Charlie T.

"Yeah, I guess, but not enough to worry about gassing them. Why do they kill them in England?" Charlie T. became more incredulous.

"They're dangerous little buggers. I can't remember why they're dangerous. That doesn't mean I think they should be killed."

"They spread TB to the cattle population," Otis commented. He still ate meat, and so kept up with the badger problem.

Lucky put his foot down. "We are not using that verse."

Nelson challenged Lucky. "Give us another verse, then."

Lucky didn't bat an eye. He rattled off a few rhyming lines and ended by saying, "Let's put in something about 'Purple Haze.'"

Nelson wrote the whole thing, then chewed the end of his pen. "I don't know about 'Purple Haze.' What if the Jimi Hendrix estate comes after us for that?"

Charlie T. sounded exasperated. "Jesus Christ, Nelson. You can't avoid every fucking song that has ever been written."

"I think I might be able to, at that, Charlie T."

Lucky wasn't going to cave on this argument so easily. "Look, it's a good line."

Nelson shook his head. "None of us have anything to do with Jimi Hendrix."

Lucky smiled. "That's what makes it funny."

Lefty and Otis had been listening to the debate.

Lefty appeared thoughtful. "You know, it's actually being used as a song title in this case. It's like advertising for the song. I don't see how it could be interpreted as copyright infringement. You can't copyright song titles, just lyrics."

Otis added, "You used 'All You Need Is Love' in a similar way in 'All Those Years Ago.' You didn't get sued for that.'"

Nelson looked pensively at Otis for a moment, his eyebrows knit. "Yeah, but I was a Beatle. I sang that song too."

Otis said gently, "But you didn't own the rights to it."

Nelson pursed his lips. "No, I didn't. And neither did Yoko and Paul. ATV did."

"So wouldn't ATV have sued you, if they could have?"

Nelson had to admit he was losing the argument. "Probably. Look, I'll call my copyright attorney tomorrow and ask his opinion about 'Purple Haze,' all right?"

"Thank you," Lucky said.

Otis contributed another verse, Nelson thought of another, and Charlie T. took a turn.

Nelson scribbled furiously. "Okay, that's enough for now. Let's see what we've got." Nelson tore off the sheet he'd been writing on and copied the keeper lyrics on a fresh sheet. The brothers congregated around and shared ideas to improve the lyrics.

"Okay," Nelson said. "And let's make this the first verse and this part the second. Here's the third and fourth. And the fifth. Now who's going to sing them?"

"Whoever wrote 'em can sing 'em," Charlie T. said; he had contributed two verses.

"We can try that, or we can have auditions." Nelson looked around the group.

Lucky snorted. "When is the last time any of us auditioned for something?"

Otis asked, "Who's going to judge the singers?"

Nelson smiled. "I will, of course."

Otis nodded. "Fine by me. Just don't make me sing right after Lefty."

"I don't know why not, Otis. You've got the best voice, after Lefty." Nelson frowned at his brother, wondering again why he always put himself down.

Otis turned it back onto his brother. "You've got the best voice, after Lefty."

"Well, I'm not auditioning, am I?" Nelson winked. "Besides, it's not about who's got the best voice. It's about whose voice sounds the best for the purpose of the song. I'm going to start it and finish it."

"Let's do a backing track before we start these auditions." Otis entered the studio and sat at the soundboard next to Don. He watched his brothers filing inside. "Play some chords."

Otis quickly organized the musicians and the studio equipment and had the backing track recorded and expanded into five verses and three bridges in no time. He recorded the bass line himself while he was at it. The whole process consumed less than ten minutes. Any other producer would have required hours.

Nelson stood at the door. "Hey, Otis, I've got an idea for an intro." Nelson played a sprightly ascending lick on his acoustic.

Otis nodded. "Let's put it on now, before the vocals."

Don cued a new tape, and they recorded Nelson's intro.

"Want any more tracks before we do your auditions for vocals, Nelson?" Otis asked.

"No, let's get started. I want to hear Charlie T. sing the first bridge, Otis sing the second verse, Lucky sing the second bridge, and Lefty sing the third verse. How does that sound to everybody?"

"Huh?" Lucky grunted.

"Which part is it that you want me to sing?" Lefty asked.

Nelson sighed and wrote each man's name on the master lyric sheet next to the part he wanted him to sing. He assigned the whole song that way.

"Then I want Charlie T. to sing the third bridge." He wrote *CTJ* next to the third bridge. "And Otis to sing the fourth verse." He wrote *Otis* in the proper place. "I'll sing the last."

Everyone donned their headphones. They listened to the intro and the first verse play through. Charlie T. approached the mic and sang the first bridge. Otis sang the second verse, and so on. Nelson listened intently and jotted notes.

When Otis finished the fourth verse, the four auditionees looked at Nelson expectantly. Nelson studied his notes.

"Lucky, I'm going to have you sit out this song. Otis, let me hear you sing the second bridge."

Lucky indignantly cocked his head. "May I ask why you don't want me to sing?"

"Your voice doesn't fit the mood of the song," Nelson replied.

"How doesn't my voice fit the mood of the song?" Lucky hadn't failed an audition since his Greenwich Village club days in early 1961.

"Your voice has such a strong character of its own that it tends to dominate. Instead of hearing the song and what it's saying, the listener would think, 'Ah, that's Lucky Wilbury singing,' and be taken out of the spirit of the song. If you were going to be singing throughout the song, it would be different, but since we're splitting it up, your voice would stand in sharp contrast to the others."

This was all bullshit, of course. Nelson just didn't like the way Lucky's voice sounded in the song, and he'd already been featured in three songs. Let someone else sing, Nelson figured.

Lucky didn't realize it was bullshit. "Oh, okay, man. I get it."

Having calmed the diva, Nelson returned to the task at hand. "Otis, you ready? Just sing the words to the next verse that comes up on the track."

Otis sang the verse, followed by Charlie T, and finally Lefty. Nelson jotted notes and looked thoughtful. He asked Otis to take a walk outside with him.

When they had gotten out of earshot of the studio, Nelson turned to Otis. "What do you think of my plan of me singing the first and last verse?"

"Sounds fine to me," Otis answered.

"You're not just saying that because I'm Beatle Nelson?"

Otis crossed his arms. "When have I ever been a yes man?"

Nelson regarded Otis for a protracted moment. "No, that's not you."

"Just so we got that straight. My priority is making the music sound pretty, not getting on your good side." Otis mustered a stern expression.

"Otis, you're always on my good side." Nelson peered through Otis's shades for a moment but gave up trying to see his eyes. "I don't expect you to be objective about your own singing but look at the other assignments."

Nelson had assigned Lefty one stanza, Otis two stanzas, and Charlie T. three stanzas, with Nelson singing the first and the last.

"Why does Lefty have only one stanza? He's the best singer," Otis inquired.

"What I told Lucky about dominating a song was mostly bullshit to get him to shut up, but it wasn't all bullshit. Lefty dominates a song too. As it is, we'll have to tell him to hold back, but his voice has less contrast to the rest of us than Lucky's does."

"I see." Otis nodded. "I think we've got a game plan then."

When Otis and Nelson returned to the guest house, they found Lucky sitting in the corner, sulking. Nelson assumed Lucky's feelings were hurt because he had asked Lucky not to sing on this song, but it was hard to determine. He decided to ignore his brother's emotional state and proceed with the recording.

"Okay, Otis and I have agreed on a plan." Nelson held out the lyric sheet for Lefty and Charlie T. to see. "Charlie T., you are singing all three bridges. Lefty, you are singing the third verse, and Otis is singing the second and fourth verse. Everyone got it?"

Three of the brothers nodded. Lucky continued to stare at the wall.

Lefty asked, "What are you singing, Nelson?"

Nelson replied, "I'm singing the first and last verse."

Lucky stood up. "I'm getting the fuck out of here if you don't need me."

Nelson looked over at his brother. "Of course we need you, Lucky. We just don't need you to sing the lead on this song. We'll be doing backing vocals later, and I'd sure like for you to sing on those."

"Fuck backing vocals. I'm a lead singer." Lucky looked angry.

Nelson sighed. He loved Lucky, and he was eternally grateful to him, but Lucky's ego could be a huge pain in the ass. "If you want to leave, go ahead, but I'd like it if you stuck around."

Nelson nudged a gentle probe into his friend's mind, calming him, but being careful not to control him. Any "Jedi mind tricks," as Lucky called them, would only anger him further. Nelson could feel Lucky repelling the psychic probe.

The corners of Lucky's mouth turned down. "I'll think about it." He walked over to the fridge. "Have we got anything besides beer in the studio?"

Charlie T. opened a bottom cabinet. "We have a good selection down here. There's vodka, scotch, rum, tequila, and gin. There's also Cabernet Sauvignon."

Lucky poured himself some premium scotch on the rocks. "I'll stay if it don't take too long."

Nelson addressed the rest of the group. "Okay, let's get this on tape. Lefty, you are only doing one stanza, and I want you to hold back your singing on this stanza. The rest of us can't match your power, so if you really sing out, you'll fuck up the song by sticking out like a sore thumb. So just really soft pedal this verse, okay?"

"Yeah, I got it." Lefty wore a dubious expression, eyebrows knit. He knew he was the best singer in the bunch, and he didn't understand how he could mess up a song.

Nelson turned to Otis and Charlie T. "The three of us have quite a burden on this song, right? Even though Lefty is not going to be singing to his fullest ability, we still have to sing next to him. Put everything you've got into this, lads. Pretend you are Lefty. Sing like you've never sung before. I know I will be."

Charlie T. and Otis nodded. They knew what Nelson meant. On the final product, the listener would be comparing their vocals with Lefty's. It was daunting to sing next to the greatest pop singer who ever lived.

Nelson directed Otis, Charlie T., and Lefty into the sound booth. "Okay, let's do this vocal. Everybody got their parts?"

Otis, Charlie T. and Lefty nodded and gathered around the microphone, joined by Nelson. "Start the backing track, Don."

Everyone donned their headphones, and Don clicked the button to start the tape. Nelson sang the first verse. Charlie T. sang the first bridge. And so on until they had the whole song recorded.

The four Wilburys hustled out of the sound booth.

"What did you think, Lucky?" Otis asked enthusiastically. "I think this song might be a hit."

Lucky couldn't muster any enthusiasm. "It was okay."

Charlie T. overheard the interaction. "What the hell is the matter with you, brother? This is a great song! Give it its due!"

Lucky rolled his eyes. "Give me a fucking break if I can't get excited about another fucking song about death. They're a dime a dozen."

Nelson, Otis, Lefty, and Charlie T. focused on Lucky.

Nelson finally broke the silence. "So what if it's about death? It explores the subject in a lighthearted way. Besides, it's not about death, it's about the last stages of life, when you're old and gray."

Lucky rounded on Nelson. "We're only middle aged. I don't see why we have to be thinking about being old and gray at this point."

Nelson calmly regarded his brother. "Death comes to everyone. If you are fortunate, you are old and gray before if does."

Lucky turned away. "I'm not ready to deal with death."

Nelson put his hand on Lucky's shoulder. "Lots of your songs deal with death. So do mine. 'He not busy being born is busy dying.'"

Lucky turned back to his brother. "They deal with death in an abstract sense. They don't deal with my own death."

Lefty joined in. "Everything we do is about our death. We're moving closer to our death with each breath. We have to think about our death with every action, every thought, every time we speak to another human being. That might be the last time we speak to them before they die. It might be the last time they speak to us before we die. Living is all about dying, man."

Nelson regarded his friend with affection. "You really get it, Lefty. Yes, everything we do is about our death. And everything we do is about moving us closer to God."

Lucky nodded his head. "I'm with you on that. I found God and moved away from him, and I'm trying to zero in on the whole God thing again."

Nelson shook his head. "You can't lose Him once you truly find Him, Lucky. We've talked about this before. You told me you found Jesus, but then you incorporated Judaism again. Faith isn't real if you keep skipping around. I honor any faith you find, but for it to work for you, it has to be real."

Lucky frowned at Nelson but didn't argue.

Lefty spoke. "I drifted away from the faith of my youth for decades, and only came back to it a couple of years ago. I didn't go back to the Church of Christ because it felt too restrictive and hypercritical, but I came back to a loving kind of Christianity. I felt reborn, renewed, like I had been taken into the bosom of the Lord. I am not afraid of death because I will be reunited with God."

Nelson took Lefty's hand and squeezed it without letting go. "You know I follow the Lord Krishna, which is another name for God. I am not afraid of death either."

Lucky looked at the floor. "You motherfuckers are making me feel bad."

Nelson dropped Lefty's hand and took Lucky's hand in both his hands. "You don't have anything to feel bad about. What's the problem?"

Lucky looked up at Nelson. "Life's too short. Here I was pissed off because you wouldn't let me sing on this song, when I really should be thinking about my spiritual development. Nelson, you are one of the most spiritual shitheads I know, and I'm totally missing out on the opportunity to soak up some positive vibes from you. Would you just go into one of those altered states of consciousness that the Maharishi taught you, so I can soak up some fucking positive karma or something?"

Nelson laughed at Lucky's joke. "I don't meditate like that any longer, Lucky, but I've some mala beads here, and we can chant Hari Krishna together."

Lucky shook his head and laughed. "Fuck that. We've got a song to record."

Nelson gathered Lucky into a big bear hug, which he hesitantly returned.

Recording wrapped at about 12:30 a.m. Eric Idle had arrived around midnight. Nelson had called and asked him to come over, to please Lefty. Nelson and Eric's relationship went back to the seventies when Nelson had admired Eric's comedy work on television and asked him to direct music videos for his songs "Crackerbox Palace" and "True Love."

Lefty was overjoyed to see Eric and pumped the comic's hand enthusiastically. "You're my favorite Python!"

Eric smiled. "Ah! You have mistaken me for John Cleese."

"No, I don't think so," Lefty said, confused. "I'm sure he's the tall one that does the silly walks."

Eric sighed and shook his head. "You can't fool a true fan."

Nelson dragged Eric by the arm down the hall and up the stairs to the bedroom that had been converted to a sitting room. "Look, Eric, that's Lucky Wilbury!"

Lucky looked up from his guitar and nodded, although an irritated expression crossed his face. He hated when Nelson did that to him.

Otis watched from the landing, grinning widely. "Look, Eric, that's Nelson Wilbury!" He rushed up to stand beside them.

Eric turned to his old friend, who still grasped him by the upper arm. He started as if surprised to notice who it was. "Bollocks, I thought it was the butler. And who the hell are you?" He drilled Otis with a Cambridge-educated stare.

Nelson grabbed Otis by his arm with his other hand. "That's my genius friend and half-brother, Otis Wilbury."

Eric scoffed. "What's he genius at? Wearing sunglasses at night?"

"No, Eric," Nelson huffed, "Otis is genius at putting records together and writing music. You've heard his stuff. Electric Chair Philharmonic."

"Oh, you mean that band that never should have changed their name from The Idle Race? That was the perfect name for a band, and they fucked it up."

"To be fair, that was a totally different group of blokes than ELO."

"I don't care. You should've kept the name."

"They kept the name."

Lucky remained upstairs. Heading to the kitchen, the three men passed Charlie T. leaving the bathroom. Nelson grabbed him with a third hand. "Eric, I told Lefty you'd play some Python material for him. Let's go jam with him."

Eric had brought his guitar. He agreed to sing some of Lefty's favorite Python songs, and three of the other Wilburys volunteered to join in. Lucky made excuses and left, but Otis and Charlie T. were happy to oblige.

The singing continued far into the night.

# CHAPTER 14

## TWEETER AND THE MONKEY MAN

The sixth day of recording dawned bright and warm, just like every spring day in Southern California. It wouldn't rain again until October. After breakfasting at home, the group arrived ready to work around 12:30 p.m. The brothers sat in the sunny front room of the main house with their guitars.

"I need to let y'all know I'm gonna be leaving a little early today," Lefty said. "Around eight."

Four heads nodded.

Lefty continued. "I've got a business meeting with the label about my album. They couldn't meet this morning before we started recording. They sure threw a fit about starting the meeting so late. I didn't tell them I was working on a different album though. I didn't want to rile them."

Nelson smiled. "Good thinking, Lefty. I haven't done anything about getting permission from your label, or anybody's, for you to appear on the Wilburys record."

Lefty nodded. "I didn't think you had."

Nelson changed the subject. "Let's get to work. You lads got any ideas for a song?"

At first no one answered. Finally, Otis spoke up. "I was working on an idea for a backing track before we started the album that I'd be happy to contribute. Actually, I've got a few of 'em."

Lefty laughed. "Otis, you always do everything bass-ackwards."

Nelson, Lefty, and Charlie T. all knew how Otis worked, since he had written and produced songs with each of them. When writing with his brothers, he had adapted to their preferences, but Otis worked in reverse from most songwriters. He came up with chord changes and instrumentation for a backing track first, then a melody, and finally, the words. If it had been up to him, Otis's records would all have been instrumentals; but he knew instrumentals rarely cracked the Top 40.

Otis played a series of chords on his acoustic guitar: A minor, G, F—a very basic progression.

Lucky wasn't interested in chords at the moment. He knew Nelson and Otis could come up with anything they needed. He looked at Charlie T. "Let's talk about a topic for a song."

They went to the recording studio and relaxed in the kitchen with a legal pad and a cassette recorder.

Lucky started the recorder. "I've been thinking about Bruce Springsteen. Let's write a song that references a shitload of Springsteen songs and is done in the style of one of his great works. He's always said he's a big fan of mine. He's done a lot of my songs in his live shows. Let's show him some love."

"That sounds cool. What songs do you want to include in the homage?" Charlie T. raised an eyebrow. "Hey, are you doing this just to fuck with Nelson and his aversion to copyright infringement?"

"What? Of course not." Lucky looked at the floor and smiled mysteriously. His eyes were twinkling when he returned his gaze to Charlie T. "How about 'Thunder Road?' 'Jungleland?'"

Charlie T. accepted the challenge. "'Promised Land.' 'Stolen Car.' 'State Trooper.'"

Lucky added, "'Randolph Street.' 'Part Man, Part Monkey.' 'Factory.' 'Jersey Girl.'"

Charlie T. smiled one of his sly smiles. "He's gonna release songs called 'Lion's Den' and 'Paradise.' Well, he's already written 'Lion's Den' but hasn't released it. Let's get those in there somehow."

"Great!" Lucky exclaimed. "Man, I am so glad you can predict the future! Sorry you had to be abused by your stepdad to get the ability."

"A simple twist of fate. This song has to be set in New Jersey," Charlie T. opined. "Let's include some place names from Jersey."

Lucky immediately popped off, "Rahway Prison, Jersey state line."

Charlie T. threw up his hands, holding his palms at angles to each other. "Let's make it a car chase."

Lucky was even more excited. "Let's have the cops be after 'em for a drug bust. And the mob has to be in it. After all, it's Jersey."

Charlie T. giggled. 'Then we have to have an undercover cop and Florida, if the mob is in it."

"Abso-fucking-lutely," agreed Lucky. "And a blown-up TV."

Charlie T. and Lucky looked at each other for a long moment.

"A sex change!" they said together and burst out laughing.

Lefty wandered into the recording studio's kitchen, having abandoned Otis and Nelson to the backing track. "What are y'all talking about?"

Charlie T. grinned. "We're writing a homage to Bruce Springsteen. Wanna help us?"

"I love Bruce. He sang 'Happy Birthday' to me last month at my party." Lefty had just turned fifty-two. "Earlier last year he inducted me into the Rock and Roll Hall."

Charlie T. showed him the list of Springsteen songs they had generated to include in the song lyrics. "Can you think of any more, Lefty?"

Lefty scanned the list. "Well, you can't have a Springsteen pastiche without 'Born to Run.' 'The River' is another classic. And I always thought it was funny that both Hank Williams and Bruce wrote a song called 'Mansion on the Hill.'"

Lucky nodded. "Those are all great ideas, Lefty. We also have a car chase, the mob, and a character who's had a sex change."

Lefty thought a moment. "Why don't you make the person who had a sex change a Vietnam veteran? That way you can kind of pull in 'Born in the USA.' I actually know someone like that. I have a friend who came back from Vietnam and then got a sex-change operation. She showed courage on both fronts, in my opinion."

Charlie T. looked impressed. "Wow, Lefty, you're a genius. That's brilliant." Charlie T. was aware Lefty's ego needed stroking after the put-down Nelson had given him yesterday by not accepting his song.

Having taken the backing track as far as they could, Otis and Nelson were smoking a joint on the studio porch. They heard some of what the other three were saying from inside the house.

"You listen to Springsteen much?" Otis asked.

"My wife does, but not me. I don't have a clue what they're talking about."

Otis shook his head. "I don't either."

Otis and Nelson stuck their heads through the doorway.

"How's it going in here?" Nelson asked.

"Great!" Charlie T. responded.

Lucky strummed an A-minor chord and sang, "*And the walls ...*"

The two Brits listened for a few moments.

"Sounds bloody fantastic!" Otis said. "We'll leave you to it."

Otis asked Don to run a line into the living room and plug a small synthesizer into the soundboard. He and Nelson had decided to lay down the backing tracks while Lucky, Lefty, and Charlie T. worked on the lyrics.

Although Nelson wanted a natural sound on this album, he figured one synthesizer wouldn't ruin it. Otis had agreed to set it on Piano or Organ, so it would sound less synthetic and more organic. Just as Otis sat down at the keyboard, Charlie T., Lefty, and Lucky exited the kitchen. They crowded into the tiny living room with the drum set, the synthesizer, and their bandmates.

Lucky announced, "Okay, we're ready to write this thing."

Nelson turned around. "I thought you'd been writing it."

"We were getting ready to write it. Now I'm gonna write it. Watch the door, man. Buster and Don shouldn't see this. I don't want my Wilbury ability getting outside the family. It was hard enough to show it to you guys."

Nelson, Otis, and Charlie T. stood in the corridor leading to the living room to guard against encroachment. They repeatedly glanced over their shoulders so they could watch the proceedings in the cramped living room. Lucky's Wilbury superpower was still new to them, and they found it fascinating.

Lucky clutched the cassette tape and their yellow legal sheet full of notes in his left hand. He extended his right hand in front of him. After concentrating for a moment, Lucky's right hand moved as if he were writing in the air.

Line after line of golden letters appeared. He got to the floor, and the lines continued to appear. Lefty started writing them down, but Lucky told him, "No, man, let me do it."

Lucky continued air writing in a new location as high as he could reach, and more golden words materialized in the air, in front of the drum kit. Finally, the song was done—ten verses in all. The lyrics had a rhyming pattern of AABB. The text contained ten of the fourteen Springsteen song titles the brothers had brainstormed and all the plot points.

Lucky grabbed the legal pad and transcribed at a furious pace in his tiny, spidery handwriting. The song's lines were long, but he managed to fit each on one line of the legal pad by writing small. Lefty stepped back to make sure he didn't block Lucky's view. Nelson and Otis stood by the entrance to the living room to guard against Buster or Don walking in and seeing the words hanging in the air. Charlie T. almost walked through the hanging words to get to the couch, but Lucky stopped him in time, explaining human touch caused the words to dissipate rapidly.

Nelson glanced over his shoulder for the twentieth time, amazed by his brother's power. "How many of your songs have you written this way, Lucky?"

Lucky didn't stop transcribing. "I don't have any fucking idea, Nelson. I don't do it when the song is short or if the lyrics come easy."

"Maybe half your three hundred songs, then, you think?"

"Maybe."

Lucky had transcribed the whole song on paper pretty quickly. Once he was finished copying, he ran the palm of his hand over the floating words. They vanished as if he was erasing a blackboard. This impressed everyone almost as much as writing the words in the air.

Lucky turned to his brothers. "What do you want to do now?"

Otis checked his watch. "I'm peckish. Let's see if dinner is ready."

Bugs had arranged another feast. This time it was burgers: turkey burgers, veggie burgers, and regular beef burgers. Cheese, mushrooms, pickles, lettuce, and all sorts of condiments were available to pile on. Side dishes included French fries, onion rings, corn on the cob, fried okra, and mixed braised vegetables.

Lucky had the lyrics sheet with him at the dining room table, tweaking them. The lyrics composed by his superpower never emerged in their final form. They always needed work before they could be recorded. Sometimes the words were too hard to sing the way his superpower had written them, as Otis had discovered. Sometimes they didn't fit the tune that had been composed. The floating golden words were never the exact lyrics that went on the record.

Bugs sat next to Lucky at dinner. "Did you write that song today or did you bring that in?"

Lucky glanced at Bugs. "No, we wrote it this afternoon. Nelson and Otis worked on the backing track, and me and Lefty and Charlie T. did these here lyrics. We don't have a melody yet. Charlie T. was working on one."

"Amazing," was all Bugs could say.

Otis, Lefty, and Charlie T. looked at each other and smirked.

Nelson diverted attention away from the subject. "Hey, Bugs, why don't you listen to how the fridge turned out on the track we did a couple of days ago? The fridge, I tell you; it's a great new sound, folks. It's happenin'."

"What's the track called?" Bugs asked.

Nelson responded, "It's called 'Rattled,' appropriately enough, since Buster was rattling around in the refrigerator."

Bugs laughed. "That's so funny!"

"We're trying to be funny on this album," Nelson commented. "Otis is about the only one of us who ever got to put any jokes on his albums, although I tried, but my jokes never seemed to be funny. He got me to put a load of funny jokes on *Cloud Nine*, and I love him for it."

"Hey," Lucky protested, "There's plenty of jokes on my albums. I'm a really funny guy." He took the last bite of his burger.

"Oh, yeah? Like what?" Nelson challenged him.

Lucky dusted his hands together and talked with his mouth full. "How about 'Stuck Inside of Mobile with the Memphis Blues Again?' That was pretty funny. So was 'Maggie's Farm.'"

"Okay, okay. Both you and Otis put jokes on your albums."

"Stuck Inside of Mobile with the Memphis Blues Again" had eighteen verses, and Nelson was sure Lucky had air written it.

"I got jokes on my albums too. I meant 'You Got Lucky' to be a joke; although I didn't know Lucky then, so it wasn't a double entendre or anything. 'Dogs on the Run' is pretty funny. 'Jammin' Me' was fucking hilarious, but I wrote that one with Lucky, so I guess it don't count." He speared another onion ring and jammed it into his mouth.

"If we're all so damn funny, this album ought to rival the Marx Brothers," Nelson deadpanned.

"Or Monty Python," Lefty said and launched into "Camelot Song" from *Monty Python and the Holy Grail*.

Nelson hissed at Lefty. "Keep your voice down so things don't start breaking."

Lefty dissolved into high-pitched giggles. There were scattered groans and grins as everyone rose to return to work.

Once they arrived at the guest-house studio, the five rock stars reclaimed their guitars from where they had deposited them in their cases. They took their places around the circle of chairs in the kitchen. Buster and Don entered the sound booth to resume their game of gin rummy on a piece of plywood laid across two chairs, waiting for the brothers to settle on their recording plans.

"Okay," Nelson said, organizing his group. "Let's rehearse this new song. Lucky should sing the lead and the rest of us do back up."

Otis asked, "What about the chorus?"

Lucky looked at his lyric sheet. "It doesn't really have a chorus."

"You were singing a chorus when we stuck our heads in the door earlier."

"I was? I don't remember." Lucky seemed genuinely surprised, his mouth gaping open.

"Yeah, it sounded like, uh …" He sang: "… *and the walls fell down all the way* … to what, Nelson?"

Nelson frowned. "It was 'came down,' I think."

Nelson and Otis recalled the rest of the chorus, words and tune, and pieced it together for Lucky.

Lucky nodded. "Okay, I remember. Yeah, that was it."

"Yeah, I like it," Otis agreed. "We could do some nice harmony on that bit."

"Let's put it after every other verse, like the verses are eight lines long," Lucky said. "Then it's like there are five verses instead of ten and the song doesn't seem so extravagant."

Nelson laughed. "There's no way this song isn't going to seem extravagant, but that's part of the beauty of it. Here's an intro I came up with." Nelson played a couple of riffs on his acoustic guitar. "And here's the chord pattern we worked out." Nelson strummed his guitar. "Suit you?"

Lucky nodded. "Yeah, that's fine."

"Were you playing a straight A minor to E minor to D minor for that chorus?" Otis asked.

"I guess so, man." Lucky shrugged. "I still can't hardly remember."

"I'm throwing an augmented E7 in there to make it interesting," Otis said.

"A naughty chord," Nelson laughed.

Otis demonstrated the chord pattern he recalled for the chorus, plus the augmented chord.

"Okay," Charlie T. drew out the words. "I think we are go-o-od to go. Lefty?"

"Ye-a-uh," Lefty drawled in his Texas accent.

Lucky suggested, "Let's just practice it like a band a couple of times before we start recording it, okay?"

"Okay, Lucky," Nelson said.

Nelson played the intro he had worked out, and the rest played their guitars. Lucky had the lyrics sheet spread out in front of him, reading from it. He used the tune for the verses Charlie T. had been kicking around, which suited the song well. They started and stopped three or four times before getting through the song.

Otis looked at Lucky. "Want to go again?"

Lucky pursed his lips. "Naw, let's just do the backing track, and I'll overdub at the mic in the sound booth. It's too hard to see my writing and play at the same time."

Otis spoke into one of the mics to Don. "Sound level check."

Don jumped at the sound of Otis's voice. He had just won his third gin rummy game in a row with Buster and wasn't expecting the musicians to be prepared to record so quickly. He hustled to the board and leaned forward to the talkback mic. "Ready."

Nelson played his intro again, and the rest of the band joined in with their guitars. Don gave a thumbs up from the soundboard.

"Okay, we aren't doing a demo this time, are we Nelson?" Otis confirmed.

Nelson shook his head.

"Nelson's intro, one verse, one chorus. We'll do a fade out on this number."

The brothers each played their guitar part. Don set up two tapes, so Otis could turn the brief section they had recorded into an extended backing track. Otis completed the operation in about thirty seconds—a long time by his standards.

"Play that back and get a time on it," Otis instructed.

Don played it back, using a stopwatch. They had the intro, ten verses, and five choruses, with the last chorus repeated. The five guitars had been doubled to ten, and the track faded at the end. It came in at five minutes and thirty seconds, so far the longest cut on the album.

Nelson looked at his brother with appreciation. "Nice one, Otis."

"Thanks, Nelson," Otis smiled. He always lit up when Nelson praised him.

"Yeah, great work, Otis," Lefty added and patted him on the shoulder.

Otis thought he would faint with so much praise from the people he admired.

"Thanks, Lefty. That means a lot."

Now it was up to Lucky to sing it. He took the lyrics sheet into the sound booth and stepped up to the microphone. Don adjusted the mic for Lucky's vocals and and cued the backing track. Buster, being a drummer, boogied out of the sound booth and into the kitchen.

Lucky warmed up his voice and looked at Don. "Are we recording?"

"If Otis or Nelson tells me to, we are," Don answered. "So far, this is just rehearsal."

Lucky addressed the kitchen through the sound booth mic. "I'd like to record this, just in case it's a usable take." Lucky was infamous for not liking to do things more than once in the studio.

"Okay, we've got plenty of tape," Nelson answered. "Don, cue it up."

It was not a usable take. Lucky hadn't learned the tune. He sang it differently for some of the verses. He stopped and started a few times. His performance improved with each verse, however.

"How was that?" he asked from the sound booth.

Lefty answered, "That was good."

Charlie T. showed a thumbs up. "I think it was good."

Neither producer answered. They both thought it sucked, but they were willing to bear with Lucky. They knew his abilities.

Lucky cleared his throat. "I'll do it again." He pointed to Don to cue the backing track again and took a deep breath.

Five minutes and thirty seconds later, he had sung the whole song through with only a few minor mistakes. But he had not matched his performance with the backing track.

All the brothers crowded into the sound booth to review the playback.

From behind the sound board, Otis remarked, "You'll have to do that one again, Lucky."

"I'm not doing that again," Lucky stated unequivocally.

Charlie T. agreed with Otis. "Yeah, your voice cracked in a couple of places, and your timing was off."

"I don't give a fuck."

Charlie T. had worked with Lucky in the recording studio on *Knocked Out Loaded*. He knew how obstinate his half-brother could be. Lucky would insist his studio musicians deliver rendition after rendition until he got the sound he wanted, but Lucky hated to repeat certain vocal takes. He'd allow substandard performances to go out to the public rather than sing some things again. His last two albums contained numerous low-quality vocal interpretations.

Nelson didn't want to bicker. "That was fine. Lucky, you don't have to do it again. We'll bury it in the mix."

Otis wouldn't let it pass as easily. "All due respect, Nelson, we can't bury errors of this magnitude in the mix."

Nelson tried to look through Otis's shades into his eyes, but it was impossible in the dim lighting after dark. "Otis, I have the deepest faith in your ability to perform miracles in the studio."

Otis knew he had lost the argument. He looked at Charlie T. and shrugged. They were the junior members of the group and less respected in the music world than Lucky and Nelson. Charlie T. shrugged in response, as if to say, *If Lucky wants his song to sound like shit, it's no skin off my nose.*

During playback, Lucky had jotted a few notes. "Hey, Otis, I made a few changes to the lyrics that will improve them. I'll do those lines again, but I'm not doing the whole song."

Otis nodded. "I can drop in the lines so you don't have to sing the whole song again."

Lefty's gaze swept his brothers. "I gotta take off. See y'all tomorrow at the usual time, okay?"

After Lefty had left the building, the four remaining half-brothers entered the sound booth to record the chorus.

Coaxing tight harmonies from those he was producing was another of Otis's non-Wilbury superpowers. Nelson had plenty of experience singing harmony with his other group, The Beatles. Charlie T. often did harmony with his group; although as lead singer, he was usually carrying the lead line. When working with Otis, he could easily sing a harmony line. Otis could sing anything: lead, harmony, tenor, countertenor, falsetto. Lucky had trouble with harmony, but it was mostly his song, and he would do his best, as long as he didn't have to sing the same thing more than once.

Otis quickly coached his fellow group members on the harmonies he deemed would sound best. Nelson didn't quibble with him. He knew Otis was much better at figuring this out than he was. After fifteen minutes of rehearsal, everyone had learned their part. They secured their headphones and recorded one chorus with consummate harmony.

Otis entered the sound booth and worked his magic with the two tape decks. He had dropped in the changed lyrics and the five choruses with final repeat in less than a minute.

Now it was time to do the backing vocals. Otis had worked out harmonies for this as well, to give the song a full, rich sound without excessive instrumentation. Being able to hold multiple tunes in his mind made remembering harmony lines and backing vocals a snap.

When they were finished, Otis listened to the playback with the harmonies and backing vocals. They still sounded a bit thin because only four of them had been singing—Lefty's rich tones were missing.

"What do you think, Nelson? Double the backing vocals?"

Nelson nodded. "Yeah, why not?"

Don cued the tapes. Otis sent sparks dancing across the console and made the four voices eight. Don switched tapes again, and Otis added the doubled backing vocals to the master tape.

"Let's have a listen then," Otis instructed the engineer.

After listening intently, he thought the track needed more instruments. "We need some horns on this baby and that keyboard we were setting up earlier. And bass and drums, of course."

Nelson looked at the clock. "Yeah, but it's twelve thirty, and we're all tired. We can do horns and keyboards when we get to Friar Park."

Otis cocked his head. "Buster's been here all day. Let's at least get a snare on it."

Nelson turned to Buster. "Your moment has come. Get those sticks out."

Buster hurried to his drum kit and took his place. Otis flipped on the mic, and Don checked the sound levels and cued the master track.

Nelson addressed the drummer, "Nothing too fancy."

Buster smiled back. "No problem."

# CHAPTER 15

## HEADING FOR THE LIGHT

I found myself back at Bungalow Palace, in The Barn again. I was determined not to go all fangirl a second time and make Otis disappear in a puff of make believe. Otis played his first guitar for me. His father had bought for it him for two pounds when he was a teenager. A few years ago, he had paid two thousand dollars to have it restored and upgraded to a decent instrument.

"*Freeeee as a bird,*" Otis sang softly, strumming the chords to the song he produced with The Beatles in 1994. The "Threatles," the press had jokingly called them, since John had been gone for fifteen years by the time they released *Anthology 1*. Charlie T. had predicted this Beatles reunion years before, and Otis hadn't believed him.

Otis looked up expectantly from his singing and guitar playing. He leaned the guitar against the plush sofa.

"You've been so generous with your time for my project."

"Any Wilbury is a friend of mine, Mavis," Otis told me. "What would you like to talk about this time?"

"I'm researching how the song 'Heading for the Light' was written and recorded."

"Ah, that one was Nelson's, you know. It had a spiritual theme." Otis smiled as he recalled his dear friend. "I wrote the melody for the bridge."

"What else can you tell me about how Nelson wrote it? I want every detail you can remember."

"That was forty years ago, you know," Otis offered.

I didn't correct his timeline again, although it had been less time than he stated.

"I don't recall very many details."

I smiled and waited for him to talk.

"Nelson came to my house the night before he showed that song to the rest of the group, I remember. I didn't live here then. I lived in another house in LA. He had been working on the song for a few days. He originally called it, 'He ...' um ..." Otis slapped his leg, trying to remember. "'He Falls in the Night,' that was it, and he had some chords, a melody, and a couple of verses written. He changed most of the original words, though."

Otis sat quietly for a moment, as if he were thinking. Finally, he spoke again. "The first version did have the lyrics 'heading for the light' in it, just not as the title. We sat down together and talked about what he was trying to say. He wanted to get across that the singer was coming out of a period of doubt about his faith."

Otis raised a finger, remembering another point. "Nelson wrote all the words to it. He just bounced ideas off me. It takes time for me to write lyrics, you know. It was much easier for Nelson.

"I helped him write the melody to a bridge he wanted and suggested some changes to the main melody. Then he wrote the lyrics up to the bridge. "He had the final version revised and typed up before he went home that night."

I scribbled on my notepad like crazy, even though I had a digital recorder going. "This is really good information. You're remembering a lot more than it sounded like you would."

"Oh, I remember something interesting. He said he had based the song on a raga. That's a concept in Indian classical music that he learnt from his sitar teacher, Ravi Shankar. It's a melodic mode kind of thing. Nelson used ragas a lot—he always said Indian musical compositions are much more subtle and complex than Western music, particularly pop music. The tune and the mood of a composition are based on the raga. Somehow the phrasing is too, but that's a bit over my head. Indian music uses a different scale and different time signatures than Western music. That means you can't adapt Indian music exactly to Western keys and timing. Nelson also said ragas are always spiritual in nature." Otis talked without being prompted. This subject was obviously of great interest to him.

I nodded and scribbled.

"He told me once there were hundreds of ragas, and each one was indicated for a particular time of day or set of conditions. He used the raga for 'Heading for the Light' that was most appropriate for a sunny day, so he joked with me that this song was his version of 'Mr. Blue Sky.' I told him surely that had been 'Here Comes the Sun.'

"Nelson believed that music was a form of worship. It was so inspiring to listen to him talk about it, even though I was never much on religion. In a way, music is my religion, so I totally get where Nelson was coming from." Otis fell silent.

"So many of Nelson's songs had a spiritual theme," I prompted.

Otis nodded. "He would write songs that were about romantic love on the surface, but they were really about his love of God."

"Did you produce any of his songs like that?" I was way off topic, but it fascinated me.

"On *Cloud Nine*, 'Fish in the Sand' and 'Someplace Else' were both love songs to Krishna. Or so he told me. He'd also mentioned his doubts about religion in "Fish." Later on in his career, he wouldn't be so obvious when he would write songs about Krishna because it seemed to keep the records from selling. 'My Sweet Lord' was the obvious exception, since it sold really well."

"What about 'This is Love' that you wrote with him?"

"That song was about both human love and spiritual love. You can see in the video where he showed family and friends who he loved."

I moved to the next topic. "It always struck me that Nelson wrote so many songs about dying in order to become one with God."

Otis's cheerful expression turned sad. "There are a surprising number of those songs. That's even what 'My Sweet Lord' is about. 'All Things Must Pass' and 'Art of Dying' were too."

"So were 'Living in the Material World' and 'Life Itself,'" I added. "Even The Beatles' song, 'Love You To,' referenced death."

Otis spoke so softly I could barely hear him. "It was hard to lose him at such a young age."

It took every bit of courage I had to ask the next question. "Do you think Nelson wanted to die young? He mentioned wanting to get to God so many times in his songs. Dying young made it come true that much sooner."

Frown lines furrowed between Otis's eyebrows. "Look, Nelson fought for his life at the end. He had every treatment that was available, even experimental ones. Some people have claimed he tried to meditate himself back to health, but that's bullshit. He certainly continued to meditate, but he sought Western medical treatments as well. Nelson wanted to live."

I swallowed and nodded, not knowing what to say.

His expression softened. "Hindus, like the Hari Krishnas, believe in reincarnation, and Nelson did too. Though he told me that he believed he might not be reincarnated into another life, but he might spend eternity with Krishna when he died in this life."

We sank into silence, thinking about the great musician the world had lost. I sensed I may have pushed too far and regretted mentioning Nelson's death.

I changed the subject. "Otis, what do you remember about how the song was recorded?"

Otis shook his head and shoulders. "What? Sorry. My mind was miles away."

"How was 'Heading for the Light' recorded?"

"Pretty much the same way the other tracks were recorded for the first Wilbury album. We laid down the acoustic guitar track first, then the backing and lead vocals. Nelson did the lead vocal on the verses, and I did the lead vocal on the bridges. Charlie T., Jnr. did harmony on the bridges. Next, we did bass and drums. We added a horn, lead guitar licks, and some percussion afterward at Friar Park."

"Anything interesting happen while you were recording that song?"

"We had the photo shoot that day."

"Neal is coming to do the photo shoot in a few minutes, so let's get ready, lads," Nelson prompted as Lucky entered the guest-house studio. "This week is probably the only time we'll all be together, so I thought we should have the pictures done now."

Lucky looked up after thumping his guitar on the floor. "Nelson, you didn't say nothing about a fucking photo shoot. I hate having my picture taken."

"I know, Lucky, but we need some photos for the album."

"Let's send the photographer down to the slums or the train yard and get him to take some pictures of some hoboes," Lucky retorted. "We'll say hoboes made this album. I don't think we should put pictures of ourselves on the sleeve."

Charlie T. chuckled. "Nelson told us he let you off the hook on the publicity angle, but you still have to be on the album cover and in the music videos, Lucky."

"You're gonna make me do music videos too?"

Nelson sighed. "Lucky, we have to do music videos if we want to sell records."

"I did a few videos for *Empire Burlesque*, but I fucking hated it. I especially hated the one where I had to act. After that fiasco with *Hearts of Fire*, I am never acting again."

Nelson remained patient. "These will all be music performance videos. I'll make them as painless as possible. There won't be any acting. Besides, you were good in *Hearts of Fire*. It wasn't your fault it tanked."

Lucky thinned his lips and scowled. "I thought this project with you guys was gonna be fun. Now it's turning into work."

Lefty joined the conversation. "Oh, quit your complaining. You know this is part of the music business as much as writing songs and singing them."

A van parked outside the guest house. Undoubtedly, it was Neal and his photographic equipment.

Lucky huffed a quick breath of air through his nose. "I'm not getting out of this, am I?"

Nelson smiled close-lipped at his half-brother. "No, you aren't. Put on your best enigmatic expression, and let's take some pictures."

Lucky pouted. "I have to get ready first."

Neal exited his van and walked into the guest-house studio. He and Nelson shook hands. "It's an honor to photograph your group, Mr. Wilbury. I was so excited when you called. Thank you so much."

"Thank Bugs. He gave me your name. He said you've worked with some great people, and he knew you from Lucky's tour with Charlie T. and the Heartbreakers. I looked at a few of your shots, and I thought they were phenomenal. This photo shoot should be easy by comparison to your usual work because we aren't going to be jumping around a stage."

Bugs helped Neal unload his photographic equipment.

"Don't take the reflective screens in yet, Bugs. The light is great outside. I want to walk around the house and find some spots to shoot in the yard. You can take the lights in, though. I won't need them outside."

Bugs nodded and removed a reflective screen folded like an umbrella. He placed it on the sidewalk leading to the recording studio. Neal approached the main house, looking for a suitable place to shoot, and disappeared around the corner.

Lucky watched him go and turned to Nelson. "We don't have time for fucking around like this. He needs to take the damn pictures and go so we can get back to working on the album."

"Okay, I'll tell him we don't have much time. Meanwhile you go get ready."

Lucky entered the guest house. His footsteps hammered up the stairs.

Nelson headed around the opposite corner of the house from where Neal had disappeared, intercepting him midway.

"Hey, Neal."

"Hi, Nelson. I was thinking you guys could stand in front of this set of French doors, holding your guitars, and over by those trees. They have a beautiful shape."

Nelson glanced at the indicated trees. "I love trees too, Neal. Look, I have to let you know that we only have an hour for this photo shoot, so you really need to speed it up. Any problem with that?

"No problem at all. I'm used to working within my subjects' constraints. Let's get busy."

Neal enlisted Bugs and Richard to help him move his reflective panels to the locations he had chosen. There was a moment's struggle as the tripod stands refused to balance on the tree roots, but Neal was resourceful, and he quickly found a way to stabilize them, using branches from the yard.

All was in place except Lucky. Nelson found him in the upstairs sitting room, strumming his guitar.

"Are you ready yet?"

"I guess so."

Lucky and Nelson joined the other three against the trees.

Neal snapped several shots in front of the trees and moved the group to the French doors on the side of the main house, where he snapped another dozen.

He jabbered the usual photographer's patter. "You guys look great. These expressions are priceless. Charlie T., give me some attitude. Otis, raise your chin. Nelson, smile, but don't show me all your teeth." *Click, click.* "Lucky, can you look a little less bored? Yeah, that's good." *Click, click.* "Lefty, turn your left shoulder out. Just like that. Yeah, that's right." *Click, click.* "Okay, we're losing the good light out here, guys. Let's go in the house. Where's Bugs? I need some help moving these panels."

Once the equipment had been relocated into the house, Neal enlisted Bugs to help move furniture. They pushed a couple of chairs together in the foyer so Neal could shoot a family portrait.

"Okay, Nelson, we've got the chairs set up," Neal called to the next room. "You guys can come in here."

The band members filed into the room, carrying their guitars.

"Is this the last photo setup?" Lucky whined.

Nelson looked at Neal. "Are you planning any more?"

Lucky wandered over to Dave's pinball machine. "I'm gonna play pinball while this photographer makes up his mind."

Neal raised his eyebrows. "That's up to you guys. I want you to be happy. We can stop after this and you can look at the proofs if you want."

"Okay, that sounds great," Nelson said. "Let's do this. Where do you want us?"

"Line up right here under the chandelier."

"Let's give Lucky a few seconds to finish playing his ball," Nelson suggested.

The sound of another pinball launching emanated from the machine under the stairwell.

Neal sighed. "I'll just take some establishing shots." *Click, click.*

Nelson looked over his shoulder just as the camera shutter clicked. "Lucky, would you care to join us soon?"

"Yeah, in a second."

The last pinball disappeared accompanied by a descending electronic tone and a synthesized voice intoning, "Loser." Lucky ambled over to join the group, leaning his head on Otis's back. "Man, I suck at pinball." *Click, click.*

Neal pointed to the chairs. "Lucky, you and Lefty sit in the chairs, holding your guitars, and the other three line up behind them with your guitars."

Neal adjusted his bright lights as the half-brothers complied. He changed the tilt of their guitars to create the most pleasing composition.

His camera clicked.

"Okay, guys, let's get a few shots without the guitars."

Lucky could contain no himself longer. "Mother-fucker."

"What's wrong ..." Neal hesitated, unsure if he should call this music legend by his first name when not giving photo directions. But if he called him Mr. Wilbury, five people would answer. "... Lucky?"

Lucky looked at Neal in exasperation. "Nothin'. Let's just get this shit over with."

Neal didn't know if he had done something amiss, but he was here to do a job, and he intended to produce a quality product. "Okay, Lucky, you change places with Otis. Yes, that's a nicer composition. Lean down and put your hands on the arms of the chair." *Click, click.* "Yes, hold it just like that. Very nice. Look at me. Yes, just like that." *Click, click.* "Oh, yes, we have something special there. Yes, very nice. Okay, just a couple more." *Click, click.* "Lucky, stand up straight. Nelson, turn your head to the right. Good." *Click, click.*

At last, Neal pronounced the photo shoot complete. One by one, he and Bugs toted the lights and reflective panels to the van.

Returning to the studio, Charlie T. and Nelson exchanged glances. They silently agreed that Lucky needed some comeuppance for acting like a diva about a necessary part of the music business. And it should involve photos. Bugs had been shooting Polaroids of the group throughout their sojourn at Dave's house and recording studio. Nelson and Charlie T. headed for the stacks of Polaroids that Bugs had stockpiled in the studio's small living room since they started.

"Maybe we could decorate his face, Nelson," Charlie T. suggested.

"That sounds like just the thing. Let's get some markers. Otis will help us. We have to hurry because Lucky is all hot to get to work on the next song."

Nelson almost collided with Otis on his way into the studio's kitchen area. "Oi, Nelson, what ya doing? Let's get back to work."

"Yeah, in a minute, Otis. But first, Charlie T. and I want to play a trick on Lucky."

Nelson grabbed the red and black markers they had been using for writing lyrics and rushed into the living room, where Charlie T. sorted photos of Lucky.

"I found five good ones that we can decorate, Nelson."

Nelson picked up a photo. "Here, Otis. Draw a moustache on him or something. We want to take the piss out of him for being such a diva about the photo shoot."

All three men drew embarrassing images on the Polaroids of Lucky. Nelson stuffed them in his pockets.

Lucky shouted into the living room from the kitchen, where he was strumming his guitar. "Are we gonna do any work today or not?"

Nelson strode into the room. "I wanted to show you the proofs for our photo session today. You'll wish you had looked a little happier about it." He handed the doctored photos to Lucky. Lefty looked over Charlie T.'s shoulder, smiling.

Lucky took the photos. "Ha, ha, very funny. Who's the artist?"

Nelson smirked. "You are, Lucky. You painted that ugly expression on your face. I hope Neal is enough of a genius to make you look good, because it was obvious you were pissed about having to do the photo shoot."

"I get the message. If the photos look bad enough, I'll figure out a way to redo them. Let's move on."

"Okay," Nelson said. "Otis and I worked on a song last night called 'Heading for the Light.' This is how it goes."

# CHAPTER 16

## NOT ALONE ANYMORE

Lefty needed guitar strings for his Gretsch. Nelson informed him they were starting a little late that day, so he had time to stop at his favorite place to buy them, McCabe's Music Store on Santa Monica Boulevard. That establishment had been there since the 1950s. They knew who Lefty was, who he had been, and they understood his musical needs.

It was still before noon when Lefty pulled his 'Vette into the parking lot down the street. As he neared the music store, he heard a masterful bass line. He initially thought it was coming from inside the store, but he saw a man dressed in shabby clothes playing an upright bass on the sidewalk by the opposite corner of the store. The bass player swayed backward and forward as he played, his gloved left hand with fingers exposed briskly moving up and down the neck of the instrument, his feet planted near the spike of the bass. The tall instrument reeled with him. His right gloved hand slapped and plucked the strings.

Wandering to where the musician stood with his double bass, Lefty loitered on the sidewalk, grooving in time to the bass. A higher-register melody line emerged as the single-note bass continued.

*How is he doing that?* Lefty wondered. He recognized the tune as a song he had written the previous year with his friend, Glenn Danzig, called "Life Fades Away." The song was an obscure one, written for a minor film with unknown actors. The bass player impressed Lefty with how well he knew his catalog.

In the film, Robert Downey, Jr. played a recent high-school graduate addicted to drugs who dies. Lefty's song about an early death and the loves the deceased left behind played over the credits. The lyrics mention December as a metaphor for death.

The double bass the fellow was playing looked exactly like one his high-school classmate, Charlie, used to play in the Wink Westerners. That band had been his entry into show business. The Wink Westerners had played all over West Texas and had appeared on the radio. Once Lefty had tasted singing in public, he craved more. He knew he would be a professional singer for the rest of his life. But he lacked the magical voice he possessed now. That came later, with a visit from beyond the stars.

Lefty tapped his toe and smiled at the brilliant street musician. "Mister, I haven't heard anyone play the double bass like that since … well, I haven't ever heard anyone play the double bass like that. I don't understand how you can play those high notes and low notes at the same time. I'll be going out on a tour pretty soon. Would you like to join my band?"

The double-bass player paused for a moment to doff his hat and shake his head. He spun his instrument on its spike and resumed playing "Life Fades Away."

Lefty chuckled. "You aren't trying to tell me something with that song, are you? I already had a triple-coronary bypass."

The music swelled on the lyric referencing peace forever. Lefty did a double take, turned his back on the incredibly talented but darkly sinister double-bass player, and entered the music store.

Nelson sat on the studio's front porch, strumming a classic red Gretsch guitar—similar to the one he had played during The Beatles' early years—as Otis and Charlie T. drove up. Bugs was right behind them.

Charlie T. got out and slammed the 'Vette door. "Why'd you want us here so early, Nelson? Are we gonna record without Lucky and Lefty?"

Nelson smiled and shook his head. "No, we won't start working on music until Lefty arrives. Lucky has a business meeting at Columbia today. I have a treat in store for us this morning. The Gretsches are coming for a visit."

Otis cocked his head and pulled his beard as he sat down beside his friend on the divan. "Guitars are visiting us?"

"Not Gretsch guitars, Otis. Gretsch people. Dinah Gretsch sent me a thank you note for featuring a Gretsch guitar on the cover of *Cloud Nine* and asked if I could think of any other ways to get the Gretsch trademark out there. They bought the company back from Baldwin a few years ago and want to make guitars again soon."

Charlie T. sat in a rocking chair opposite Otis and Nelson. "Did you have any ideas for her?"

Nelson played a couple of chords on the unplugged electric guitar and nodded. "As a matter of fact, I did. That's what they are coming to talk about."

Otis couldn't stand the suspense. "Hey, what was your idea?"

Nelson retrieved an envelope from the porch floor. He opened it and removed a color pastel drawing on tissue paper. "I commissioned this from an artist friend of mine in England. It's for a Wilbury Gretsch guitar line." He passed the paper to Otis.

Otis examined the drawing and whistled. "Lovely colors. So do we get anything out of this?"

Nelson nodded. "A cut of sales. Promotion for the album. We can sign a few and auction them off for charity. Mostly, I wanted to give Gretsch a leg up on their new guitar line. That's why we got the classic Gretsch guitars from Norman's Rare Guitars to use in the photo shoot yesterday. Now we can keep them until we're done with the album."

Charlie T. raised one eyebrow. "It's been seven or eight years since Gretsch stopped making electric guitars. I know the Gretsch family bought the company back from Baldwin, but are they sure they can just jump right back in and make quality instruments?"

Nelson opened his mouth to answer, but a Chevrolet with a rental sticker on the bumper rolled up the driveway before he could respond. A man and a woman emerged.

The woman strode right up to Nelson with her hand extended. "Oh, Nelson, it's so lovely to meet you at last. This is my husband, Fred." She enthusiastically shook hands. Her voice carried a Southern accent undertone.

Fred appeared behind her and muttered an indistinct greeting.

Sensing his nervousness, Nelson stood to welcome Fred. "Hello, Dinah. Hi, Fred. It's quite an honor to meet the owners of Gretsch Musical Instruments."

Otis stood to shake hands, but Dinah had already moved on to Charlie T., Jnr. "Oh, Mr. Wilbury," she gushed. "I have all your albums, too. I think your music is brilliant."

He shook hands. "Thank you. Nice to meet you, Dinah. Fred. This is my assistant, Alan Weidel." Bugs stepped up and shook hands with Dinah and her husband.

Otis remained standing. Nelson took the cue and tapped Dinah on the shoulder. She turned to face him.

"This is Otis Wilbury, our half-brother, co-composer, singer, multi-instrumentalist, and my co-producer for the current album project."

Dinah peered into Otis's face as if she were trying to place him.

Fred whispered, "You know, dear, Electric Light Orchestra."

"Oh, yes," Dinah said, nodding and smiling. "So pleased to meet you, Otis."

Nelson suggested they convene in the big house because the furnishings were more suitable for a business meeting. Once they were seated around the large dining table, Dinah announced she had gifts for all the group members—black T-shirts sporting the Gretsch logo. She handed them to the members present and gave two extras to Nelson to pass on to Lucky and Lefty. Nelson noted the size of the one she had brought for Lefty—medium. He knew that wouldn't fit him and decided not to mention it. Lefty was very sensitive about his weight.

"These are lovely. Thank you."

Dinah smiled at Nelson. "I don't want you to think T-shirts are the only gifts we will bestow in return for the enormous favor you are doing for us. We can't give you guitars right now, but are there other musical instruments any of you would like right now?"

Otis leaned forward. "Would Gretsch ever make drums? If you do, I'd love a set of those."

"We can provide Gretsch drum sets for all five of the musical Wilburys. Just give us the addresses where you would like them delivered. It will take a couple of weeks for them to get to California from South Carolina."

Charlie T. arose from his chair and summoned Bugs from the kitchen. "Would you make a list of all our addresses for the Gretsches, please?"

"Right away, boss."

"Anything else we can provide?"

Nelson smiled, "Dinah, Fred, I think you've made us happy. Let's talk about the Wilbury guitar."

Dinah and Nelson spread their two copies of the drawing for the front of the proposed Wilbury guitar. Dinah's was larger than Nelson's—five feet by three feet— and had been folded multiple times.

"This design is really quite special," Dinah gushed. "It'll make a distinctive motif and will signal the return of Gretsch to guitar making. At this point, we have no American shop that can make a quality instrument. I assume we're on a time crunch, because we want the guitars available at about the same time the album is released."

Nelson sat back in his chair, across from Dinah. "That's correct, Dinah. The Wilbury guitar won't carry the same impact unless it comes out at the same time as the album. We expect the album to be released next fall, maybe September or October."

Fred added, "It's essential that we put out a quality product for Gretsch guitar's reintroduction to the world. Otherwise, we blow our best chance. I notice your design conforms to the classic shape of Gretsch guitars. How would you feel about the Wilbury guitars having a different shape, more similar to a Danelectro?"

Nelson sat upright and put two arms on the table. Charlie T. and Otis looked sharply across the table at each other. They were letting Nelson answer this one. "I don't know, Fred. Danelectro has a reputation as a real cheap brand. Why did you choose that one as a model?"

Fred had overcome his initial nervousness and was all business now. "Frankly, Nelson … may I call you Nelson?"

Nelson nodded.

"Frankly, Nelson, the equipment Gretsch once used to make guitars is long gone. We have to start all over from scratch. The startup costs will be enormous. That's why we're so grateful for your help. The only good lead on a manufacturer we have is one in Korea that acquired the machine tools from Danelectro after it went out of business. We wouldn't use the same cheap materials they used, like Masonite or plywood. We'd produce quality instruments. Well, we might have to skimp on the machine head. But it would save a hell of a lot on startup costs if we could reproduce that old body shape. As I'm sure you know, the Danelectro was a three-quarter guitar, so we'd have to scale this drawing down to get it to fit."

Nelson nodded. "I get what you're saying. As long as the Wilbury guitar doesn't have a cheap feel to it and makes a good sound, I'm on board with it. You could even use Masonite, like the original Danelectro. How about you, Otis? You, Charlie T.?"

Otis and Charlie T. exchanged another glance.

Otis said, "I'll support whatever decision you make, Nelson."

Charlie T. nodded.

Nelson stood. "Okay, let's do it. You can adapt that drawing to whatever guitar shape you end up with. We'll still want final approval before you begin manufacture. Will you contact me when you have a prototype ready?"

Dinah and Fred stood, taking the cue from Nelson that the meeting was over. Fred nodded. "As soon as we have a prototype, we'll make arrangements to get it to you for approval."

Charlie T. stood, stretching a little. "Sounds good."

Otis was the last to stand, holding the drawing for the Wilbury guitar in front of him. "Could we ever change this, Nelson? Like after the first year? Maybe keep the same colors and do a different design?"

Nelson put his hand on Otis's shoulder and smiled at his half-brother. "I always like the way you think. I'll speak to the artist."

As they exited the house, Lefty's 'Vette approached. The day's musical work was about to begin.

Fred and Dinah slid into their rental and drove away.

Charlie T. touched Nelson on the arm. "I get why Lucky wasn't here, but why didn't you invite Lefty?"

"Lefty brings Barbara with him. Too many cooks ... You know."

Lucky had scheduled a meeting with his road manager, Victor, that day, so he couldn't record with his half-brothers. Lucky didn't like Victor coming to his house, and he had to parlay with executives at Columbia about his next album. He might as well kill two birds with the metaphorical stone, so he scheduled both meetings at Columbia in LA. The four-story white building was small and unassuming compared to the towering steel and glass home base in Manhattan.

As Lucky pulled his van into the covered employees-only parking lot, the guard waved and smiled at him. He waved back without smiling. The boom barrier flew up, admitting him to the parking area. He parked as close to the door leading to the elevator as he could. He never liked being outside the car or walking unescorted. He was always afraid of being recognized or accosted, especially since John Lennon had been murdered.

Lucky found a spot ten spaces from the elevator. When he opened the door of his vehicle, he heard the music of an acoustic guitar. Lucky stood at the van and peered past the elevator foyer. He saw a shabby-looking man playing a worn-out guitar near a column.

*Might as well listen a minute. Victor knows I'm always late.*

Lucky slammed the van door and locked it. He headed in the direction of the man standing by the column of the indoor parking structure. He wasn't as afraid of other musicians as he was of the general public, whether it was sensible or not.

As Lucky approached the player, he noticed writing on the man's battered guitar: *This machine kills ...ists.* The picker's right arm covered the rest of the word. Lucky recognized the song—Woody Guthrie's "Bound for

Glory," a song that had inspired Lucky on his journey of words and music.

Lucky strode right up to the guitar player and looked at his worn, whiskered face. "You aren't Woody, but you look kind of like him. You sound kind of like him too."

The guitarist changed the song in mid-bar. Now Lucky recognized a song he had written but hadn't yet recorded. He didn't plan to ever record the song because it told too much about him and his secrets.

"How do you know that song?" Lucky demanded.

"... *when the deal goes down*," the guitarist sang. He swayed as he strummed the battered guitar and closed his eyes as he sang the provocative lyrics. His gloved hands showed exposed fingers.

As Lucky stood before him, he noticed a faint glow around the navy-blue Dodgers baseball cap on the musician's head. Lucky did a double take and looked the fellow over again.

"You aren't who you seem to be, are you? We've met before. You were out in the forest, near Woodstock in the sixties; although you didn't show me a face then. You gave me my gift of air writing. I've written some of my greatest songs that way. Have you come for me?" Lucky fell to his knees. "Take me, if it be Your will."

The being held his guitar in one hand by his side. "I'm not going to take you. I'm here to tell you the next part of the deal."

"I'll do Your will."

"I'm only an emissary."

"Okay, I'll do His will."

"Stand up. Twenty-five years ago, in exchange for the ability to write extraordinarily poetic and moving song lyrics, you agreed to record those lyrics and share them with the world. That was your part of the deal. That contract has expired. I'm here to renew it if you wish, but also to add a new rider. You are to play more live shows."

"I'm leaving on a tour next month. I can book as many shows as you want. And I definitely want to renew the air-writing contract."

"You are to take your music to the people. Get it out there. Stop hiding in Malibu. In exchange, the powers that be will make sure you don't get shot on tour. Deal?"

"Of course it's a deal. How many shows do you want me to play?"

"That's up to you. More shows than you're playing now. Just make sure you reach a wide audience. In addition to protection during the tours, you'll receive continued success and adulation."

"You could actually slack up on the adulation a little."

"I'm afraid we can't do one without the other."

Lucky's face drooped. "I guess that's how it works."

The emissary nodded.

"I'll start planning a bigger tour. I'm meeting with my tour manager today. This is going to be great."

The emissary smiled benevolently. "You can still 'air-write,' as you call it. We'll be in the front row at your next concert."

"Could I hold that guitar? Was it really his?"

"Sure, you can hold it. It was one of his guitars. He had dozens."

Lucky strummed a few chords on the strings his idol, Woody Guthrie, had touched. He had never heard sweeter music.

It was day eight at the recording studio. The Traveling Wilburys had been working without a break. They weren't running out of steam because they enjoyed what they were doing. Work isn't work when it's play.

Everyone except Lucky congregated on the studio's front porch with coffee. Lucky was at his meetings with Victor, the Columbia execs, and another fateful meeting he hadn't foreseen.

Otis gulped his second cup of coffee, although he was usually a tea drinker. He hated coffee, but today he needed the extra caffeine. Plenty of milk and sugar made it more palatable. He had been up late two nights in a row, working on his least-favorite thing: lyrics. It was imperative that this album include a song featuring Lefty's gargantuan voice, and he intended to make certain it did, so he wrote it himself. Otis had the chords and five melodies for the song. The lyrics always slowed him down. He had chained himself to the desk for the last two nights to write them.

So far, Otis had two pages of scribbled, rewritten lyrics. His efforts weren't going well. He had crumpled up the first two pages and discarded them. The second night, Lefty dropped by his house to help him after recording ended. He had added to a bridge Otis had composed. He thought what Lefty had written was better than anything he had managed.

Otis revealed the latest version of the lyrics. "Lefty and I worked on this for him to sing. I've got the music, but you know how I am with lyrics."

Nelson sniffed. "Let's have a look at that. Sing us what you've got."

Otis sang the four verses and the bridge he and Lefty had completed together, using the tune he thought would best showcase Lefty's range and timbre.

"It's got potential," Nelson admitted. "It's certainly a good story for a Lefty song. Boy leaves girl because he wants something better, then tries to come back, and she's taken." He reached for a legal pad and began scribbling lyrics.

Charlie T. looked over Nelson's shoulder and made suggestions. After an hour, Nelson had three pages of rewritten lyrics, but none of them were spectacular.

"Hmm, this is a hard one," Nelson fretted. He reviewed Otis's original sheet. "Maybe we were too quick to discard these."

"I wish Lucky was here," muttered Otis.

Charlie T. patted Otis's shoulder. "If Lucky was here, we'd just get a ten-verse epic about shadows at midnight. We're all world-class songwriters, and we can do this."

Otis nodded; Charlie T. was right.

"Hey, Otis," Nelson said. "Let's lay down the backing track and let the lyrics simmer for a bit. Maybe we can summon great words while we eat." He looked more closely at his brother. "You look tired. Have you been sleeping?"

It's hard to tell when someone hasn't been sleeping if his eyes aren't visible. Nelson's clue had been Otis's slumped shoulders, which were normally straight.

"Well, some," Otis answered. "I've been working on this bugger."

Nelson admonished him. "Don't kill yourself on one song. We can write others."

Charlie T. and Lefty had already proceeded toward the kitchen to get their guitars from the cases.

Otis leaned close to his brother so the others wouldn't hear him. "I want to make certain that Lefty has a song all to himself. It has to be one that really shows off his voice."

Nelson nodded. "You are absolutely right, Otis. We have to make certain of that. This song could be the one that does that. But it has to be good enough and fit with the rest of the album."

Otis couldn't agree more. He struggled to his feet and fetched his guitar.

The song as Otis had written it was simple enough. It only had three basic chords: two minor and one major.

"All right then," Otis said, assuming his role as producer. "Same as usual. Play one verse and one bridge. We don't yet know how many verses we'll have, but that don't matter. I can zap in more verses later."

Don cued the tape and set the recording levels for the acoustic guitars. He started the click track. The brothers strummed their acoustic guitars with little rehearsal. Otis sang a guide vocal. In less than five minutes, the recording was done.

"Okay, I'll do a bass line now." Otis sighed. "Lay this down on a separate track so I can zap it to the master."

Otis could play bass in his sleep. He donned the headphones, plugged his guitar into the direct box, and played a bass line for one verse and one bridge while seated at the soundboard. He zapped the tape into a backing track of eight acoustic guitars and bass with a verse-bridge-verse-bridge-verse pattern.

"Is it time to eat yet?" Otis was always hungrier when he didn't have enough sleep.

"Are you 'peckish?'" Charlie T. teased as they walked to the big house.

Bugs had made efficient use of the thousand dollars Nelson had given him for food. He had engaged a pizza caterer to provide dinner today.

Barbara had dropped her sons off at the library for a few hours, and decided to observe the recording. When she arrived, she saw the caterers at the big house, and decided not to interrupt the musicians at their work. She helped the caterers unload the food and prepare the meal instead.

"About twenty minutes on the pizza, boys," the caterer called. "There's salad and bread on the table."

Barbara scooped greens into a bowl for her husband. She passed him his favorite dressing. Nelson, Otis, and Charlie T. helped themselves.

Bugs sat down next to Nelson. "So, how's it going?"

Nelson crunched his salad and swallowed before answering. "Great. We're right on schedule. I think we're gonna finish in time. Lucky isn't here today, as you can see. We're working on a song for Lefty."

"What's it called?" Bugs remained astonished at the brothers' ability to write and record a song a day.

"I don't know." Nelson turned to his brother. "Otis, what's this song called?"

Otis, chewing on a piece of garlic bread, held up a finger to signal he needed a moment to ponder a title and swallow. He looked at Lefty for suggestions.

"I like that line at the end of the bridge," Lefty answered. "'You're not alone anymore.'"

"I like the shorter titles," Bugs teased.

Otis swallowed. "Maybe just 'Not Alone Anymore,' then."

"That title's a little shorter," Bugs laughed.

Don wondered if Bugs knew about what Otis and Lefty could do, but he had promised not to say anything. He didn't have to wonder long.

"So, Don—" Bugs turned to him. "—what did you think of Otis's light show? It sure freaked me out the first time I saw it. I thought the board was on fire." He liked to get the reactions of people the first time they were exposed to Otis's abilities.

Don laughed. "No wonder they call him a wizard in the control room."

Bugs laughed too. "No kidding. But he's a really talented producer too. He's one of the best, if not *the* best."

Charlie T. looked at Nelson. "I heard George Martin is losing his hearing."

Nelson nodded grimly. "I'm afraid it's true. The last time I talked to him, he said he couldn't hear in the high range at all. He hasn't retired, but he can't do what he used to do for us. He has to rely on his engineer for a lot of things he used to do himself." He winked at Otis. "Since George Martin is out, you were next in line, so that makes you the best."

"Oh, bollocks," Otis said. "There's plenty better than me. What about Phil Spector?"

Nelson snorted. "He's not a producer, he's an over-producer!"

"You've said the same of me," Otis persisted.

"I'm just teasing you when I say that, Otis. But I do have to tell you to stop sometimes. I tried to tell Spector to stop on *All Things Must Pass*, and he wouldn't listen to me. 'One more string track!' he'd say, and the next thing I'd know, there'd be six more string tracks. 'Wah-Wah' wasn't a wall of sound. It was a neutron star of sound. It was John's and my idea to get him to produce *Let It Be*, and he sure ruined that, didn't he?"

Otis shrugged. "Well, I like it."

"You would!" Nelson laughed again.

Otis didn't want to let go of this bone. "What about Brian Wilson?"

Nelson frowned. "Brian's out of the game too, isn't he? But it's not his hearing, it's his mind. He can't focus well enough to produce a bowel movement, much less an album, poor chap."

Otis nodded. "I had the honor of working with Brian on a song just a few weeks ago. That doctor who's supposed to be helping him is just making it worse. He got along much better when Dr. Landy was out of the room. He even takes credit for Brian's musical work. Wanker. His family should fire that useless prick. He prances around Brian's house wearing a cape and carrying a cane."

Nelson agreed, "That's what I heard, too. You met that arsehole? You saw how he treats Brian? Wow." Nelson raised his eyebrows and grimaced.

"Brian Eno's a better producer than me," Otis said, refusing to admit he was the best in the world.

Nelson scoffed. "Brian bloody Eno? You are shitting me, Otis. I mean, his stuff for U2 is pretty good, but you don't think Bono gave him much control, do you? And Talking Heads? Same deal. You know David Byrne was pulling those strings." Nelson was demonstrating his inborn persuasiveness superpower. He wasn't going to let Otis avoid the acknowledgement of his mastery as a music producer. "Just admit it, Otis. You're a musical genius."

"Eno was pulling the strings on his own albums," Otis persisted, ignoring Nelson's title of "musical genius."

He could usually resist his half-brother's influence for an extended period.

"Yeah, Otis. And his albums weren't nearly as good as ELO's. Who came up with that symph-pop sound first, I'm asking you?"

"Well, Eno is a bit more techno pop, don't you think? With some avant-garde thrown in."

"More like avant-garde a clue. ELO was streets better." Nelson waved his hand in dismissal of Brian Eno.

Lefty had been following the conversation from the end of the table. "I agree with you about Otis. He's the best producer I've ever worked with, and I've been through at least thirty of 'em. What do you mean by 'avant-garde a clue?'"

Otis leaned over the table and shot Lefty a grin. "Many thanks, mate. Nelson means most experimental music types 'aven't got a clue about what they are doing."

Those seated around the table erupted into laughter.

"Anyway, I'm not as good a producer as Quincy Jones."

Nelson stared at his brother. Otis had him; Quincy Jones had produced some of the greatest pop, soul, and jazz albums of the twentieth century. He had Grammys out the wazoo. Quincy Jones was at least as good as Otis, although Nelson had no desire to work with him. He figured Otis was a lot more fun.

The pizzas arrived at the table.

"All right, Otis. You're tied for best producer in the world with Quincy Jones. Pass me a piece of that vegetarian pizza, will you?"

Otis felt a little smug about winning the argument. He didn't quite realize he had admitted to being the best working music producer on the planet, even if it was a dead heat.

Back in the recording studio, the brothers set themselves to the task of refining lyrics. Nelson picked up the original lyric sheet from Otis.

"You know, most of these are not bad. I think we can just rework them. Let's see ... This first line is good." Nelson read the next line. "'That you would always be my only friend.' That line's weak. Anybody got something else?"

"Well, he's coming back to her, right? How about a line that says that?" Charlie T. suggested.

Nelson snapped his fingers and pointed at Charlie T. in one motion. "Perfect!"

"Well, Otis, this doesn't make any sense." Nelson had moved to the third line of the song. "You've got 'Hanging around, you're not alone.'"

"You know lyrics aren't my forté." Otis was quite tired now and didn't have the patience to try to account for what he considered his lacking words. "Just fix it for me."

Lefty had been staring at the sheet. He offered an alternative line that fit the story the lyrics were telling.

Nelson laughed. "And again, that's perfect. And that's the first verse! This bridge looks fine to me. Any suggestions to improve it?"

Charlie T. said, "You don't need the 'and,' but other than that, it looks pretty good to me. I thought it sounded good when Otis sang it too."

Otis and Lefty reviewed the tune they had chosen for the new song. Lefty decided to adjourn into the yard to run through the lengthy song several times. He promised to sing softly to preserve the flora. Otis, Nelson, and Charlie T., Jnr. took a joint break on the porch. Since Lefty didn't smoke marijuana, they took every opportunity to indulge when he wasn't around, out of respect for him.

Otis took a hit off the joint and passed it to Nelson. Charlie T. decided to speak to Otis about a matter that had been on his mind.

"Brother, I've been meaning to ask you. Why are you so damn down on yourself?"

"What do you mean?" Otis's voice was strained as he held the smoke in his lungs.

Nelson added his opinion. "Charlie T. is right on target. Like that conversation we had about what a brilliant producer you are. We had to argue with you about it."

Charlie T. passed the joint back to Otis, who dug out his keychain and attached his roach clip to stall. He took too deep a hit and wound up in a prolonged coughing fit.

"Well?" asked Charlie T. when the paroxysm had ended.

Otis folded his hands and stared at his fingers. "I dunno, fellas. I've always been shy, you know. It makes me feel uncomfortable when I get too much praise."

Lefty interrupted their conversation, returning to the studio with the lyric sheet in hand. "I think I've got it. Let me run through it once with the backing track, and we can turn on the recorder." He sniffed the air. "Smoking some herbs, eh?"

Nelson snuffed out the joint. "Yeah, we know you don't approve. Thanks for not making a big deal of it."

Lefty took his place at the microphone, and Otis situated himself at the soundboard. Don sat beside him, running some equipment checks. Otis turned to Don. "You've already seen what Lefty can do, so set the recording level low. He wants to do a run through. Don't start recording right off, and don't base your levels on the run through. He won't do it at full volume."

"Okay," Don answered. Nothing surprised him at this point.

Lefty taped the lyric sheet to the mic. He pointed to Don to cue the backing track. Lefty sang the first verse. He was not at full volume, as expected. Otis checked the sound levels. The needles were nowhere close to optimal. He didn't touch the levels.

Lefty completed the song as they had written it and addressed Otis. "I think it would be better if the bridge was repeated at the end. I think it would make a nice ending."

Otis nodded and activated the talkback mic to the kitchen. "Nelson, Lefty has an idea to improve the song." Otis flipped the switch off to address the occupants of the sound booth. "Tell Nelson what you told me."

Lefty cleared his throat and stood at the door of the booth. "Nelson, I think I should sing the bridge over at the end of the song and make it a chorus."

Nelson entered the sound booth to look at the lyrics. "Yeah, that sounds good. Hey, can you do a big Lefty Wilbury ending?"

Lefty looked puzzled. "Like what?"

"Like a swelling vocal. Come on, you know. Climbing the ladder, keep going up the scale." Nelson sang an ascending scale. "*Not alone, not alone anymore, anymore, anymore.*" His voice cracked at the end when he tried to hit the highest note.

Lefty glanced at the lyrics sheet. "Yeah, I can manage that." He looked at Don. "Can you cue up the last verse? I think we'll have to extend the guitar part. Otis, can you do that?"

"Without a doubt," Otis responded. He was determined to project some self-assurance after the reaming the others had given him.

Lefty sang the second verse, lengthening it after the guitars stopped as Nelson had requested. Otis took note of how the backing track would have to be extended to provide musical support for the newly developed vocal.

"Don, would you put a blank tape on the second deck?"

Otis's task was to preserve the two tracks they had made—acoustics and bass—while chopping a portion of the chorus and appending it to the end of the last chorus.

Once Don had mounted the tapes, Otis held his hands over the board and concentrated. He had no doubt he could do this. He had done it before. It would be done just as an engineer would splice an ordinary tape onto the end of another, except Otis wouldn't physically cut the tape. Sparks of electricity left his fingers and entered the board. The tapes spun, and fifteen seconds later, a tape with an extended coda sat on the deck.

Otis didn't even test it. He instructed Don to mount the new tape and asked Lefty. "Are you ready for a real take?"

"Sure, I'm ready. Aren't you going to make sure the tape is right?"

"I don't need to check it. It's right."

Nelson and Charlie T., Jnr. exchanged glances in the kitchen. Maybe Otis had heard them and was working on his confidence already.

Lefty put on the headphones. "I'm ready then."

Don rolled the tapes.

Lefty let loose with his full volume. A small crack formed in the corner of the glass separating the sound booth from the kitchen. Lefty lifted off the ground. He grabbed the microphone at the last moment.

Lefty's tone and cadence swelled. He spun slowly in the air, holding the microphone. The wire twisted beneath his feet. He sang hypnotically, closing his eyes when he didn't need to consult the lyric sheet. Like Otis, Lefty perpetually wore shades, and it was hard to determine when his eyes were open or closed, except from the side.

Lefty's singing transported Otis into another realm. He forgot to watch the board. He forgot to do his producer's job and think about what the track needed. All he could think about was how beautifully Lefty could sing.

Fortunately, Don kept half an eye on it, and everything was under control.

When the newly devised coda ended, Lefty sank to the floor, and Otis jumped to his feet. "Brilliant! That was great! We got a lot of good stuff there!" His extension of the backing track had been right on the mark.

Nelson and Charlie T. entered the sound booth to listen to the playback. When it was finished, Nelson remained silent. Everyone looked at him.

Finally he said, "It's not as exciting as it ought to be with that tremendous vocal."

Otis put his thumb and forefinger to the bridge of his nose beneath his shades. "What the hell, mate? It's Lefty singing. It's magnificent."

"Listen to it, Otis. It's flat, dull." Nelson rewound the tape and played it again.

Otis listened as objectively as he could. "The whole effect is a bit brittle and gray, ain't it? Shit. I can add a bit of wobble."

Nelson lowered his chin and regarded his friend through his eyebrows. "Otis, I know you are the master wobbler, but wobble is not going to help this track."

Charlie T. said, "Maybe we could add some instruments and backing vocals."

"Yeah, let's try that," Nelson agreed. "What do you think, Otis?"

"Sure. Backing vocals might liven it up." It was obvious where the backing vocals needed to go, so that was no problem. "Let's do *sha-la-la-la, sha-la-la-la* behind the second verse and third verse and 'not alone, not alone' behind the bridge."

"Do you want me on backing vocals?" Lefty asked.

"Oh, yeah," Otis replied. "Just sing real soft-like."

Otis conducted the group on the backing vocals. The whole thing went off without a hitch. They listened to the result through the monitors. Again, it seemed lackluster despite Lefty's soaring vocal.

"There's something wrong with it that I can't put my finger on." Otis was tired, and he was getting a headache.

"I can put my finger on it," Nelson said. "It sucks, and we can't bloody use it."

"Man, we have put so much work into it," Lefty said. "Especially Otis. I can't believe we have to throw it out."

"Maybe Lucky will have something tomorrow," Charlie T. said.

"Don," Otis said. "Can you put this on a cassette for me? I'm going to take it home and try to work on it there. I can't stay here another minute."

At home, Otis listened to the cassette recording of "Not Alone Anymore" over and over. The melody was good. The lyrics were good. The vocal was dynamite. The backing was … That's what was wrong with the track. The backing track was lifeless. All the other Wilbury tracks had been put together the same way with simple chords. This song demanded loftier accompaniment.

Otis felt too exhausted to think about it anymore. Cracking the doors to his two daughters' rooms, he observed them sleeping peacefully. He stumbled into his bedroom, dressed for bed, and collapsed beside his wife.

Three hours later, he awoke with a start, sitting upright in bed. A dream of suspended chords lingered in his memory.

"What's wrong?" Sandi asked, struggling awake and rubbing her eyes.

"I've figured it out. I know what to do." Otis was already out of bed and throwing on his clothes.

"Where are you going? What time is it?"

"I'm going back to the studio. I have to do another backing track to the song."

"You're crazy." Sandi's head fell back onto the pillow.

Otis laughed. "I know."

Otis grabbed his Telecaster on the way out of the house.

When Otis reached Dave's, all the lights were out, and a violet dawn gleamed on the horizon. All the studio doors were locked. He circled the guest house, looking for a way to enter. Only Nelson and Bugs had keys to the house and the studio, and he hadn't wanted to disturb them to pick up a key. But his parents sometimes used to latch the front door from the inside when he'd come in late from gigs, thinking to teach him a lesson; Otis knew how to get into a house without damage.

After testing every port of entry, he found a bathroom window opened a crack. It was small and high off the ground, but with his tall, slender frame, he could manage it. First, he had to remove the screen, which was no mean feat. He shoved the Telecaster guitar through the opening and held it by the neck end of the case, longways, gently dropping it six inches into the bathtub. It landed leaning against the wall and teetered. He hoisted himself by the window frame, climbed the wall, and dropped into the bathtub feet first, being careful not to jar the guitar.

Otis flipped on the studio lights and powered up the board. He plugged in his Telecaster and cued the tape labelled *Master Not Alone Anymore*. He readied a second tape.

"Gotta pull off this backing track and leave the vocals and drums," he muttered.

He held his hands over the board and shot lightning into it. The knobs and levers rotated and clicked, and the tapes spun and whirred. He created a tape with only lead and backing vocals and the snare. He cued a third tape and played the new guitar part he had heard in his dream. The progression was much more complex and contained several of the "naughty chords" he and Nelson loved so much.

He laid down a verse and a bridge. Now he could hear in his head a downward-spiraling synthesizer riff that mirrored the crash and burn of the hero in the song, but he wouldn't add that yet. Now he could hear in his head a keyboard playing with the Telecaster, but he wouldn't put that on yet either. Those parts could wait until they got to Friar Park.

Otis cued the new guitar recording and the stripped-down vocals/drums tapes. He sent lightning through the board and made a new master tape that incorporated the emotional chords from his dream. He played back the results ... and loved it.

"This is just what it needed."

With energy renewed, he added some guitar licks on the new track. He was a lead guitar player, after all. Nelson had been doing most of the lead guitar work on this album, so this was Otis's chance to contribute a few riffs.

He also laid down a new bass line suited to the revised chord structure. Satisfied, he keeled over onto the sofa for a few more hours' sleep.

Nelson was the first to arrive at 12:30 in the afternoon. "What the bloody hell are you doing here asleep on the couch, Otis? You have a row with the wife?"

"No. Although I might when I go home tonight. I came in to work on a track. Jesus, I need a toothbrush. Let me play you something."

"Sorry I didn't make you a key, Otis. I'll have Bugs see to it. How'd you get in?"

"Window."

Otis started the new tape for Nelson and trudged toward the main house. He hoped to locate a toothbrush, having scored the keys from his friend. He anticipated there would be leftover pizza in the fridge for breakfast. He waved at Don, who arrived as Otis traipsed across the grass.

Behind him Nelson pounded to the studio door and bellowed across the lawn. "Jesus fucking Christ, Otis. I told you that you're a genius. This is exactly what that track needed."

Otis turned back for a moment and dismissively waved his hand at Nelson. He wasn't having that conversation again.

Otis found an unopened toothbrush and some toothpaste in one of the guest bathrooms. He figured these items would fit under the production cost budget. To his delight, plenty of leftover pizza remained from the day before, affording him a passable microwaved breakfast. He grabbed a box of mixed pizza slices to carry to the studio for the other group members.

Lefty intercepted him on the way back. "Come to my car with me, Otis. I've got some treats in the trunk."

Otis followed Lefty to his red Corvette. Lefty opened the trunk and proudly displayed an outsized pink box full of breakfast goodies, looking much more appealing than his leftover pizza. Inside the box were éclairs, Danish pastries, bear claws, palmieres, little sponge cakes and crème puffs.

"Otis, I want you to have first pick of the cakes. You worked so hard on that track. I want you to know that I don't think it's your fault we can't use it." Lefty held the open box toward Otis.

"Lefty, that is just bostin."

The kindness Lefty showed Otis in giving him first pick of the breakfast cakes truly moved the producer. For the rock-and-roll legend to bring breakfast snacks to the recording session at all was extremely considerate, but to single Otis out and offer them to him first really touched him.

Lefty looked puzzled. "What's bostin mean?'"

"It means fantastic. I think the track is fixed. Come on down to the studio and listen to it." Otis took the yummiest-looking chocolate éclair and rested it on top of the pizza box.

The two headed toward the studio and saw Charlie T.'s 'Vette cruising down the driveway, with Lucky's van not far behind him.

As they walked, Lefty asked, "How did it get fixed, Otis? Did you zap it?"

"Well, in a manner of speaking. I changed the chords and put a different backing track on it," Otis said, while munching on his éclair.

Lefty looked puzzled. "When did you do that?"

"This morning," Otis said through the half-chewed treat.

"How long have you been here today?"

"I got here about dawn, but I slept a bit on the couch." Otis shrugged. "I felt like I had to get it done, you know."

As they walked through the studio door, Lefty said, "I really admire your commitment to this project, Otis."

Otis turned to Lefty as Nelson exited the sound booth. "Lefty, this is the most thrilling thing I've ever done in my life, getting to work with you lot. I am not only committed, I am devoted. I am so chuffed to be here." He put down the pizza box; he had already finished the treat.

Charlie T. and Lucky entered the kitchen behind Lefty and Otis, completing the brotherhood. Nelson hurried toward Otis and grabbed him around the shoulders, embracing him. He let Otis go with one arm and seized Lefty in the same hug. "I'm really excited about working with you lot too. Come here, Lucky and Charlie T. I have to give you hugs as well." He gathered them both up.

"Come in here and listen to what Otis has done," Nelson said, visibly enlivened. "We aren't going to have to junk this track after all. It sounds bloody brilliant. Otis saved the day."

Otis laughed. "I'll tell you what Olivia would tell you if she was here, Nelson. 'Cheer down.'"

Charlie T. cocked his head. "Good song title."

Lefty, Lucky, and Charlie T. crowded into the sound booth. Don was already there, and he started the tape Otis had made during the early morning hours. After listening, they congratulated Otis on a job well done.

Otis hung his head, visibly uncomfortable with the praise the others were heaping on him. "I wouldn't have had to fix it if I'd done it right in the first bloody place. I'm just a Brummie git."

Charlie T. took the opportunity to nag his half-sibling further about his self-deprecatory habit. "Look, Otis, you need to work on a more realistic self-concept."

Otis jerked his head up. "This old chestnut again?"

"This is what I was telling you earlier. You lack self-confidence. Look at everything you have accomplished, and still you act like you're a piece of shit. Maybe you should get some therapy."

"Working-class people don't believe in therapy." Otis felt defensive now. "Besides, after seeing Brian Wilson with Dr. Landy, I'm really off the whole idea."

"You know that guy is incompetent and hoodwinking Brian," Charlie T. said.

Nelson took up the cause. "Otis, you aren't working class anymore. And getting therapy is nothing to be ashamed of. I've done it."

Otis was taken aback. "You have?"

"So have I," Charlie T. added. "I'm in therapy now because of my marital problems. See, I'm saying 'marital problems,' because that's what the therapist calls them. I used to call it 'wife problems,' but I learned it wasn't all her."

Nelson leaned in toward his friend the way his therapist had leaned in toward him when he had shown empathy and understanding. "Otis, you are one of the most brilliant and musically talented people I have ever known, yet you fend off every attempt at compliments. You pretend like you can't write songs, but you've had dozens of hits. At least you acknowledge you can play a bit of guitar and sing, but even that you seem shy about. I wouldn't like it if you got a big head, but at least admit what you're good at."

Otis was tired from days of little sleep. The love his brothers were showing him overwhelmed him. "Okay, I'll think about it. Do you have any suggestions about who I should see?"

Charlie T. rummaged through his wallet. "Here's the woman I'm working with." He handed Otis a card— Lenora Sharp, Ph.D., Licensed Psychologist. "She'll help you see things more clearly."

"It can't hurt," Otis admitted and put the card in his own wallet.

He looked at Nelson, who showed him a warm smile—the smile Nelson saved for those he really cared about.

Otis could barely see straight when he left their recording venue that night. He didn't relish driving the twisty, windy road that was Mulholland Drive, so he chose straight, flat Ventura Boulevard instead. It took him twenty minutes longer to make the trip home by that route. As he came upon the huge Pier 1 store in Studio City, now closed for the night, Otis thought his eyes must be deceiving him. He spotted a man playing a violin. At this hour, he had no audience. Even more oddly, Otis felt compelled to stop and listen to the street musician. He pulled over and stood on the sidewalk near the violinist.

Otis had worked with several classical violinists in his day, but he had never heard anyone handle the instrument like this musician. The player had mastered bowing and vibrato to a degree Otis had never imagined possible, even for virtuosos like Perlman and Heifitz. The sweetness of the notes hypnotized Otis.

He didn't notice the tune the maestro was playing until he had been listening for a few minutes. It was one Otis had written a couple of years ago, called "Destination Unknown," which had been featured as a C-side on a twelve-inch single released only in the UK two years before.

*Blimey, how did this bloke get ahold of that record?*

The song was Otis's farewell to Electric Light Orchestra. He had purposely recorded it using sax instead of strings, as a way of showing he had gotten the "strings out of his arse." The song's words described his disillusionment with the music business, the record industry, and his manager. He was leaving the cash cow of ELO behind, and he had no idea where he was going. Wherever he would end up had to be better than where he had been when he had disbanded ELO.

The itinerant violinist let loose a flying spiccato, the likes of which he had only heard in rumors repeated by less-talented violinists. The player bobbed his body with the bow, bending and twisting like Mulholland Drive. The bow bounced lightly off the strings, executing a flawless seven-note combination. His body straightened as he reached for the summit of the instrument's range. He ended on a three-octave dive from the top of the instrument's range to the bottom. He bent over backward as he bowed the lowest note the violin could produce.

Otis stood in open-mouthed disbelief. "That was bloody marvelous, mate. I've never imagined the song played like that. So that's how it would have sounded on strings. Would you like a job?"

The violinist flashed an enigmatic smile and shook his head. He played a few notes on his violin that sounded exactly like the question Otis had just asked him, in tone and inflection. *Would you like a job?*

Otis laughed. "What's that? I already have a job, mate. I'm a Traveling Wilbury."

The realization hit Otis like a freight train. The Traveling Wilburys—his half-brothers and fellow musicians—were the unknown destination he had been headed for when he had abandoned ELO. He was having fun with music again, like he had when Woody convinced him to join The Move in 1970 and they wove ELO together with Bev Bevan.

Otis spied the open violin case on the sidewalk. "Here, let me reward you for that fantastic performance." He slid his wallet from his front pocket and dug for a ten-dollar bill. He also found a twenty and extracted that as well. "There isn't enough money in the world to equal the satisfaction you have given me, but here's thirty dollars."

# CHAPTER 17

## BLOWN AWAY

I returned to The Barn in Otis Wilbury's home. He had been by far the most willing to give me interviews for developing the story surrounding the creation of the album. We sat on grey velvet couches opposite each other. He explained that velvet couches provided the perfect acoustical absorption for recording in the cavernous room. He tried leather couches, but they didn't sculpt the sound to his liking.

I was much less nervous with Otis this time. I felt less like a fan and more like a friend.

"Thank you for granting me another interview," I said. "I found I couldn't finish the book without talking to you again."

"What can I help you with today, Cousin Mavis?" Otis smiled as he poured me a cup of tea. "Rum with your tea, right?

"I'll take it straight today, thanks. The tea, not the rum. I'd like to ask how you met your half-brother, Nelson. Also, Charlie T. mentioned meeting you for the first time during a hurricane in London."

He sat down opposite me with his own tea balanced on his knee, placing his right arm along the back of the couch.

"How much detail do you want about how I met Nelson?"

"I want it all," I replied, smiling.

He smiled back. "It started when I was having dinner with Dave Edmunds in, uh, I don't know what year it was. You know how I am with timelines. I've never been able to remember when something happened or how long ago it was. But I can remember what happened pretty well."

"Give me some anchoring events, and I'll figure out when it was."

"It was after *Riff Raff* flopped and before *Shanghai Surprise* flopped."

I recognized the name of the second album Otis had produced with Dave and the name of one of the less-successful ventures produced by Hand Made Films. "So about 1985?"

"Yeah, I guess. I was having dinner with Dave, and as we were walking away from each other down the sidewalk to go to our cars, he yells out at me, 'Oh, by the way, Nelson Wilbury asked me to ask you if you'd like to work with him on his new album.' I said, 'Oh, okay, thanks,' but I'm thinking, *Oh, by the way? Wouldn't you normally say something like that at the beginning of the evening?* I had loved Nelson and The Beatles since I was a kid, you know. I always wondered if we were related."

"Nineteen eighty-five was before ELO broke up."

"Yeah, that's right. Anyway, the next time we were in England, Dave took me round to Friar Park and introduced me. It turned out we were half-brothers, at that. We wrote a couple of minor songs together for *Shanghai Surprise,* but we didn't really get friendly until we took a vacation to Australia to see the Grand Prix. We hit it off really well and decided we could make an album together. We wrote 'When We Was Fab' in Australia. Called it 'Aussie Fab' for the longest time before it was finished.

"Hanging out with Nelson was, like, the best thing. Of course, when you're with Nelson, you can get in anywhere. And get anything you want. 'What would you like?' people ask you." Otis chuckled and shook his head.

"And we went to the Grand Prix track in a helicopter. You didn't mess about."[8]

Otis stopped talking. Behind his shades, he appeared to be staring into space. He moved his left hand to pull his beard. He was probably reliving old memories with Nelson, his teenage hero turned good friend. A smile played around the corners of his mouth. In almost every photograph of Nelson and Otis together, Otis is smiling.

I gave Otis a few moments with his reveries and prompted him with a question. "Why do you think you and Nelson became so close?"

Otis took a beat to reorient himself to me and my question. "Close? Yeah, I suppose we were. Well, we enjoyed the same things, especially music. And laughing. We both enjoyed laughing quite a bit."

"You and Nelson each wrote a few songs about the environment and about saving the earth."

"Which songs are those? I don't recall ..." I could see Otis's eyes sparkling behind his shades. He was teasing me. I played along.

"You don't remember 'Jungle?' The 'big blue ship?' That meant the Earth, didn't it? And going even further back, there were the evocative lyrics to 'In Old England Town—Boogie Number 2' about choking on the air."

Otis had just taken a sip of his tea, and I thought he would do a spit take, but he managed to swallow before he started laughing uproariously. Gasping for breath, he wheezed. "You gonna hold me responsible for that shite?"

I didn't conceal my indignation. "You wrote it."

"Yeah, I did, but I was only twenty-two when I wrote it, trying to impress Woody."

---

[8] Adapted from remarks in *Mr. Blue Sky: The Story of Jeff Lynne & ELO*

"You weren't twenty-two when you wrote 'Save Me Now.'"

"Okay, okay, Cousin. You've got me on that one. I quite like that song. And it is important to take care of the only planet we got. Nelson thought so too. Some try to make it a political issue, but I don't see it like that. I see it as a human issue."

Otis rested his teacup on the coffee table between us. He glanced at his lap and returned his gaze to me. "You asked me why Nelson and I hit it off. There weren't many people in Nelson's life he could trust, and he trusted me. I trusted him too. ELO was nowhere near as big as The Beatles, but we had our share of sponges and sycophants. It was nice for me to have a friend who understood … the life."

I nodded and waited to see if he wanted to add anything else. When he remained silent, I asked, "So, tell me about your relationship with Charlie T. after the hurricane."

"That's a funny story. It was the Thanksgiving after the hurricane in London when I first met him, and I had gone home to L.A., where my wife and daughters lived. There was a lot of family at our house, and they were carrying on, like families sometimes do. I said I was going out for a pack of cigs and was just driving around the neighborhood. I stopped at a light and heard someone tooting the horn over and over. I looked at the car next to me, and it was Charlie T. We pulled over to chat. I said, 'What are you doing here?' He said, 'I live around here, and I'm buying some equipment for yard baseball.' I said, 'I live around here too, and my family is driving me crazy. Can I come home with you?' He let me come home with him, and I didn't leave for six months!"

We laughed at his joke.

"By that time, Charlie had heard Nelson's album that I'd just produced, and he loved it. He actually called me up one day and asked, 'Do you fancy writing some songs with me?'" Otis laughed. "'Yes, please.' We wrote 'Free Fallin' and 'Yer So Bad' that first day."

## CHAPTER 18

## MARGARITA

The brothers finished "Not Alone Anymore" by dinner time on the ninth day. They spent more time on that song than any other so far, but the results were well worth it. Lefty's vocal sounded sensational, and now the instrumental portions also sounded spectacular with Otis's new backing track.

Bugs outdid himself with a catered vegetarian South Asian dinner. The wine and beer poured freely. Otis declared the curry tasted almost as delectable as he could get back home in Birmingham. Aloo baingan, vegetable biryani, and vegetable curry were on the menu. Non-alcoholic beverages included yogurt-based lassi and Darjeeling tea. Dinner continued longer than it should have, and everyone devoured too much. No songwriting happened.

Lefty picked at the curry on his plate and gulped lassi after every bite. "This stuff sure is hot," he commented during a lull in conversation.

Nelson chuckled. "I've had Mexican food in Texas, Lefty. It's really hot too."

"Yeah, I like hot Mexican food, but this is a whole different kind of hot. I've been to the Indian restaurant in Nashville too, but it's not nearly this fiery. What do they spice this stuff with?"

Nelson was something of a connoisseur of Indian food. "I imagine they serve mildly spiced food in Nashville, Lefty. This catering place is run by an Indian family, and it's strictly authentic. There are lots of different spices in Indian food: cumin, coriander, ginger, turmeric, cardamom, uh, let's see …"

"I've heard of ginger before, but I never heard of those other ones. Which one makes it so hot?"

"That would be red chile pepper."

"Well, why didn't you say that first?"

Nelson and Otis giggled at Lefty's discomfort. Otis passed Lefty the serving bowl of basmati rice, and Nelson handed him the vegetable biryani.

"I think your delicate palate can handle these dishes," Nelson joked.

Bugs placed the platter of poori bread next to Lefty. "This fried bread isn't spicy at all."

"Yeah, but Barbara will kill me if she knows I'm eating a bunch of fried stuff."

After dinner, the brothers retreated to the porch of the guest-house recording studio.

Charlie T. lounged in a rocking chair. "Well, our next to last day to work. When we get done with this, I'm a gonna get me a big, ol' margarita."

Otis stood on the steps and gave Charlie T. a bemused smile. "Do you mean a beverage or a woman?"

Nelson bumped against Otis as he walked past. "He means a cocktail, you wanker. It's a sweet mixed drink made with tequila. You wouldn't like it." Nelson plopped on the divan on the porch.

Otis walked over and bumped him back with his knees. He flopped next to him. "I like beer, red wine, and aged scotch. None of that sweet shit."

"Well," Charlie T. paused to stretch his arms over his head. "When we get done with this, I'm gonna get me a whole big-ass pitcher of margaritas. When does the plane leave for London?"

"We can't leave until after the twenty-fifth," Nelson answered, "When Otis is producing a session for Del Shannon. Bugs is joining us in England, right?"

Charlie T. nodded. "I've never made an album without him. But you got your own engineer at Friar Park?"

Nelson nodded. "No offense to Richard, but I want to use Phil. He used to work with The Beatles and has engineered most of my solo albums. He knows my studio equipment inside and out, and he's seen Otis work, so no surprises."

Lucky climbed the three steps to the porch. "Phil-fucking-Spector?"

Nelson smiled. "No, Lucky. Phil-fucking-McDonald."

Lucky let out a sigh. "Thank God. I don't want that guy working on our record."

Lucky entered the studio, and they heard his footsteps pounding up the stairs.

"And we'll still have Buster and Ray?" Otis asked.

Nelson nodded. "And Jim for horns."

"How long do you think it'll take us to turn what we've done into a record?"

Nelson turned to face his brother. "Otis, that's a question I was going to ask you."

"I think we have to give everything a final listen before we can take a guess at that. But we don't have to be in a hurry, like we are now."

Charlie T. sang, "*Mar-ga-ri-ta*," over and over. He was eagerly looking forward to drinking at least half a dozen of the sweet, frosty drinks. The others turned to look at him.

"Is that a real song?" Otis asked.

Charlie T. stopped. "It's a real song I'm making up."

Nelson hopped to his feet to retrieve his guitar and returned to the divan; he strummed a C chord. "Sing it some more."

Charlie T. continued singing the single word while Nelson changed to an F chord. Charlie T. sang, "*Aaaaahhhhhh.*"

Nelson's hands came to rest. "It's gonna be a reach to get a song out of this shit."

Lefty exited the guest house just in time to hear Nelson's remark. "Yes, but we only have one more day. We can turn it into something good. Let's get to work. What have you got?"

Rather than playing the snatch of tune they had worked out so far, Nelson looked around. "Where's Lucky? We need all the talent here for this. Who's got the notepad?"

Otis retrieved the notepad and Lucky from inside the studio.

"Okay, Charlie T., sing what you've got," Nelson said.

Nelson played his guitar, and Charlie T. sang, "*Mar-gar-eeet-aaah. Aaah, aaah, aaah.*"

Lucky scribbled lyrics while Nelson played a three-chord progression.

"Okay, how's this?" Lucky sang his brand-new lyrics: *"She came to my table, to take down my order. She'd come from the back way, from over the border."*

"Needs work," Nelson said.

"I got more," Lucky said and continued singing.

"Sounds a little too much like Lucky Wilbury," Charlie T. objected. "Maybe you can use that for your next album."

Lucky looked at Charlie T. in exasperation. "Just how do I not sound like myself?"

Nelson could see friction developing between these two old workmates. "Let's keep going. What else you got, Lucky?"

Lucky looked at the ceiling. "Hmm."

He scribbled two more lines on the tablet and handed it to Nelson. "You sing it, and maybe it'll sound less like Lucky Wilbury."

Nelson looked at the page for a few moments. Another pair of arms snaked out from under his shirt so he could hold the tablet and play his guitar at the same time. He sang what Lucky had written, using his own melody: *"Slowly now the days go by, with Margarita still on my mind."*

Nelson continued playing the chord progression and sang some new nonsense words he had made up on the spot.

Lucky asked Nelson, "What the fuck's that supposed to mean, man?"

"Well, I don't know about shoebox soup, but the second line was something I heard some kids singing in India once," Nelson said.

Otis laughed. "I love it."

Nelson wrote the lyrics he had just sung and continued scribbling on the tablet with his first right hand.

He shifted the tablet to his second left hand and strummed his guitar with his original pair of hands. "*I been up all night with my radio broke. Since I met her, I've been a joke.*"

Lucky objected. "That section has an entirely different meter than the parts I wrote."

Nelson was smooth. "Then we'll use it for a bridge. Who else has some words?"

Lefty extended his hand for the tablet. He wrote for a few moments and turned to Nelson, who had retracted his extra set of arms. "Sir, would you do me the honor of playing an accompaniment?" He sang, "*Her name is Taloobla. She lives in the back room. I used to go see her. Once in a Blue Moon.*"

"I like that, except her name is Margarita," Charlie T. corrected.

"Oh," Lefty said and crossed out the first line. "Margarita doesn't have the same number of syllables as Tallulah."

Otis looked over Lefty's shoulder. "That's spelled t-a-l-l-u-l-a-h."

"Thanks, Otis. I knew there was an aitch in it somewhere."

Charlie T. held out his hand for the tablet. "I've got an idea." He wrote down the new words and signaled for Nelson to accompany him on guitar. "*She sent him a letter. And promised to return. On a slow boat from China. You'd think that I'd learn.*"

"I like the first two lines," Lucky said.

Charlie T. handed the tablet back to Nelson.

Nelson ruefully scanned it. "This song is gonna need an arseload of work, and we don't have a reliable tune or a backing track."

"We have some chords, Nelson," Otis said encouragingly. "The ones you've been playing will do just fine."

"Yeah, thanks, Otis. It's a place to start, just like these lyrics. Shall we work on a tune? That's your bailiwick."

Otis scratched his head and pulled his beard. "Okay, I got three tunes. Do you want to hear them now?"

"Otis, how do you do that so quickly?"

"Tunes are always tumbling around in my head. All I have to do is pull out the ones that will work for what I'm doing at the moment." Otis smiled at Nelson's consternation. "I always wonder how you pull lead-guitar licks out of your arse, and that isn't so different."

"You aren't too far behind me on that, Otis."

Nelson looked over at Lucky and Charlie T. They were discussing the verses both had written earlier. Nelson was doubtful that much of them could be salvaged. He heaved a deep sigh and waded in, hoping they would have a song to record by tomorrow.

Lucky pointed to the mangled lyric sheet. "If we take that section here and put it at the end, it would work better."

"We need a new opening verse."

"What about Pittsburgh?"

"What *about* Pittsburgh?"

"What about setting the song in Pittsburgh?"

"That sounds great. Let's do that."

"Then we can have him go to New York."

Nelson interrupted. "You write that verse, Lucky. You can sing it too."

At midnight, the song consisted of three verses and a bridge. Lucky had written the first one about Pittsburgh and New York and the second one about the waitress. Nelson's bridge featured the lyrics he had heard the children singing, and Charlie T.'s final verse described the letter from China. Lucky's singsong tune would grace the verses, and they planned to use something Otis had composed for the bridge. They would resume recording tomorrow.

Tuesday brought another bright, clear day for Southern California on their tenth and final day to work. Nelson arrived first, right before Bugs. Charlie T. and Otis drove up in Charlie's 'Vette. Next came Richard, and Lefty followed behind him, with Barbara. Lucky's van wasn't far behind. Buster arrived last. The entire crew was present and accounted for by 12:45 p.m.

Nelson intercepted Otis at the door and steered him around the side of the guest-house studio. "Do you think this last song is going to amount to anything?"

Otis shook his head. "It's not as good as the rest."

"I don't think so either, but this is the last day we have Lucky, and we need at least one more song. What are we gonna do?"

Otis shrugged. "I'd say we get Lucky's vocal and try to punch it up as best we can when we get to Friar Park."

Nelson looked through Otis's shades, searching for his eyes. "I can't think of a better plan. Let's go with it."

Otis put his hand on Nelson's arm. "We don't have anything for Lefty to do on this song."

"Background vocals," Nelson retorted.

"Lefty would dress it up a bit."

"We decided not to use his verse," Nelson pointed out. "It was about the wrong woman."

"Can't we just change it a little and include him? Margarita, Tallulah. What difference does it make?"

"Well, all right. If it doesn't work, we can cut it later. Give him ... erm, the verse after the bridge." Nelson pursed his lips. "I know you're protective of him."

"Great! Thanks, Nelson. You won't regret it." Otis flashed one of his wide, winning smiles.

The half-brothers strode to the studio to find the other three in the kitchen with their guitars. Otis and Nelson unpacked their instruments.

Barbara, Lefty's wife, was ensconced on the love seat in the living room, out of the way. She hadn't said anything during any of the sessions she had attended, quietly observing instead.

"Okay, here's what we're going to do," Nelson said. "Four verses and the bridge after the second verse. Lucky's singing the first two verses, we're all backing Otis singing the bridge, Lefty's singing the third verse, and Charlie T. is singing the last verse. Otis hasn't given us the melody for the bridge yet. I assume he's got a great one, since he had all night. Let's do the acoustic track. Everyone ready?"

Otis entered the control room to set the sound levels and flipped the talkback mic switch. "Strike up."

Four guitars strummed a C chord, and Otis showed both thumbs up.

Lefty frowned. "Nelson, what third verse am I singing?"

Nelson smiled a little at his brother. "The one you wrote."

"I thought you said we weren't using it because her name was Margarita and it didn't have the right number of syllables."

"Just change it a little." Nelson picked up the tablet.

"Instead of 'Her name is Tallulah,' sing, 'Her name's Margarita.'"

Lefty nodded. "Yeah, sure. I coulda thought of that."

Otis spoke from the control booth. "Everyone ready?"

Four heads nodded. Four voices said, "Yeah."

Otis exited the control booth and reclaimed his guitar. "One verse and the bridge. C, F, G, then C minor, F minor, G minor for the bridge."

Lucky said, "Let's run through it once."

Charlie T. disagreed. "I'm not really clear on the whole thing."

Otis draped his arms over his guitar. "Well, we don't have to sing it yet."

Lucky shook his head. "No singing, just play the verse and the bridge."

Nelson looked at the ceiling in exasperation; the instructions were so simple. What was Charlie T.'s problem? "Okay, Lucky, you sing the guide melody for the verse. Otis, will you sing a guide melody for the bridge?"

"Be happy to," Otis answered. "After four. One, two, three, four."

Once the five guitar players had completed the rehearsal, Lucky said, "I want to sing my verses to minor chords. It'll add more drama to being in Pittsburgh."

Nelson laughed. "I've been in Pittsburgh, and drama isn't the word I'd use, but we'll do it your way."

Lucky said, "Let's run through it again with minor chords in the verse"

When the music had finished, Otis said, "Yeah, Lucky. I like that better."

Lucky scoffed. "Of course you do. I thought of it."

Nelson and Charlie T. giggled; Lefty and Otis joined them. Lucky lengthened his neck and his shoulders lowered. He jerked his head an inch to the right, all to express he was insulted. But when he saw the others laughing, he chuckled as well.

Once the laughter died, Otis asked, "Everyone ready to record?" He waved at Richard in the control room.

Richard gave a thumbs up. "Ready to record." Came through the talk-back mic.

Otis counted off. "One, two, three, four."

Five guitars played C minor together as Lucky softy sang the guide melody for the verse. Five guitars switched to C major, and Otis assumed the guide melody for the bridge. Five guitars went silent. Richard switched off the recorder.

Otis put his guitar aside and entered the control booth. "Let me hear a little of it, Richard. I may want to double the guitars."

Richard clicked the primary tape machine to Play.

Otis tapped his foot a little as he listened to the playback. "Yes, I think double-tracking the guitars, as well as expanding the number of verses, will do nicely."

After working his magic, Otis exited the sound booth and addressed his brothers. "Does anyone need any rehearsal for the vocals?"

"Hell, yes, smartass," Charlie T. answered. "I'm sure we all do."

Each Wilbury took his turn in the sound booth with their headphones and rehearsed his portion of the song. It didn't take more than a couple of turns for each one to perfect his section. After an hour, all three were ready to perform their solos. Only the bridge that the five would sing together remained.

Otis sang the three best tunes he had composed. All agreed the one he had used as the guide melody was the best, so they employed it for the song. The five gathered around the microphone and sang it twice, with Otis taking the lead.

"I think we are ready," Nelson said.

During the recording, Lefty lifted off the ground and bumped his head rather hard on the frame of the skylight in the control booth, stopping the take. Barbara rushed in to make sure her husband wasn't injured. He reassured her, and they were able to move on to the next take.

An hour later, the finished song was on tape, and it was time for dinner.

Bugs had ordered a vegetarian Mexican feast this time; although he had snuck in some beef dishes for the meat eaters. Beer and wine poured in abundance, and Bugs even supplied a pitcher of margaritas. Nothing was lost on Bugs. That attentiveness was one of the reasons Charlie T. wanted him around when he was working. He was heedful and thorough and saw to all the band's needs, including, when necessary, margaritas.

Charlie T. was ecstatic when he saw the margaritas emerge from the big refrigerator. "We finished the bitch! It's time to celebrate! Margaritas all around!"

Only Charlie T., Lefty, Barbara, and Nelson wanted margaritas.

"More for me!" Charlie T. punched the air with his fist.

Once everyone had their food and beverages, Otis remarked, "I had a strange experience last night."

"What happened?" Barbara asked.

"There was a street violinist playing one of the last songs I ever released with ELO. The funny thing was, it had only been released on the back of a twelve-inch in a couple of countries. It couldn't have sold more than two thousand copies in Europe. I don't know how this fella ever could have learnt it."

Lefty looked up from his enchiladas and listened with interest. "I saw a street musician a couple of days ago. He was playing a little-known song of mine too. How was this guy dressed?"

"Tawdry-like. Wearing a beat-up baseball hat and gloves with no fingers. I thought that was odd because gloves would make it harder to play the violin. And he played that violin like I've never heard before."

"This guy played a standup bass like nobody's business, and he was dressed the same, with the fingerless gloves. I thought he had four arms like Nelson because he was playing a high line and a low line at the same time." Lefty shook his head. "I offered him a job, but he said no."

Otis scoffed. "I offered him a bloody job too. He said no and offered me one, by making his violin talk. I think he was trying to tell me something with that song as well."

Nelson put the last bite of a tofu taco in his mouth and brushed his hands together. "I saw the same fellow playing a uke out in front of the Griddle Café the other day. He was making music come out of the instrument that I didn't think was possible. More than a couple of thousand people couldn't have ever heard that song of mine he was playing either. I thought it was really odd at the time because there was no way that fellow could have shelled out the hundreds of pounds for the book set that included the record. And it was just what I needed to hear at the moment. I've been away from Friar Park too long and needed a reminder."

It was Charlie T.'s turn to be incredulous. "Y'all got to be kidding. I saw the same guy out in front of Guitar Center. He was playing one of my songs with a really … personal meaning to me. It was on an album that sold okay, so it's no mystery how he learned it. He didn't talk to me at all. Did he talk to you, Otis, except with the violin?"

Otis shook his head.

"Come to think of it," Lefty added, "he didn't say a word to me either. He just shook his head when I asked him if he wanted a job. Did he talk to you, Nelson?"

Nelson shook his head as well. "No, he barely looked at me. He only spoke to me with the music."

Charlie T. continued. "Amazing that the same street musician can play the electric guitar, the standup bass, the violin, and the ukulele like a master, and none of us have ever heard of him before. How is that even possible? Have you seen him, Lucky?"

All eyes turned to Lucky.

Lucky heaved a deep sigh and looked down. He moved the tamales around on his plate. He cut one with his fork and shoveled a bite into his mouth. Glancing up, he returned the steady gaze of the seven pairs of eyes focused on him as he chewed and swallowed. After a long pause, he answered, "Naw."

Nelson found an opportunity to walk behind Lucky as he refilled his margarita. He bent down when the others were engaged in conversation and whispered, "That ukulele-playing bloke was the same as the light in the cave, wasn't he?"

Lucky jumped in his seat. He twisted in his chair to face Nelson and whispered, "How'd you know that?"

Nelson shrugged. "I got a vibe off you."

Lucky frowned and spoke in a low voice. "You know I hate it when you go rooting around in my fucking head."

"It's just between us. Always has been." Nelson returned to his seat.

Dinner ended just shy of 10:00 p.m.

Nelson surveyed the group seated around the table, holding his margarita aloft. "I want to take this opportunity to thank all of you for lending your valuable time and inestimable talent to this project. I think we have a really great recording and at least two hit records. It was so fantastic to spend this time with you. You are all my friends and a significant part of my life. And most importantly, I've never had this much fun in my life!" Nelson stood and raised his glass even higher. "Here's to the Traveling Wilburys!"

Everyone raised their beverages and clinked glasses with those around the table.

"The Traveling Wilburys," they said in unison.

"Now, let's go back to the studio and give a listen to what we have so far," Nelson rose from the table and gestured for all to follow suit.

Otis interrupted. "You know it's rough. You know it needs lots and lots of work. Don't get your expectations up."

Lucky dismissively moved his hand back and forth. "I like it rough, Otis."

Lefty nodded to Otis. "You're going to make it sound beautiful, Otis. I trust you as a producer."

Charlie T. echoed the sentiment. "Yeah, when I can get you to finish work on my solo album, I see in the future that it's gonna be the best thing I ever did."

Otis looked at the floor and blushed. "Thanks, mates."

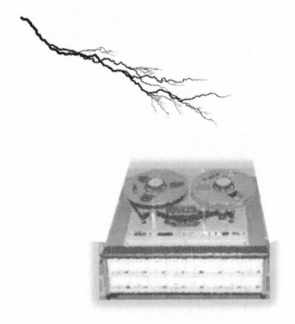

# CHAPTER 19

## A LOVE SO BEAUTIFUL

The weather was clear and much cooler than California had been when they arrived at Friar Park. Almost everyone was jet lagged. Nelson's manor home and his gardens revitalized him. Once there, he felt invigorated and alive. He invited Charlie T. to row out with him on the lake but was rebuffed; Charlie T. preferred to sleep.

Olivia left a note saying she had gone into London for the day while Ayrton was at school. Barbara was the only one of the Wilbury troupe with any energy. She hustled around the kitchen, making a grocery list.

Barbara opened one of the enormous wood-paneled refrigerators. "Don't you have a cook, Nelson?"

"Yeah, but she's not arriving until Monday. We can make do."

"We'll have to go grocery shopping."

"Let's go."

Nelson and Barbara drove into Henley-on-Thames in one of his dozen expensive automobiles. Everyone in town knew Nelson. "Welcome home, Mr. Wilbury," said the townspeople they met. Nelson nodded, smiled, and called them by name. He had lived at Friar Park since 1970.

Barbara laughed. "I hope they don't think I'm your girlfriend."

"They've seen me with enough of them," Nelson replied.

Barbara looked nonplussed, blinking her eyes and raising her eyebrows.

They filled a shopping cart with staples—flour, rice, fruit, vegetables, noodles, chicken and fish—enough for all of them for several days. Nelson's cook would buy more provisions to suit her own needs when she arrived. Nelson bought the meat for his meat-eating visitors.

When Nelson and Barbara returned from their shopping expedition, they found Lefty fidgeting in the immense kitchen. He nodded when he saw the bags of groceries and got up to help them carry in the rest.

"I wondered where you'd gone with my wife, Nelson."

"I wouldn't lead her astray, Lefty."

"This is quite a place you have. When was it built?" Lefty had never seen a house like this. The Belmont Mansion in Nashville wasn't nearly this big. He'd never seen the Biltmore House in Asheville, North Carolina, but he figured this house was almost as big.

"Around 1889, by Sir Frankie Crisp. He left messages all over the house and grounds. I'll show you some of them when we do the tour."

"How many bedrooms does it have?" Lefty asked.

Nelson shrugged. "We don't use the whole house, so it depends on how you count them. The architect's plans indicate a total of a hundred and twenty rooms. We have ten furnished bedrooms to sleep in. Plenty of room for our Wilbury guests to be comfortable." Nelson led his guests toward the voluminous entryway.

Ayrton, Nelson's nine-year-old son, arrived home from school and ran across the foyer to hug his father. "Mother said you'd be home today! It's so good to see you! How long will you be here?"

Nelson hugged and kissed his son. "I'm home for the summer, Ayrton. I've missed you so much."

Ayrton noticed the guitars and luggage that hadn't yet been put away. He spotted the tape boxes among the stacks. "What are you working on? How many people did you bring home with you?"

Nelson laughed. "I can't put a thing past you, can I? I brought home three of my brothers, Lefty, Otis, and Charlie T. We're working on a new album. This is Lefty and his wife, Barbara."

Ayrton became the proper country gentleman, shaking Lefty's hand and nodding his head in a sort of bow to Barbara.

"Pleased to meet you, sir. Ma'am." He turned back to his father. "Mother said you were working with Uncle Lucky. He didn't come? I always wanted to meet him."

"No, Uncle Lucky is going on the road. Maybe you can meet him some other time." Nelson hugged his son again.

"Where's Uncle Otis? I want to give him a big hug and a kiss. I haven't seen him in a long time either. Did Uncle Charlie bring Adria? I'd love to play with her."

"Uncle Otis and Uncle Charlie are upstairs asleep, recovering from jet lag. No, Adria didn't come. She stayed with her mother in Los Angeles. Buster and Ray are here too."

"Uncle Buster! Uncle Ray!" The small boy's voice echoed in the cavernous space.

"Shh, not so loud." Nelson laughed. "People are sleeping."

"Then I guess I can't hear any of the album until everyone wakes up," Ayrton said slyly.

"Come on into the studio, and I'll play some of it for you through the headphones. Remember, it's far from finished."

Nelson noticed Lefty and Barbara heading upstairs. He guessed they were going back to bed.

Nelson and Otis made runs into London for blank tape and other recording supplies. Decompressing from the rushed recording schedule, the brothers indulged in stoned and drunken nights of revelry—except Lefty, of course. He and Barbara didn't enjoy altering their consciousness, but they did enjoy sitting up with the others and playing music until late into the night.

Nelson took each brother, one after another, for rides on the lake in the rowboat. He paddled them through the cleft in the rocks alongside the waterfall and into the pitch-black water caves. Nelson invoked each rider to "grip with his bum" because hands on the side of the boat could result in scraped fingers as they bumped into the sides of the cave in the darkness.

Inside the cave, it was pitch black. The walls were not visible, and visitors couldn't even see their hands in front of their faces. Water dripped from the ceiling all around. Sounds echoed from the walls of the cave. Most visitors remained silent to preserve the sanctity of the place.

After rowing for several minutes, Nelson and each of his guests entered a large area that shimmered with blue light from prismatic panes of colored glass that had been placed in the dome of the chamber. The glass filtered sunlight from above so that the entire area was illuminated in blue. When Nelson took Charlie T. through the water caves, he remarked, "This reminds me of the Blue Grotto on the island of Capri off southern Italy."

"Sir Frank built it with that place in mind."

Rounding a corner in the caves revealed an area with eerily lighted statues of swans and white owls, followed by bats, frogs, and toadstools. After the small creatures, they found stone statues of crocodiles with eyes lit by electric lamps. The caves under the upper lake transported their visitors to a land of make-believe and wonder.

The final treat the water caves had to offer was an array of gnomes next to an underground rainbow at the exit waterfall. Each guest at Friar Park applauded the impressive sights of the underground lake and thanked their host profusely.

On May 28, Nelson said during a late breakfast, "Here's the schedule for today."

Otis reviewed it. "This seems doable. How do you want to approach Lucky's vocals on 'Tweeter?'"

"They are kind of shit, aren't they? I mean, they don't really match the backing track."

"Let's work with it and see what we can do," Otis said, sounding confident.

The four Wilburys climbed the stairs to the first-floor studio in Nelson's mansion (the "first floor" in England being the "second floor" in American parlance).

Phil, the engineer, joined them. He touched a few buttons, and "Tweeter and the Monkey Man," recorded at Dave Stewart's home studio, played through the monitors.

All four brothers listened intently to the more than five minutes of the song. When it ended, they exchanged glances and shook their heads.

Charlie T. spoke first. "It makes your heart feel like it ain't beating right."

Lefty shook his head. "I don't know if we can use this. How can it possibly be fixed?"

Otis turned to Phil. "Could you play that again, please?" Otis picked up a pair of headphones and fitted them over his unruly mop of hair.

Phil directed the output to the headphone jack.

Nelson knew better than to talk to Otis when he was diagnosing a production problem. It was as if his brain was analyzing the shape of the music. Somehow, Otis could draw a topographical map of any music he heard and identify its incongruous features. Nelson had no idea how he did it. He thought Otis had been born with this ability, and it wasn't an electrocution-based superpower.

After the song ended, Otis removed the headphones. "Lucky is out of synch with the backing track. He's not out of synch all the way through, but for most of the song, he's about an eighth of a second behind the backing track."

Nelson looked at his friend with widened eyes. "You could figure that out just by listening?"

"Yeah, sure. Just concentrate on it. You can hear it too."

Nelson smiled proudly at his friend. "Now that you know what's wrong, can you fix it?"

"I think so. I'll have to separate the vocals from the backing and alter the speeds by hand. It won't be any problem to separate them because they're on different tracks, but it'll take a bit of time to synch them up."

"Take all the time you need."

The next morning, Otis played his finished product to his three half-brothers. They were delighted with the results.

Nelson was especially complimentary. "You are fucking brilliant, Otis. I swear, you could synch anything."

Otis smirked and didn't say anything. He'd had to adjust Lucky's vocals by holding both reel-to-reel tapes with his finger and changing the speed in multiple places.

Charlie T. whistled a couple of bars of "Free as a Bird," which only Yoko Ono would hear for another six years.

Lefty turned to Charlie T. "That's a catchy tune. Did you write that?"

Charlie T. looked out the window and didn't answer.

Otis, Nelson, and Buster added additional layers to "Dirty World," "Not Alone Anymore," and "Last Night." It was a good day's work.

Over the next few weeks, the brothers took their time. Otis and Nelson listened attentively to the tracks they had laid down and decided what each one needed. Sometimes it was additional vocals and backing vocals, and sometimes it was additional musical instrumentation or percussion. Lefty and Charlie T. were ever present to pitch in. The Sideburys stood by with their horns and kit to contribute brass, percussion, and drums when needed. Otis added his "fairy dust." They artfully added keyboards, Jim's horn, tympani, and even a few synthesizers. The compositions took shape.

Nelson and Otis decided to switch the first two lines of the last two verses on "End of the Line." Now Nelson sang the half the fourth and fifth verses and Otis sang the other half.

Eventually, "Margarita" rose to the top of the work schedule.

Nelson studied Otis. "This one's a mess."

Otis nodded. "The tune and them verses are really bad. I think we can keep the first one that Lucky sang, but that tune is monotonous."

Nelson sat back. "Why can't we dress up the first verse with background vocals and write a different tune for the rest of the verses?"

Otis shook his head. "That's not standard practice."

Nelson looked at his brother. "Who gives a donkey's arse? Do you?"

Otis smiled and shook his head.

"You write a verse, and I'll write a verse. We'll have three verses, all with different tunes."

An hour later, Nelson and Otis played their melodies for each other. Nelson used the Hindi nonsense lyrics he had composed when they were still in L.A. Otis only had a couple of lines of lyrics and three tunes.

Otis looked at what they had written down. "I quite like that line Charlie had about the letter and the piece of paper. Let's add that verse."

"No, let's just add that couplet," Nelson rebutted.

"More non-traditionalism. I love it." Otis laughed and scratched his head.

Nelson helped Otis finish his lyrics, and they were ready to add the vocal track. Phil set up the recording equipment, and the brothers went to work. They dropped in the vocal Charlie T. had already recorded, and Otis zapped the backing track to suit the new ending. Phil announced he was going for a walk on the grounds, since they wouldn't need him for a while.

Otis and Nelson were listening to the newly reconstituted track when Charlie T. entered the studio. "Hey, I don't remember those verses. Or those melodies."

Nelson looked up. "That's because we just wrote them."

Charlie T. plopped down on the divan. "You rewrote the song so it has different tunes for different verses? That's funny. Oh, you've got my verse at the end so it circles back to the original tune. Hey, where's the rest of it?"

Otis answered without looking up from his watch. "It isn't there ... Hey, Nelson," Otis finally regarded his brothers. "This track is only two and a half minutes long. We need to add something to make it longer." He picked up the bass guitar leaning against the console and absentmindedly picked out a circular rhythm.

"How about the rest of my fucking verse?" Charlie T. asked.

"We aren't using that, Charlie T." Nelson turned to Otis. "How about that bass line you're playing, combined with some guitar licks?"

Nelson hoisted his acoustic onto his lap and picked out a riff that blended so perfectly with what Otis was playing on the bass, one instrument could hardly be distinguished from the other.

"Get Phil, would you, Charlie? We want to do some more work on this track."

"Where'd he go?"

"He's taking a walk."

"You've got thirty-five fucking acres here, and he could be in at least four of those outbuildings. I'm not wandering all over creation looking for him."

"Okay, I know how to run my own board. Let's do this, Otis."

When they dropped in the intro and the outro, the song clocked in at three minutes and fifteen seconds.

"Okay, that part's done." Nelson turned to Otis. "This song needs a higher-pitched voice in the backing vocals."

Otis smiled. "How high do you want me to sing?" Otis sang a scale into the falsetto range until his voice broke. He coughed and laughed.

Nelson whacked his half-brother on the knee. "I'm not talking about *you* singing, you wanker. I'm thinking of getting Ayrton to sing."

Otis wiped his mouth with the back of his hand. "I love that idea. Has he ever sung on any of your records before?"

"No, this would be the first time. I'll talk to him and see if he wants to do it."

Nelson met his son at the door after school. "Hey, Beaver, want to sing on this record we're making?"

"You want me to sing on your record, Dad? That's brilliant! Show me what you want me to do!"

Ayrton had just begun to understand who The Beatles were. A kid at school had taunted him about his famous father, and Ayrton had no idea what the kid was talking about. When Ayrton got home from school that day, he asked Nelson, who told his son, "Oh, yeah, I was in that group."

"Okay, Ayrton, sing this part after me, only in a key that is comfortable for you."

"Okay, Dad."

"*Ah-ah-ah* and *mar-ga-ri-ta.*"

Ayrton practiced the parts his father had demonstrated for him.

"It sounds like you have it. Are you ready to rehearse with the track through headphones?"

"Yes, Dad."

Ayrton needed an hour of rehearsals to perfect the backing vocals. He was only nine years old, after all.

The time had come to add his backing vocals to the mix. Otis positioned himself behind the mixing board with Phil. Ayrton perched on a white leather bar stool before the vocal mic, wearing headphones, singing sweetly in his high-pitched voice. After three attempts, Otis obtained an adequate sample to zap onto the master tape.

"Great work, Ayrton." Nelson hugged him. "I hope you don't become a recording artist, but you could if you want to."

"Thanks for asking me to sing, Dad. It was fun." Ayrton ran off to practice with his skateboard.

During dinner break, Otis approached Lefty. "We've finished the Wilburys work for the day. I brought the basic track we made of 'A Love so Beautiful' for your album. I've overdubbed a few more tracks on it when I wasn't working on Wilburys stuff. You fancy doing the vocal?"

Lefty said, "Yeah, I think we should."

Charlie T. inquired, "What are you talking about?"

Otis said, "Well, Lefty and me want to put a vocal on 'A Love So Beautiful.'"

Nelson asked, "Can we go?"

Otis and Lefty looked at one another.

"No," Otis said. "We'll do it fast, just me and Lefty. We'll be back before you know it. I'd like you to add a bit of guitar later, Nelson. It'll need strings as well, but those will go on last at Rumbo Records in L.A."

Nelson clicked his tongue. "I knew you'd have to put something posh on that album."

Wanting to hear the session, Barbara entered the courtyard and stood outside the studio, as Otis had asked everyone to let them record the vocal track unobserved. Few people have heard a voice like that give a live, unamplified performance. The earth seemed to stand still.

Barbara spun slowly outside the studio's open windows, the enchantment of her husband's voice transporting her. The water in the pool near Friar Park's greenhouses surged up to form the shape of a woman's head resembling her face and hair. She stared at the apparition open-mouthed, wondering what it meant, and stunned that her husband's full-volume singing had not caused the physical damage that usually transpired.

Lefty's voice floated through the grounds of Friar Park like a susurrus of butterflies. The song ended. Barbara waited for him to start another take, but only silence ensued.

He had delivered his single most transcendent performance on a recording, requiring only one take. Moreover, his gift of creation with his voice had supplanted his curse of destruction. Lefty was happy once again.

# CHAPTER 20

## RUNNIN' DOWN A DREAM

After working on two continents, the recording was complete, and the Wilbury brothers were thrilled with it. They'd had the time of their lives making it. Now the question was: would anyone ever hear it? No permissions had been obtained from Lucky's, Lefty's, or Charlie T.'s respective record labels.

Four of the brothers were gathered in Charlie T's living room in L.A., where the journey had started several months before. Lucky was still on tour.

"We didn't clear this with any of our record companies except mine," Nelson said. "We may be stopped in our tracks, but I think I can convince them."

Charlie T. leaned back in his chair and drew on his cigarette. Smoke escaped his mouth as he spoke. "I have every confidence in your persuasive abilities, Nelson. You've only got to convince MCA, Columbia, and Virgin. At least you and Otis are on the same label."

Nelson gave Charlie T. a long gander. "I thought I'd start with MCA. They should be the easiest nut to crack. Then Columbia, then Virgin. That sonofabitch Richard Branson may not give in and release rights for Lefty, since they only recently signed him. His first album with them hasn't even come out yet."

"I've had a shitload of battles with MCA Records and won them all. Good luck."

"Can't you foresee if I prevail against the record companies, Charlie?"

"Nope." Charlie T. snuffed out his cigarette.

Nelson opened his pocket phone book and punched the numbers on Charlie T.'s phone. When the receptionist answered, he put the call on speaker. "Hello, I'd like to speak to Irving Azoff, please."

A female voice came on the line. "Who is calling for Mr. Azoff, please?"

"This is Nelson Wilbury."

"Oh, Mr. Wilbury. I'll see if he's available to speak to you."

Charlie T.'s most recent album served as the hold music. "Runaway Train" sounded tinny through the phone speaker. Charlie T. raised his eyebrows.

Irving's gravelly voice interrupted the music. "Nelson, my good friend. How in the hell have you been? What the hell can I do for you?"

"Well, Irving, as a matter of fact, I've been thinking about putting a little project together, and I want Charlie T. Wilbury to be involved. We've already done a good deal of work on it."

Irving was cagey. "Nelson, that sounds just fine, as long it's on MCA."

"Sorry, Irving. I've set up an independent record label called Wilbury Records."

"Damn, Nelson. I should've known you'd be one step ahead of me. You know I can't let one of my best artists loose to make money for another record label."

"Come on, Irving. This is just a small project among family."

Irving's cackle came through the phone line. "Nelson, nothing involving you is small."

"Are you looking for a cut?"

"You know it."

"I'll give you two percent."

"Don't insult me."

"If you think the project's not small, that's not an insult."

"Five percent."

"Three percent."

"Three and a half."

"Done."

"Okay, then you can have my boy, Charlie. I'll send over the papers. Say, how's that record coming along that Otis is producing for him? Why don't you write a song for that?" Irving was always looking for an angle.

"That record is coming along just fine without me, Irving. I'll play on a couple of tracks if you like." Nelson rolled his eyes.

Otis grinned broadly.

"That would be terrific."

Both hung up the phone.[9]

Charlie T. lit another cigarette. "Well, that was easier than I thought. I figured he'd want a bigger cut."

Nelson shrugged. "Oh, he always wants something more." He was already looking in his phone book for Columbia Records.

Columbia was the oldest record company in the world, and Sony of Japan had just acquired it. The phone rang ten times before anyone answered.

"CBS Records, I mean Sony Corporation of America, I mean Columbia Masterworks Records," a female stuttered.

Nelson laughed. "Well, make up your mind. May I speak with George Daly?"

"I'm sorry. He's no longer with us."

"Who is in charge of the Columbia Records Division?" Nelson asked.

---

[9] None of the discussions with record company executive are known to have happened in your universe except with Richard Branson

"I don't really know. There have been lots of changes around here. I'm kind of new." The receptionist sounded rattled.

"Is Tony Martell still there?" Nelson asked. Tony was a record label vice president Nelson knew from many years ago. He thought Tony might at least be able to tell him who he could talk to.

"Who is calling for Mr. Martell?"

"This is Nelson Wilbury."

"Oh, I'm so sorry, Mr. Wilbury. I didn't recognize your voice. I'll put you right through."

A male voice answered, sounding high pitched and stressed. "Tony Martell."

"Hey, Tony. This is Nelson. What the hell is going on over there?"

"Hi, Nelson. Good to hear from you. I don't know what the hell is going on over here. No one is telling me anything, and I haven't been invited to any meetings. I'm probably going to be fired."

"Sorry to hear that. Look, can you help me with something?"

"Sure, anything, Nelson." Tony's pitch dropped slightly.

"I want to talk to a high muckety-muck about using Lucky on an album. Who's important enough over there now to okay it? The receptionist said George was gone."

Tony hemmed and hawed for a minute. "Hmm, look, people are dropping like flies around here. Behind a big wooden desk one minute, out the door the next. Last week I would have said George, but I don't even know who to tell you this week. I heard someone was about to be promoted to record label president, but I'm not on the memo-distribution list."

"No wonder you're so paranoid," Nelson said. "Well, life goes on within you and without you. I'm sure it'll all work out for you whether you get fired or not."

"Thanks, Nelson."

"Say, could you transfer me back to the receptionist?"

"Columbia Masterworks Records." Apparently, someone had coached the receptionist how to answer the phone.

"Hi, is Clive Davis there?" Even though Clive was with the Arista subsidiary and not Columbia, Nelson figured Clive would know what was happening now that Sony had taken over.

"Mr. Davis isn't taking calls."

"Tell him Nelson Wilbury is calling."

"Hi again, Mr. Wilbury. I'll see if he wants to take *your* call."

The hold music was *Faith* by George Michael, the current number one Billboard album—on Columbia, of course.

Clive answered the line. "Nelson, I'll talk to you anytime. What's cooking, baby?"

"Hi, Clive. It seems like there's been a bit of a shake-up since Sony took over."

"Boy, you can say that again. Nobody knows which way is up."

Nelson heard Clive puffing on his cigar.

"Look, Clive, I've just finished a project with Lucky, and I don't want to have a fight with a bunch of lawyers over putting the record out. Who do I have to talk to about clearing the way?"

Nelson saw Charlie T. sit bolt upright in his chair. Nelson put his hand over the receiver and mouthed, *What?*

Charlie T. sat back in his chair and relaxed again. "It won't happen for another seven years. Tell you later."

"Everything all right there, Nelson?" Clive asked.

"Yeah, yeah, everything's fine, Clive. You got a name for me?"

"Well, the memo I got yesterday said Tommy Mottola had just been appointed president of Columbia Records; although, I don't think they're going to call the records division by that exact name anymore. Hell if I can remember what they're calling it."

Nelson scribbled on a piece of paper. "Got it. Can this Tommy Mottola release Lucky to appear on an album with me on a different label?"

"Yeah, I don't see why not. He's the head of the whole shebang. Tell him you'll owe him a favor. Be vague. He's new enough to think that'll be worth something."

"I never say something I don't mean, Clive. You ought to know me well enough to know I'm not like most people in the record business." Nelson furrowed his brow.

"I'm not saying you are, kid. You don't have to do anything unsavory. Just play guitar on one of his artist's records. Yeah, he'll love that."

"Good talking to you, Clive."

"Always a pleasure, Nelson. Give my love to Olivia."

"And give my regards to Frank." Nelson hung up the phone and turned to his half-brother. "What got you so excited, Charlie?"

"Oh, I got a flash that guy is going to negotiate the purchase of The Beatles' catalog for Sony in 1995. Paul's going to try to outbid him, but he can't do it, just like he couldn't outbid Michael Jackson three years ago. It just seems a crying shame that The Beatles don't own their own songs."

"Yeah, it's all too much. I own some of mine. The best ones, any road. Sony isn't getting their paws on those. It's a little bit of revenge for having so many songs rejected for The Beatles albums.

"I'm going to call back and try to get hold of this Tommy Mottola fellow. Let's hope he's too preoccupied with figuring out what he's doing running a record company to care about Lucky appearing on our album."

Otis and Lefty whispered in the corner. "Wow, I'm glad I'm not on Columbia anymore. Except it was called 'CBS Records' in America when I was on it because of a trademark dispute. Sounds like it's total balls up over there," Otis observed.

Lefty nodded. "Yeah, I know what you mean. Wait, what? Did you say, 'balls up?'"

Otis chuckled. "Sorry, mate. It means 'all messed up.'"

Lefty smiled. "Oh, okay. You English guys are hard to understand sometimes. I've never been on Columbia. Monument and MGM and now Virgin, but never Columbia."

Otis leaned his head against the wall and lit a cigarette, which he offered to Lefty. "It was a good label when I was on it, except for that *Secret Messages* cock-up, erm, I mean fiasco."

"What fiasco was that, Otis?"

"I recorded enough songs for a double album, and Columbia said they wouldn't issue a double album because of the bloody oil crisis and the cost of making vinyl. Can you believe that excuse? They just didn't want to let me out of my contract because a double album would have finished it off."

Lefty shook his head. "Record labels, huh?"

"It's just as well the double album didn't come out. It would have included that embarrassing 'Beatles Forever' song, and I would have to explain to Nelson why I wrote that."

Lefty smiled. "What was embarrassing about it?"

"I sounded like a half-soaked teenage wench went 'round the Wrekin over The Beatles. I'd hate it if Nelson thought I'd lost the plot. The song sounded yampy, y'know."

Lefty did a double take. "What did you say?"

Otis suppressed a smile. "Nothin'."

"Will you ever release that song?"

"Never in a rain of pig's pudding."

"Otis, you talk funny as all get out."

Otis laughed and slapped his half-brother on the shoulder. "So do you, Lefty."

Nelson dialed the number for Columbia again with the speaker on. The same receptionist answered. "Hello, it's Nelson Wilbury again. This time I'd like to speak to Tommy Mottola. I understand he's been put in charge of the recording division."

"Oh, Mr. Wilbury. I didn't know. Okay, let me see if I can find an extension for him."

The same George Michael album played as hold music again.

"I can't stand this shit. I'd rather listen to *Give My Regards to Broad Street* on repeat." Nelson said to no one in particular.

Lefty answered. "It's not so bad, Nelson. It's soothing."

If it had been anyone else on hold, the receptionist doubtlessly would have "accidentally" disconnected the call. Because it was Nelson Wilbury on hold, she called department after department in the huge building, looking for Tommy Mottola. After ten minutes, she found his brand-new secretary. She connected her to Nelson without a warm handoff.

"Hello? Tommy Mottola's office," the secretary-of-the-newly-minted-president-of the-record-company-now-owned-by-a-Japanese-megacorporation answered.

"Thank God I don't have to listen to George Michael sing any longer," Nelson said with the phone still on speaker. "Do you have Mr. Mottola for me?"

"No, I'm sorry. He's out of the office. May I take a message?"

Nelson inhaled a long breath. "This is Nelson Wilbury. I'm calling …"

Before Nelson could get any more words out, the secretary screamed. "Oh my God. Oh my God! You're my favorite Beatle!"

Nelson looked around the room at Otis, Lefty, and Charlie T. He dropped his head into his hands and rubbed his face. His half-brothers covered their mouths to stifle their laughter.

The secretary regained her composure. "How can I help you, Nelson—er, I mean Mr. Wilbury?"

"What's your name?"

"Angela," she giggled.

"Well, Angela, are you sure Mr. Mottola is out of the office?"

"No, that's just what he told me to say when anyone called for him."

"Do you think he might be willing to talk to me?"

"I'll ask him." Angela giggled again.

"Thank you, Angela."

Angela must have dropped the phone on her desk without hitting the hold button, because she could be heard calling out, "Mr. Mottola, Nelson Wilbury is on the phone for you!"

A male voice responded, "Good heavens, Angela. Why didn't you put him through? What line?"

"Line one."

Through the speaker, the Wilbury brothers heard, "Hi, Nelson, great to hear from you. What can I do you for?"

Nelson smiled. Sometimes being him had its perks. "Tommy, we haven't met, but may I be one of the first to congratulate you on your promotion to record label chief?"

"Thanks, Nelson. Yeah, I'd love to remedy that situation of us not meeting. Can we have lunch soon? It can't be this week because things are crazy here, but maybe next week?"

"I'm in L.A. right now. I'm not sure when I'll be coming to New York next, but I'll call you as soon as I know, if you'll give me your direct number. Listen Tommy, there's something a little urgent I need your help with."

"Anything, Nelson, anything."

"I want to do a project with Lucky Wilbury. He's signed to Columbia, you know. I need your okay to use him for a recording on another label."

"Uh, what label?" Tommy suddenly became protective of his act.

"It's a label I'm setting up. Wilbury Records."

Nelson closed his eyes and focused his mind. *I see my light come shining,*

"Aren't you on Dark Horse?" Tommy still sounded suspicious.

"Yeah, but I didn't want this project with my brothers getting intertwined with my own, so I set up an independent label."

Tommy clicked his tongue against the roof of his mouth. "No problem, as long as Columbia can be the distributor."

"Oh, that's a tempting offer, Tommy. Really it is. But Warner Brothers has already beat you to the punch." Nelson rolled his eyes for the third time.

"Yeah, I should have known. After all, Warner Brothers distributes Dark Horse."

"Tommy, you are going to be really good at this job," Nelson said wholeheartedly.

Nelson concentrated. *From the west down to the east.*

"Well, I don't know. Lucky is our biggest name, even though he's not our biggest seller. If we let another label have him, it could jeopardize our standing with some of our other artists. I may have to discuss this with the board."

Nelson slowed his breathing further. *Any day now, any day now.*

"That sounds like a lot of red tape, Tommy. What can I do to make this project move ahead? Got any favors I could do for you?" *I shall be released.*

"Well, as a matter of fact, Billboard is going to have its first awards show this December, and Columbia has been asked to join as a major sponsor of the show. It would be great if you would be there and maybe perform or be a presenter."

"If that's what it takes for you to release Lucky, I'll be happy to."

Charlie T. burst out laughing and hurried into the next room.

"Thanks, Nelson. You can have Lucky. And don't forget about our lunch date. I'll transfer you back to my secretary so we can exchange numbers."

"I won't forget, Tommy. Bye." Nelson hung up the phone; he'd get the number later.

Charlie T. returned to the room, still laughing. "Wait until you find out what you just committed to."

"What?" Nelson asked.

"George Michael is going to win that first Billboard award for best album, and you are going to present it to him!" Charlie T. guffawed, and the Otis and Lefty joined him.

"Well, shit," Nelson said and shrugged. "Two down and one to go." Nelson gazed pointedly at Lefty.

Lefty put his hands in the air. "I have no ideal what Richard Branson is going to say. I can tell you the receptionist's name is Natalie."

Nelson searched through his phonebook. "Let's find out what he says." He dialed the number for Lefty's record company.

"Virgin Records."

"Hi, is this Natalie?"

"Yes, it is. Who's this?"

"This is Nelson Wilbury. I'd like to speak to Richard Branson."

"Hello, Mr. Wilbury. I'll see if he's available." Nelson could hear her smiling through the phone, pleased that a famous musician knew her name.

Steve Winwood's album, *Back in the High Life*, played as the hold music.

Nelson nodded his head in time to the beat. "That's more like it."

A few minutes later, Richard Branson's deep voice came on the line. "Hey, Nelson. What's up?"

"Hi, Richard. There's a project involving Lefty I'd like to speak to you about."

"Oh, is that so? What kind of project?" The familiar suspicious tone entered Branson's voice.

"I want to put out an album with Lefty. We've already laid down a few tracks."

"Who else is on this album?"

That was a question none of the other record company execs had asked. Nelson was a touch taken aback. "Well, there's me, and my brothers Otis, Lucky, Charlie T., Jnr., and Lefty."

"That's quite a collection of talent. A bonafide supergroup."

"World's greatest singer, world's greatest songwriter, world's greatest music producer, world's greatest rock front man, and me." Nelson smiled as he spoke.

"Lefty is all yours," Richard said. "Who am I to stand in the way of history?"

# CHAPTER 21

## INTO THE GREAT WIDE OPEN

I suppose y'all are wondering what happened to the brothers after they made their album. The four surviving members recorded one other album after Lefty passed. They never thought of replacing Lefty; how could they find a substitute for a voice and a spirit like his? Rumors abound that they asked Del Shannon, but the rumors weren't true. Both Otis and Nelson denied it in recorded interviews. Charlie T. stated, "[Lefty] was what made the Wilburys the Wilburys, really, what made it such an unusual, special thing. He was our ace in the hole."

Most critics and fans agreed the second album lacked the heart and the cohesion of the first, but it was still quality music. After that, the surviving brothers each had his own path. It would take a book apiece to tell their stories, so I'll give you the short versions.

Lefty Wilbury's life was filled with tragedy. He lost his first wife to a motorcycle accident and two of their children to a fire at their home. His career peaked early and spent a long time in the doldrums before finally beginning to rise again just months before his early death. Another tragedy of his life was that he had the incredible gift of being able to affect the world around him with the sound of his voice. Yet, he never quite learned to control it. His voice caused destruction when it had the potential to bring forth beauty. If he had lived, perhaps he could have perfected shaping beauty from the elements with his voice, like he did that day at Friar Park while recording "A Love so Beautiful."

Otis accepted his underrated status. He never fathomed that he was a true musical genius, even since the resurrection of his career. He had produced the "Threatles" songs "Free as a Bird" and "Real Love," and was criticized for making them "sound like ELO," although others praised his work, dubbing him a worthy successor to George Martin. Except for a few producing gigs, his career lay fallow for twenty years, including a failed album and a cancelled American tour in 2001. But in 2014, he appeared as the featured performer in BBC Radio 2's Festival in Hyde Park before 50,000 fans. This show put his career back on track. As of 2018, he's playing to sellout arena crowds and includes "Handle with Care" as part of his show. Loss has followed Otis too. He has lost family and friends, including three of his Wilbury brothers, Del Shannon, Birmingham mate Marc Bolan, and others he would probably prefer I not mention.

Lucky eventually disclosed the visit from the emissary to Charlie T. and the contracts that gave him his superpower. Charlie T. told me the story of the promise Lucky had made to the "commander-in-chief" during one of our many talks, on the condition I never reveal the information in our universe. Immediately after working on the first Wilburys album, Lucky started his Never-Ending Tour. As I write this, thirty years later, he's still on the same Never-Ending Tour. He kept his word to that emissary, and he kept on writing those long-ass songs until the contract was up in 2013. Lucky's last album of originally composed songs was *Tempest* in 2012, so the emissary must not have renewed the air-writing clause. Lucky remains as secretive and enigmatic as he has been throughout his career. He didn't even collect his Nobel Prize in Literature in person.

Charlie T. and Otis made two more albums together. The solo album was easier to record than the one with the Heartbreakers because some of Charlie's backing group weren't crazy about Otis's meticulous recording style of layering the instruments; however, that album was wildly successful, so they probably enjoyed the profits. The death Charlie T. never saw coming seized him when he was sixty-six. He had fractured his pelvis immediately before a humungous tour, and he had started using great quantities of pain medication. When he toured and didn't rest, he widened the fracture in his hip bone, and even more pain troubled him by the time the tour ended. By using excessive amounts of pain medication, he tried too hard to kill the pain and accidentally killed himself instead.[10] His life became that runaway train.

Nelson stopped making records after his work with his half-brothers, but he didn't stop recording in his studio at Friar Park. He oversaw a reissue of his first solo album, *All Things Must Pass*, and contributed to albums of friends until just a few weeks before his death. His last appearance on record was with Jools Holland, singing on a song he co-wrote with Ayrton, "Horse to the Water," about the difficulty of abandoning addictions. Perhaps it was about the cigarettes that contributed to the lung and laryngeal cancer that lead to his death or other dependencies he had suffered. Otis and Ayrton completed Nelson's last album from the recordings he left behind. They became Nelson's posthumous producers, working from his notes and their own knowledge of his musical preferences.

Lefty, Nelson, and Charlie T. are gone as this book is prepared for publication. The world is a less joyous place without them. Lucky and Otis carry on, each in his own

---

[10] http://www.tompetty.com/news/statement-petty-family-1764366

way. The two surviving Wilburys were never close. Nelson and Charlie T. were their connections, and without them, Otis and Lucky don't get together. We probably won't see them reunite to make music, but you never know, do you?

Virgin Records head Richard Branson's prediction about history came true. The brothers' albums didn't set any sales records, but the group and the albums they produced are beloved like no supergroup before or since. When one of the half-brothers sings a Traveling Wilburys song in concert, the audience responds warmly, as to an old friend. Mention the Traveling Wilburys and the faces of every music fan in the room, except perhaps the youngest, light up with recognition and fondness. Mention the Wilbury name at a music event and a round of applause inevitably results, in both our universes.

The group represented four generations of rock music: the fifties, the early sixties, the mid-sixties, and the seventies. Each era had its own style and audience, but the brothers melded them perfectly. The younger members learned from the veterans, and the veterans respected where the younger members took their styles of music.

Some have pointed to the three "Elder Statesmen"— Lefty, Lucky, and Nelson—as the most significant members of the group. *The New Rolling Stone Encyclopedia of Rock & Roll* (1995) even calls them "three indisputable gods." One reason I wrote this book was to demonstrate to the reading public that Otis and Charlie T. Jnr. were just as indispensable to the songwriting and recording process as the other three. Otis's inborn abilities as a producer brought that special sound to the Wilbury records, though he has always suffered from being underrated. Perhaps, in 2018, with his resurgence as an artist in my universe and that of his counterpart in yours, the trend is finally waning. Charlie T.'s brand of Heartland Rock had the strongest influence out of the five half-brothers on the style of the albums.

In your universe, musician and prominent rock commentator Jeff Slate wrote to me about the Wilburys. "They were arguably the only true supergroup in the history of recorded music, and so everything that's come since has certainly been measured against that." Slate observed that the greatest lesson of the Wilburys is "... that having fun—especially with friends—and not taking things too seriously is the key to making great music."

In response to the question, "Would the Wilburys have had the same impact if they had come five years earlier or later?" Slate examined the greater context of the music industry at the time. "The early 80s was a weird time for rock and roll, with the aftermath of punk and New Wave, and many of the 60s era artists were still finding their way in that landscape, so five years earlier wouldn't have worked as well, I don't think. Five years later was still pre-Brit Pop and the *Beatles Anthology*, and so much of the nostalgia that came out of those things, so I'm not sure later would have been better, either. With *Cloud Nine* and *Full Moon Fever* and everything going on in the world and the Wilburys' lives, 1988 feels just about right."

When asked if there could ever be another phenomenon like the Wilburys, Mr. Slate replied, "There aren't many artists of the stature of those five artists anymore, and certainly not any who are friends and fans of each others' work—and who could come together without ego—so I just don't see it. There was also a certain magic to the Wilburys that's impossible to recreate."

In my universe, I interviewed famous rock critic Herve Wilton about possible extra abilities the Wilburys might have possessed that allowed them to record an album so quickly. "It has long been rumored that some members of the Wilbury clan have superpowers, but even without magic, this supergroup has superpowers of their own. Nelson Wilbury brings the power of The Beatles to the project, and that's no small contribution in itself. Lefty Wilbury brings his super-powered voice he alone can boast. Lucky Wilbury is the greatest living songwriter of our time, perhaps of all time. While his talent seemed to have dried up, he came back strong with contributions such as 'Tweeter and the Monkey Man' and 'Congratulations.' Charlie T. Wilbury's superpowers have got to be the down-home quality of his vocals, and the hypnotic gaze of his oh-so-blue eyes. Otis Wilbury's productions bring this music together like magic, without sounding similar to any of his earlier work. Surely his production expertise smoothed the way to getting the record made so fast."

The foremost reason I wrote this book was to capture the spirit of fun and camaraderie the five friends enjoyed as they created music together. Despite their fame, fortune, and privilege, when they joined together, they became down-to-earth musicians who loved making music and loved each other.

I, Mavis Wilbury, am grateful for the opportunity to take a deep dive into the Wilbury story. I learned things about each brother, about composing, playing, and recording music, and about the recording industry I had never imagined.

I even learned a greater lesson about life. The Beatles said it decades ago: "All You Need Is Love." Love is the most powerful force in the multiverse. That's what the Wilbury brothers felt for each other. That's what the world feels for the Wilburys and their music. That's what I feel for the Traveling Wilburys, as individuals and as a group.

The Wilburys made music for the sheer love of the music and not for the hope of making money or being popular. These musicians were of the highest standing and ability level, and something potent permeated the resulting musical product. When the musicians are fast friends who feel love and mutual admiration for each other and their work, the music they make can release the resonance of that love far into the future.

Every time I play the Wilburys albums, in my universe or yours, I hear love coming through every note, every layer and harmony. Don't you? Love is the only antidote for the endless stream of negativity pouring into our minds and hearts in the modern world. All that hate is bad for us and for the humanity of the future. Let's each be a channel that increases the amount of love in the world. We don't have to go full-on Mother Teresa to do this. It's easy enough to play music that promotes love and avoid music that feeds division and disrespect.

Nelson once said, "Someday, everybody gonna be a Wilbury." I'd like to think he meant that the spirit of universal brotherhood would finally permeate the planet. We'd one day share a sense of love and family with the whole human race the same way the Wilburys did for each other.

I expected to encounter a coterie of arrogant rock stars who wouldn't give me the time of day, much less lengthy interviews. Instead, I met unpretentious men eager to talk about the work they had done together. Let me remind you this happened in my universe and not yours, so you would call these interviews fictional. That's okay. I can't help but believe that our Nelson, Otis, Lefty, Lucky, and Charlie T. are an awful lot like George, Jeff, Roy, Bob, and Tom in your universe when it comes to levelheadedness and humanity.

In echo of the toast on their final day of recording the first album:

*Here's to the Traveling Wilburys.*

Please take a moment to review this book on Amazon or Goodreads. Reviews help independent authors immensely.

Thanks.

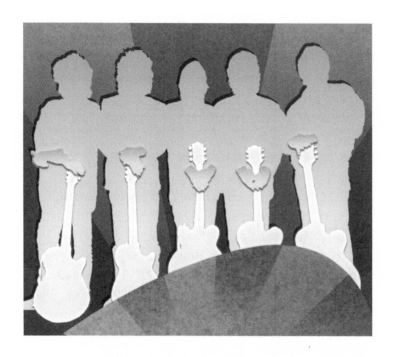

## BIBLIOGRAPHY
### Books

Amburn, Ellis. *Dark Star: The Roy Orbison Story*. New York: Carol Publishing Group, 1990.

Badman, Keith. *The Beatles: After the Break-up* 1970-2000. London, New York, Victoria: Omnibus Press, 1999.

Cott, Jonathan (ed.), *Bob Dylan: The Essential Interviews*. New York: Wenner Books, 2006.

Dylan, Bob. *Chronicles, Vol. 1*. New York: Simon & Schuster, 2004.

Genesis Publications. *The Traveling Wilburys*. Surrey, England: Genesis Publications. 2009.

Giuliano, Geoffrey. *The Private Life of George Harrison, Dark Horse*. New York: Dutton, The Penguin Group, 1990.

Greene, Joshua. M. *Here Comes the Sun: The Spiritual and Musical Journey of George Harrison*. Hoboken: John Wiley & Sons, Inc., 2006.

Harrison, George. *I, Me, Mine*. New York: Simon & Schuster, 1980 edition.

Harrison, Olivia. *George Harrison: Living in the Material World*. New York: Abrams, 2011.

Heylin, Clinton. *Still on the Road: Songs of Bob Dylan, 1974-2006*. Chicago: Chicago Review Press, 2010.

Lehman, Peter. *Roy Orbison: Invention Of An Alternative Rock Masculinity*. Philadelphia: Temple University Press, 2010.

Leng, Simon. *While My Guitar Gently Weeps: The Music of George Harrison*. Milwaukee: Hal Leonard Corporation, 2006.

Maymudes, Victor. Another Side of Bob Dylan. New York: St. Martin's Press, 2015.

Muir, Andrew. *One More Night: Bob Dylan's Never Ending Tour*. Andrew Muir, 2013.

Orbison, Alex, Roy Orbison, Jr., and Wesley Orbison, with Jeff Slate. *Roy Orbison: The Authorized Biography*. New York: Hachette Book Group, 2017.

Osbourne, Sharon. *Extreme*. New York: Springboard Press, 2005.

Ostin, Mo. "Introduction." Booklet for *Traveling Wilburys, Vol. 1*, by The Traveling Wilburys, Rhino reissue CRE39516-0, 2016, two compact discs and one digital video disc.

Rotondo, Andrea. Tom Petty: Rock'n'Roll Guardian. London, New York, Paris, Sydney, Copenhagen, Berlin, Madrid, Tokyo: Omnibus Press, 2014.

Romanowski, Holly and George-Warren, Patricia *The New Rolling Stone Encyclopedia of Rock & Roll* . New York: Touchstone,1995

Scott-Morgan, David. *Patterns in the Chaos*. Lifeware Publishing, 2012.

Thomas, Nick. *The Traveling Wilburys: The Biography*. Guardian Express Media, 2017.

Thomson, Graeme. *George Harrison: Behind the Locked Door*. London, New York, Victoria: Omnibus Press, 2016.

Van der Kiste, John. *Jeff Lynne: Electric Light Orchestra – Before and After*. Foothill Media Limited, 2015.

White, Timothy. *George Harrison Reconsidered*. Larchwood & Weir, 2013.

Williams, Paul. *Bob Dylan, Performing Artist 1986-1990 & beyond: Mind out of Time*. London, New York, Paris, Sydney, Copenhagen, Berlin, Madrid, Tokyo: Omnibus Press, 2004.

Wright, Gary. *Dream Weaver: A Memoir; Music, Meditation, and My Friendship with George Harrison*. New York: Jeremy P. Tarcher/Penguin, 2014.

Zanes, Warren. *Petty: The Biography*. New York: Henry Holt,

2015.

Zollo, Paul. *Conversations with Tom Petty*. London: Omnibus Press, 2005.


**Audio, Video, and Film Media**

Bright, Skot and Drakoulias, George (Producers). *Runnin' Down a Dream*. Streaming. Directed by Peter Bogdanovich. Los Angeles: Penn/Bright Entertainment. 2007.

Cardinal, Scott. Friar Park Garden Audio Tour #2. Carrboro, NC: Campfire Entertainment Network. 2018. http://audibleadventures.com

Harrison, Olivia, Scorcese, Martin, and Sinclair, Nigel (Producers). *Living in the Material World*. New York City: HBO Productions. 2011.

Hewitt, Don and Fager, Jeff (Executive Producers). Interview with Ed Bradley for *60 Minutes*. Retrieved from YouTube. http://www.youtube.com/watch?v=m_wAZ02JUtM &t=7s

*In The Studio - Tom Petty "Full Moon Fever"* (Interview), CD medium, 1989.

Jeff Lynne from E.L.O. on supergroup Traveling Wilburys | Top 2000: The Untold Stories. http://www.youtube.com/watch?v=GEO-chM5h48. 2014.

Orbison, Alex, Roy Orbison, Jr., and Wesley Orbison (Producers). *Mystery Girl Unraveled*. (Included in the Mystery Girl Deluxe boxed set) Sony/Legacy Video, 2014.

Pluta , James (Producer). *Mr. Blue Sky: The Story of Jeff Lynne & ELO*. (Included in the Hyde Park DVD boxed set). Directed by Martyn Atkins. Los Angeles: Daft as a

Brush. 2012.

Smax, Willie, and Olivia Harrison (Producers). *The True History of the Traveling Wilburys*. (Included in the Deluxe Traveling Wilburys boxed set). Burbank: Rhino Records. 2007.

Traveling Wilburys - Full, Uncut & Unedited MTV Interview. http://www.youtube.com/watch?v=W-qJ0TMzSJg, 1989.

Watch "Jeff Lynne-Rattled(demo) TRAVELING WILBURYS Rare" on YouTube. http://youtu.be/KyGTDZVH7rs

**Web pages**

http://archive.org/details/UNCUT_April_2016_UK/ An Audience with Jeff Lynne.

http://americansongwriter.com/2012/01/tom-petty-on-bob-dylan/

http://www.beatlesbible.com/

http://www.cnn.com/interactive/2017/10/entertainment/neal-preston-cnnphotos/

http://www.jefflynnesongs.com/

http://somethingelsereviews.com/2015/11/02/jeff-lynne-george-harrison-traveling-wilburys/

http://theeventsoundslike.wordpress.com/2015/02/13/the-mostly-true-history-of-the-traveling-wilburys/

http://thefederalist.com/2018/10/18/the-traveling-wilburys-debut-holds-up-as-extraordinary-30-years-later/

http://thequietus.com/articles/10299-jeff-lynne-favourite-albums-2?page=1

http://www.billboard.com/articles/columns/rock/8480749/jeff-lynne-traveling-wilburys-vol-1-30th-anniversary-elo-album-tom-petty

http://www.dailymail.co.uk/news/article-

4985704/Snapper-tells-secrets-pics-Nicks-Petty-Rose.html

http://www.emusician.com/gear/classic-tracks-the-traveling-wilburys-handle-with-care

http://www.google.com/amp/s/theeventsoundslike.wordpress.com/2015/02/13/the-mostly-true-history-of-the-traveling-wilburys/am

http://www.irishnews.com/arts/2017/12/08/news/elo-man-jeff-lynne-on-upcoming-irish-gigs-his-music-and-new-dvd-1204740/

http://www.mixonline.com/recording/jeff-lynne-366370

http://www.mojo4music.com/22257/jeff-lynne-bob-dylan-traveling-wilburys/

http://www.rollingstone.com/music/lists/elos-jeff-lynne-my-life-in-15-songs-20160121/the-traveling-wilburys-nobodys-child-1990-20160120

http://www.tompetty.com/news/statement-petty-family-1764366

http://www.travelingwilburys.com/

http://www.vintagerock.com/index.php?option=com_content&view=article&id=161:my-evening-with-roy-orbison&catid=1:all-features&Itemid=2

http://www.washingtontimes.com/news/2008/jul/04/top-5-98304083/  Top 5: Knob Twiddlers

**Personal Communication**

Slate, Jeff. Email Interview. 12-3-18

Made in the USA
Coppell, TX
16 December 2020

45556436R00177